Praise for *Love Comes Calling*

"Quirky and fun, *Love Comes Calling* is fresh fiction that sparkles and shines with humor and heart, a delightfully dizzy romance brimming with smiles and chuckles from beginning to end."

—Julie Lessman,
award-winning author of
THE DAUGHTERS OF BOSTON and
WINDS OF CHANGE series

"*Love Comes Calling* is fast-paced, funny, and sweet—with enough action and wisdom to be irresistible. I loved it."

—Mary Connealy,
bestselling author of *Fired Up* and
THE KINCAID BRIDES series

"Sweet, fun, and thought-provoking, *Love Comes Calling* brings the Roaring Twenties to life. Step onto Siri Mitchell's stage and watch the story of an impetuous, aspiring actress unfold. You'll be swept away by the skillful blend of description, humor, and emotion."

—Lorna Seilstad,
author of *When Love Calls*

Love Comes Calling

Books by Siri Mitchell

The Messenger
A Heart Most Worthy
She Walks in Beauty
Love's Pursuit
A Constant Heart
Unrivaled
Love Comes Calling

Love Comes Calling

SIRI MITCHELL

BETHANYHOUSE
a division of Baker Publishing Group
Minneapolis, Minnesota

Published by Bethany House Publishers
11400 Hampshire Avenue South
Bloomington, Minnesota 55438
www.bethanyhouse.com

Bethany House Publishers is a division of
Baker Publishing Group, Grand Rapids, Michigan

Printed in the United States of America

Library of Congress Cataloging-in-Publication Data
Mitchell, Siri L.
    Love comes calling / Siri Mitchell.
        pages cm
    ISBN 978-0-7642-1036-5 (pbk.)
    1. Actresses—Fiction. 2. Families—History—20th century—Fiction.
3. Brothers and sisters—History—20th century—Fiction. 4. Boston (Mass.)—
History—20th century—Fiction. 5. Domestic fiction. I. Title.
PS3613.I866L65 2014
813'.6—dc23   2013039152

Unless otherwise noted, Scripture quotations are from the *Holy Bible*, New Living Trans-
lation, copyright © 1996, 2004, 2007 by Tyndale House Foundation. Used by permission
of Tyndale House Publishers, Inc., Carol Stream, Illinois 60188. All rights reserved.

The Scripture quotation in chapter six is from the King James Version of the Bible.

This is a work of historical reconstruction; the appearances of certain historical figures
are therefore inevitable. All other characters, however, are products of the author's
imagination, and any resemblance to actual persons, living or dead, is coincidental.

Cover design by Jennifer Parker
Cover photography by Mike Habermann Photography, LLC

Author is represented by the Natasha Kern Literary Agency

14 15 16 17 18 19 14   7 6 5 4 3 2 1

For everyone who has ever wished
they could just be like everyone else.

MAY 1924
BOSTON

D id you not study, Miss Eton?" Professor Whitmore was looking at me over his terribly large, badly smudged, and completely old-fashioned wire-framed glasses. The tufts of wiry white hairs that sprouted from his ears looked like billowing clouds of smoke, and a red stain was beginning to spread along the tops of his sharply angled cheeks.

"I . . . well . . . I . . ."

He looked at me as if hoping I had something of interest to say.

I *had* studied. I was almost positive I had. This time, I'd really meant to. I curled my toes up inside my old T-strap shoes.

"Because, frankly, it doesn't seem as if you did." He was looking, quite pointedly, at the big black *D* he'd scrawled across the top of my Theory of Consumption economics exam.

9

Hadn't I studied? I had. I *know* I had.

That's what I'd been doing in the dormitory when I'd heard someone out in the hall. Thinking it was Martha, I'd opened the door, but the only person I saw was Irene Bennett slipping into the room we used to share halfway down the hall.

I hadn't had the chance to talk to her very much since Mother and Father had decided a room of my own might help me concentrate more on my studies, and now here the year was, almost over. I liked Irene. She was an orphaned scholarship girl whose grandparents lived somewhere far enough away that she never had to see them during the school year, which left her with scads of time to fix her bobbed hair and roll her stockings so the seams were exactly straight and keep her membership in the honor society, all at the same time. She looked just like the actress Colleen Moore, and she behaved like Louise Brooks. She was everything I wanted to be.

Though Irene had always been perfectly nice to me, she'd gotten in trouble several times this past term with the dean. I'd been hungry, so I left my textbook lying on the bed and went to find out how she was and if she had anything in her room to eat, only she hadn't. But what she did have was a *big black eye*! Only I hadn't known it at first because she kept turning away from me whenever she spoke, but I couldn't hear her, so I finally went to stand in front of her, and that's when I saw it.

So I went downstairs to see if I could find any steaks in the kitchen that she could put on her eye, only the cook wasn't there anymore, so I rummaged through the icebox. I didn't find any raw ones, but I did find a cooked one left over from supper, but when I got back to Irene's room, she wouldn't open the door. I had to pull a bobby pin from my hair and jab it around the lock until it opened, but then Irene told me to go away and leave her alone and yes her eye hurt like the dickens and no she didn't want to talk about how she'd got it.

I offered her the steak, but she said she didn't want it, which made me wonder if she might be ill because back when we'd been roommates, she used to eat everything, just like me, and sometimes we'd even go raid the kitchen at night. I couldn't bring myself to believe her, so I left the plate on her dresser. Once I got back to my room I studied, I truly did . . . until Martha came by. She gave me several pieces of divinity candy she'd brought from home at the start of the week and then told me the girls were getting up a game of mah-jongg down in the lounge and wouldn't I like to come play a match or two.

Wouldn't I! At least for a while.

And so I dove into my closet to look for my silk kimono, did up my hair with a scarlet-colored ribbon, and colored my lips with the new lipstick I'd bought down at the drugstore. When I went down to join the girls, Irene was there dressed in Chinese pajamas. She'd put so much powder on her face and used so much kohl pencil around her eyes you couldn't really tell anything had happened to her. She was sitting in an open window, smoking a cigarette from a long-handled holder like she was some flapper.

When I complained about the smoke and tried to ask about her eye again, she said something about paying attention to my own potatoes, which made me think maybe I'd been wrong about our being such good friends. I convinced the girls to open the rest of the windows to keep the smell out, but the wind was blowing the wrong way, so the smoke actually came back inside with a bunch of gnats and mosquitoes. Then Irene's cigarette ashes made a mark on the floor and someone said Mrs. Smith, the housemother, was coming, and we dumped the tiles back into the box, clapped the lid on it, and . . . well . . . I just . . .

"You can't tell me you studied for this test."

"I tried to . . ."

"If you would only apply yourself, Miss Eton."

"I did try." I had. Truly. This time I'd tried. It's not as if I hadn't meant to study.

"Not hard enough!" His voice was like the rap of a ruler. My toes curled even more. Enough to give me a cramp in the arch, making my bones feel like they were breaking in half. Ow! I reached down to massage it.

"Miss Eton!"

I sat back up. "Yes, Professor Whitmore."

"If you won't be courteous enough to give me your time and attention, then I will not be able to pass you this term."

Not pass! "But—"

"A D is not a passing grade."

"But you can't—"

"What is it you're hoping to accomplish here at Radcliffe?"

Hoping to accomplish? Great things, just the same as my grandmother had as a member of the very first graduating class, and just the same as my mother had and my sister had . . . before she left school in such a big hurry to get married and then went on a year's honeymoon to Europe and came back with a baby in her arms. He'd been such a *big* baby. I never had been able to work out why, because Julia wasn't that tall and her husband wasn't either, and Marshall himself had grown out of being so big and now he was on the small side compared to the other five-year-old boys I knew. It must have been all the traveling they'd done while she was pregnant. In any case, in spite of the proximity of other more fashionable colleges, the Eton girls went to Radcliffe. Everyone knew that. And it was up to me to graduate because my sister hadn't. And it's not like I wasn't trying, but I still had two years left, and the two years I'd already done had been pure torture. So what did I actually think I'd accomplish at Radcliffe? Very little, just the same as always. "I try, Professor Whitmore. I really do." But somehow, it never seemed to work.

"I suppose you're just like the others, hoping to catch a fine young man from across the Yard at Harvard."

I felt my mouth drop open. "I am not—"

He raised a hand as if to stay my reply. "Quite frankly, I find the whole point of a college education entirely irrelevant when all of you girls graduate and proceed directly into matrimony. It's the rare young woman who can withstand the rigors of a college education. You would not be the first to find yourself unsuited to the academic environment."

I would be in my family. Except, of course, for my sister. Which made it even more important that I prove myself able to withstand the rigors of a college education.

"I have said before and I will never cease saying that I never supported the idea of Radcliffe College. But it can't be helped now. And neither, I suppose, can your family's gift of funding for the new dormitory building."

Maybe, just maybe . . . I held my breath.

He cleared his throat as he looked at me with doleful eyes. I hated that look, though I'd be deceiving myself if I said I hadn't gotten used to it by now. "I have to say I'm disappointed. I had high hopes for you. I don't think it's a lack of ability, Miss Eton. I think it's a lack of commitment. But until you buckle down with your studies, you're wasting my time and your own. As well as your family's considerable resources."

I fixed my eyes on my hands, which had somehow become entangled in the hem of my Nile green silk blouse. "I promise you, Professor Whitmore, on the next test—"

"The next test for you, Miss Eton, will be in the fall, next term, when I expect to find you repeating Theory of Consumption. Even if you happen to have written a perfect final, it still won't be enough to pull up your grade."

"Repeat . . . ?" Had he said *repeat*?

"If I can't pass you, then I have to fail you. You can repeat the class in the fall. I hope a summer away from school will help you reflect upon your failings and give you reason to greet the new school year with a better attitude."

"I *can't* fail this class, Professor!" My mother would murder me, and my father would look at me with such disappointment. Such soul-wrenching sadness. I couldn't let them down. Not again.

"That's the best I can do . . . unless you'd like me to recommend you for disenrollment?" He looked at me, brow raised.

"Disenrollment!"

"We professors see more than you might think, as we travel back and forth between the yards. I'll wager you have more than one young fellow you could talk into proposing." He winked. "I do believe there's a prince of a man out there just

14

waiting for you to beckon. And I truly believe matrimony would be the best thing for you. Think about it, Miss Eton. And let me know what you decide next week. You don't have to come back in the fall." He handed the test to me.

Matrimony! Of all the—! I rose, grabbing the test. "Professor Whitmore, I don't think—"

"But I hope you do, Miss Eton. In any case, I hope you start to soon. Good day, now."

Matrimony! I kicked at a stone on the walkway that led away from the school building, then had to bite back a cry when it failed to yield. Ow! Matrimony, my eye! And to a *prince* of a man. Oh, I could just . . . just about . . . *do something*! I crumpled up the hateful test and threw it at a flock of geese. Or tried to. A spiteful gust of wind blew it right back into my face. I thrashed at it, managing to knock my hat off in the process. And the geese were interested in that, all right! One of them latched onto it and waddled away. I might have tried to chase him, but geese are mean.

Oysters and clambakes! I stamped my foot and splattered mud all over my stockings, so I stomped again for good measure. What did it matter anyway? Who had ever expected anything else from me but disappointment and failure?

Well . . . me, I suppose.

But I always ended up disappointing myself by my failures too. Why couldn't I just think things through before I did them? Why couldn't I just sit still and concentrate? Professor Whitmore was right; if I could just apply myself . . . why couldn't I? Why did I have to be so stupid all the time?

One thing was sure. In fall, I wouldn't be here. But not for the reason the professor thought. Getting married? Ha!

I stamped again. The mud gave a satisfying splat.

Double ha!

I wouldn't come back to Radcliffe because I wouldn't *be* in Boston. Next fall, I planned to be in Hollywood.

I know something you don't know." Louise was smiling like a cat who'd swallowed a canary.

I eyed her as she stepped into the dormitory hall with me. As editor of the *Radcliffe News* and a member of Phi Beta Kappa and the Radcliffe Guild, there was probably quite a bit she knew that I didn't know. Or at least quite a few things I'd once known, but hadn't been able to remember. Like the answers to the economics test.

"Ask me what it is." Her brown eyes were sparkling beneath her green straw cloche hat. "Go ahead, ask me!"

I walked right past her toward the stairs. "I think I'd rather wait."

"For what?" Mary was coming down the stairs I had planned to go up. "What are you waiting for? Prince to put his fraternity pin on you?"

"*I* was going to tell her that!" Louise stepped past me to take a swipe at Mary with her pocketbook.

I caught Louise by the forearm. "What?"

"Prince Phillips. He's going to pin you."

Oh no, he wasn't! Not if I could help it.

"He was talking to Roy about it yesterday. And Roy told Helen."

Roy told Helen everything.

"And Helen told Myrtle. And Myrtle told me—"

"And me!" Mary was smiling so widely her teeth were gleaming.

Louise shrugged. " . . . and there you are."

"Griffin Phillips and I are just friends." And oh, how I wished he wouldn't try to change things.

Louise frowned as if I'd insulted her. "How can you say—"

"The Phillips family has lived next door to us for ages."

"Honestly, Ellis! I don't know why you always say that. If we truly thought you might not have him, any one of us would be on him in a minute. What's not to like about him?"

"I don't *not* like him." I did like him. Very much. Too much to let the captain of the Harvard football team, president of the mandolin club, vice president of his fraternity, and heir to all that Phillips money put his pin on a dumb Dora like me. People said Griff was going to be a congressman someday like his father. Or maybe even governor. He didn't need me going around failing economics tests and losing perfectly good hats.

Mary smiled. "That's better." She reached down and threaded an arm through mine, pulling me up the stairs. "Let's decide what you're going to wear when he pins you."

"I can't—I'm not—"

Louise swatted at me from behind with her pocketbook. "Hush, Ellis. This is important."

They hauled me up the stairs to my room and began pulling dresses from my closet.

18

"Listen: Griff is not going to put his pin on me, because I won't let him."

"Of course you will. Why wouldn't you?" Mary held a pink and blue sailor-collar dress up under my chin as she squinted at me. "I don't know . . . what do you think, Louise?"

"I won't let him because . . ." Because I couldn't bear to tell him no even though I couldn't possibly say yes. It's not that I didn't like him. On the contrary, ever since he'd gone and gotten so tall and started talking to me in that deep, low voice as if I were the only one he wanted to hear him, it was hard not to think of him practically all the time I wasn't thinking about anything else. And ever since that fraternity dance back in autumn when he'd laughed at something I'd said and then looked right down into my eyes and said, "That's why I like you so much, Ellis" . . . at least . . . I think that's what he said, although it was hard to tell because the band was playing so loudly. But that's what it had sounded like, and after that I couldn't stop ignoring the funny feeling I got way down deep inside whenever I saw him. And that was the problem. I liked him far too much to let him ruin himself by getting involved with me. And why would he want to be pinned to the Eton girl that could never quite manage to do anything right?

If I avoided being pinned, then I'd be able to spare Griff's pride when I ended up leaving town. I'd been humiliated enough in my life to know how it felt, and Griff didn't deserve that. The sooner I could get to Hollywood, the better! I'd been thinking about it since the summer of my freshman year, when I realized college wasn't for me. Being pinned— and then leaving Griff behind—was one thing I didn't want to have to regret when I left. I just had to figure out how to get enough money to buy my train ticket.

"This one or this one?" Mary was holding up my drop-waisted orchid satin dress and my maize Chelsea-collared chiffon.

"Neither." I stepped beyond her and pulled my white tennis jumper from its hanger.

She grabbed it from me. "You can't wear *that*!"

"Good grief! I've got the play tonight. Besides, I've already told you he's not going to pin me. And even if he did, I've known Griff for . . . a long time. It's not as if he hasn't seen me in a plain old skirt and sweater. Or nothing at all, for that matter."

Mary's eyes grew wide, and Louise looked at me as if I'd suddenly sprouted horns.

I might have laughed, but I couldn't resist the temptation to give them the person they so obviously imagined me to be. I smiled a long, slow, smoldering smile as if I were the actress Theda Bara. And then I gave a languorous shrug of my shoulder as I prowled toward my bed, throwing in a shimmy for good measure.

Mary gasped. "You didn't." She turned to Louise. "She didn't! She couldn't have; she wouldn't, would she? You don't think they've—"

I broke into laughter. Peals of it. I couldn't help it. "No, I never—! I was talking about when we were *babies*. Our families have gone to the shore together every summer for practically forever."

Louise blushed so bright she looked like a strawberry with that green hat on her head. "I wasn't thinking *that*.

My goodness! How could you even . . . but . . . you almost . . . you seemed so *vampy* there for a second. I never quite know what to think about you, Ellis. You might want to pretend to be Mary Pickford once in a while or people might start to wonder . . ."

Our own Mary was looking at my tennis jumper, nose wrinkled. "Honestly! You'd think you weren't even an Eton, with clothes like that."

Which is what I said whenever I went home on the weekends. But Mother only sighed and talked about whether my old things were still serviceable. *"Just think how many orphans can be fed and clothed with the money you're thinking of spending."* I undid the buttons on my skirt and let it drop to the floor, and then I pulled my blouse off over my head. "Do either of you actually know when this pinning is supposed to happen?"

"Now."

"Now!"

"Sure. Just as soon as the boys get done with class."

"But he can't! Tonight's the play." And I had to head over to the theater soon . . . where Griff would eventually be meeting me. I'd just have to make sure he didn't catch me between here and there alone. I pulled the tennis jumper on over my head and tugged the skirt down smooth.

There was a knock at the door.

The girls shouted "Come in" while I shouted "Go away!" Two voices beat one, for Irene Bennett opened the door and thrust a tall glass jug in our direction. "Just look what I bought!"

If she weren't still standing in the door, I would have slipped around her. "Looks like a very nice jug, Irene."

21

"It's not just a jug. It's a jug filled with *grape juice*."

I pulled her into the room so I could get around her. "Why don't you go drink it somewhere, then?"

"Because, look: right there. Read what it says."

I obliged her. "'Warning. If left in a dark place, will ferment.'"

"See?"

"So don't leave it sitting around. Drink it now." Somewhere else. So I could leave!

"I'm going to turn it into *wine*!"

Mary gasped. "You can't!"

"Of course I can. If I leave it in the dark, it'll ferment. So . . . ?" She looped her arm around mine as she looked at me, brow cocked.

She wanted to be my friend now, after practically ignoring me at mah-jongg that night before the economics test? "So . . . what?"

She offered the jug up to me. "Will you?"

"Will I what?"

"Put it in your closet for me? I was really hoping it would be done by now. I've had it in mine for a while, but your room is so much stuffier, I was hoping it would work better here. If I can figure out how to make my own wine, then I won't have to depend on the boys downtown to buy it for me."

She had people buying wine for her? Since when?! "If you want to make wine so much, even though it's positively *illegal*, then put it in your own closet."

She rolled her eyes. "It's not illegal. Legally, me and you and everyone here is allowed to produce wine in the privacy of their own house—"

22

"But this is a dormitory."

She threw an arm around my neck. "Why do you always have to be so literal, Ellis?"

"I'm not." Irene had changed, and not for the better. I felt my nose wrinkle. Had she already been drinking? "Why can't you just obey the rules like everyone else?"

"Because they're only made for the benefit of the poor fools who can't figure out how to break them."

"By which, I suppose, you meant me?" Was she trying to be mean on purpose?

Mary and Louise were watching us with wide eyes.

"Of course I don't mean you. Everyone knows rules weren't made for the first families of Boston! You're above the law."

"No one's above the law."

She held up the jug. "Come on, Ellis. Will you keep it for me? Please? No one would dare expel you, but if they catch me . . ."

If they caught Irene, then the dean of the college would throw her out on her head. After having been caught smoking in her room and out in the Yard with a boy after curfew, it was a miracle she'd made it through the term at all.

"Please?" She batted her long, dark, incredibly thick eyelashes at me. They were the only thing I envied about her. That and her closet full of silk dresses. And her beaded handbags. And matching shoes. Come to think of it, she'd improved herself quite a bit lately. For a poor girl, she had a lot more nice things than I did!

"Don't do it, Ellis!" Louise was glaring at Irene. "Don't you know what will happen if they catch you?"

Of course I knew what would happen. The dean would

call me to her office for a talk. She'd be ever so disappointed and encourage me to apply myself and buckle down and then everything would be forgiven. Just like it always was. I wouldn't be coming back next autumn anyway. "Oh . . . go ahead. Put it in my closet." I waved her toward it, then slipped out the door.

"But, Ellis! You can't just—" I stomped down the hall so I wouldn't be able to hear Mary and Louise calling out behind me. I was so tired of people telling me what I couldn't do! And what I wouldn't do! And what I was supposed to do!

As I went down the front stairs, I heard the sound of chanting. It was coming from outside.

I tiptoed to the door and took a peek out the window. A big bunch of fraternity boys was coming across the Yard, waving their flag and singing one of their dippy songs.

For crying out loud!

Now I'd have to think of some other way to get to the theater unseen. At least no one else had heard them.

As if on cue, one of the freshmen popped out of the dining room.

"Don't you dare answer that door!"

She plastered herself against the wall. "I won't. Promise."

Spearing her with a Pola Negri glare, I ran back up the stairs and down the hall to Martha's room. I might have been an Eton, but she was the one who'd received the honor of the corner room.

She didn't answer my knock.

Please, please, please!

"I'm coming!" She opened the door, her hair already set in water-wave combs and tied up in string.

"Can I borrow one of your windows, Martha?"

"One of my . . . windows? Why?"

Pushing past her, I strode to one. Unlatching it, I pushed up the sash, then hitched up my skirt and sat astride the frame.

"Ellis! What on earth—?"

"Hush, Martha. I need to concentrate."

She sprang through the door and out into the hall. "Help! Help! Ellis Eton is committing suicide."

Oh, for heaven's sake. "I am not!" I raised my voice so it could be heard over hers. "But I might just have to murder you, Martha Davis!"

She came back into the room and shut up her mouth as she clutched her collar tight about the throat.

"Wish me luck." I hoped this would go more like a Douglas Fairbanks movie than a Charlie Chaplin one. Leaning forward, I swung my other leg over the window ledge. Then I pushed off the sill as I grabbed at the edge of the gutter. As I hung there, I wrapped my legs around the downspout. I'd seen Buster Keaton do it once in a movie; it had looked so easy as I was sitting there in the theater, but now I couldn't quite figure out how it worked.

I loosened my hold on the pipe and started to slide, then tightened my grip and stopped. Nothing to it! And much easier than climbing down a tree.

Only . . . those voices sounded louder. Were they getting nearer?

I loosened my grip again and started to slide, when my thighs got hung up on something sharp and pointy.

Ow!

It probably would have worked just fine if the pipe hadn't

separated from the building just then and swung me out away from the dormitory like a ride at Salem Willows Park. I tried to hold on as long as I could—I really did—but with the pipe peeling off and then curving down toward the ground, suddenly I was sliding along the gutter in the wrong direction, upside down. And before I knew it, I'd reached the end of the pipe and sailed off through the air.

I closed my eyes.

There wasn't anything else to do, and I really didn't want to see where I was headed.

3

My landing wasn't quite what I'd expected. It was much softer, and it was also accompanied by a grunt. A very masculine grunt. Which was followed by a laugh and the scent of black licorice. "Fancy seeing you here, Ellis."

I'd shut my eyes up so tight it took me a moment to open them. And another long moment to believe what they insisted on telling me. Apparently, my attempt at escape had been spotted, and when I'd fallen it had been straight into the arms of Griffin Phillips.

He was staring down at me, his blond hair flopping forward into those gorgeous blue eyes he had. "Are you all right?"

Someone started up a Harvard fight song, and all the fraternity brothers joined in.

Griff slung me over his shoulder as if I were some damsel in distress and ran several yards down the grass before stopping and setting me carefully down on the ground. Everyone cheered as if he'd just scored another touchdown.

Rah-rah. Sis-boom-bah.

I pushed through the boys and headed out toward the street.

Griff jogged to catch up with me. "Hey—you headed to the theater? Can I come with you?"

"Sure." Why not? I would have done better just to have opened the front door to him in the first place, but that's about the way things had been going this term, and there was no reason to think they might change now.

We walked together, Griff whistling the way he usually did and me wishing I were anywhere but there. He shot a glance over at me. "What were you doing on that gutter anyway?"

"I was trying to leave."

He squinted at me. "Wasn't the front door working?"

"I wanted to make a quick getaway."

He smiled that old Griff smile, which always made me want to smile too. So I did. And then I started to laugh.

"That's what I like about you, Ellis. You're always doing things no one else would ever think of."

Then he was the only one who liked that about me. But that's exactly why I liked him too. He'd never once, in all the time I'd known him, said, "Oh, Ellis!" or shaken his head over some dumb thing I'd done . . . or tried to do.

He slanted a look over at me. "There's something I've been meaning to ask you."

Oh, crumb. "And there's something I've wanted to ask you too."

"Then go ahead. Please. You first."

I knew I could count on him to be a gentleman!

"So . . . what was it?"

Oh. Well, now I had to think of something to say. "I was wondering . . . wanting to know . . . what do you think about . . . ?" What? What would make him go on and on long enough to

28

make him forget about his fraternity pin? And me. Harvard?
No. Bad idea. That would just make him think about his fra-
ternity again. Football? No, the season was long over. Baseball!
"What do you think about Roy Powell?"

"You mean about the trade?"

"You can't really call it a trade if he refused to be traded."
That's what my brother Lawrence had taken to saying.

"Well, now . . . I don't know if I agree with that." He
talked up and down and around both sides of the issue until
we reached the theater, just as I'd known he would. He was
studying to be a lawyer, after all.

I ran up the steps ahead of him and opened the door.
"Thanks for walking me over. There sure is lots to do to get
ready. . . ."

He caught up with me and took hold of the door, pulling
it open wider. "But I wanted to ask you if—"

One of the freshman girls came toward us. "There you are!
One of the curtains won't work, and I can't find the flashlight
and—"

"The curtain always catches. You just have to know how to
pull it the right way." I sent a glance back over my shoulder at
Griff as I gave a shrug. "Come with me, and I'll show you."

After I'd taught her how to coax the curtain open and
closed, I went on a search for the missing flashlight. Without
it, the props girl would never be able to see in the dim light
backstage. There were always a million things to do the afternoon of a performance, and they kept me busy enough to
avoid Griff, who finally decided to change into his costume
and then take a seat out in the auditorium to wait.

About forty-five minutes before show time, my assistant

walked up as she consulted a clipboard. "Everyone is here except for two of the trolls, the maid, and the queen."

The queen: Irene. I could have torn my hair out. This play was mine. I'd written it for my English 47 class; my professor had let me direct it, and I was also acting in it. Lots of the girls had wanted to play the queen, but I'd chosen Irene because she was the person I'd imagined as I wrote the part back at the beginning of the year. Since I'd cast her, however, she'd been nothing but trouble.

I told her to send someone over to the dormitory to look for Irene.

As she left by way of the stage, I saw Griff back in the far corner of the theater, talking to a man with hair so slick it might have been patent leather. Though he was too old to be a student, he looked too young to be a parent. As I watched, he laid a hand on Griff's arm.

Griff shrugged it off and turned away, walking down the theater toward me.

The man darted in front of him, putting a hand to Griff's chest. "It's not like we're asking for the whole season. Just one game. A couple of plays. That's all."

Sidestepping the man, Griff continued on toward me.

"Tell me you'll at least think about it! He won't take no for an answer."

"I already told you: I can't."

"You mean you won't, that's all!" The man turned on his heel, jammed his hat on his head, and stormed away.

"What did he want?"

Griff shrugged. "He just wanted to talk about football."

Football! That's all anyone ever seemed to talk about.

Another reason to be glad I wouldn't be here in September. "Forget about football." I pulled him over to the props table and . . . was that the flashlight? Squinting, I grabbed at it. It was! I switched it on.

Unfortunately, it was pointed right at Griff.

He put a hand up in front of his eyes. "Watch it!"

I swung the light toward the table as I switched it off. "Sorry." I grabbed his crown and stood on tiptoe to set it on his head. Then I pressed a mustache to his upper lip. Pulling his cape from a chair, I handed it to him. "Could you put this on?"

A growing murmur from the other side of the curtain told me the audience was starting to arrive.

"Do I have to?"

"You're the king. Of course you have to."

He grimaced. "I'm only doing this because you asked me to."

Oysters and clambakes! You'd think I'd asked him to fly to the moon and back instead of giving him the starring role in my play. "Do you remember your lines?"

"Of course I remember my lines!" He scowled and walked off, muttering to himself.

Normally, Griff wasn't involved with theater, but I'd begged him to do my play. If truth be told, he wasn't very good at acting in general, but I knew he'd be terrific in this part because all he had to do was be himself: strong, kind, smart, loyal, handsome, steadfast, resolute, considerate, and . . . well . . . perfect.

I went and put my costume on. I was the court jester, providing the comic relief for the tragedy through a running gag and a series of misunderstandings. It wasn't a big part, but it was important, and it left me free most of the time to supervise. When I returned to the props table, my assistant was standing there with Irene, clutching the clipboard to her chest.

"Have you seen the trolls and the maid yet?"

"They're in the washroom, changing."

Good. I opened the curtains and took a peek. People were starting to come in, although my parents weren't yet among them. I looked the scenery over. One of the trees had a precarious tilt. I sent a stagehand out to fix it. Then I found the prompter's copy of the play, sent the actors for the first scene out, and made sure the props girl stood at her station beside the table. I checked my watch, signaled the boy in charge of the lights, and . . . the lights dimmed.

I held my breath as the curtain opened without a hitch and the play began.

At the end of the first act, I came off the stage to the applause of the crowd and then, backstage, to the applause of the girls. Most of them, anyway. All of them except for Irene. She was scowling. "It's easy to act when you're not really acting."

Not acting! I'd given everything I had to be a perfect—if silly—jester. And at least I was making people laugh. When she was on stage she just sat on her throne, looking as if she'd rather be somewhere, *anywhere*, else. "You should know. You hardly bothered to show up to half the practices. Why did you accept the part if you didn't want to play it?"

"To keep you from making a complete fool of yourself. Only it hasn't worked, has it?"

"What is it with you? Why are you being like this?"

"I could have a perfect life, too, if I had parents like yours and money coming out of my ears and—and an adoring boyfriend. You're just so—so—*good* sometimes. I could just about scream!"

Good? Me?

"Not all of us are as lucky as you. Sometimes you have to figure out what it takes to get ahead and then just do it. Sometimes you have to put your inhibitions aside."

What was she talking about?

"Don't you ever get tired of doing the right thing all the time?"

"I'm not like you think I am, Irene! I mean—"

"Just let me be."

A hand on my shoulder stopped me when I would have replied. As she turned away, Griff pulled me to his side and gave my shoulder a squeeze. "Don't let her get to you. She's just jealous."

"Of . . . me?"

"Who wouldn't be?"

Who wouldn't be? Who *would* be was the better question.

"Besides, it takes someone really smart to pretend to be so stupid."

I didn't have time to respond because one of the trolls needed a costume repair. I sent him to the costumes girl to have it patched, then helped the stagehands move the scenery. Once everything was in place, I put the actors and actresses in their positions. But then Griff came up to me, his mustache dangling.

I swiped the jar of spirit gum from the props table and applied some more to the dent above his lip. "Don't breathe so hard! You're making the mustache move."

His nose had wrinkled. "That smells terrible!"

Over to my left, one of Griff's fraternity brothers was pacing behind the curtain, out of glimpse of the audience.

"Stage right is actually to the left only when you're looking up at the stage. Remember?"

"What?" Griff was looking down his nose at me.

"Not you. I'm talking to Richard." I pressed my finger to Griff's lip and motioned for his fraternity brother to go across to the other side. To the real stage right. How on earth did any of them ever catch a football if they couldn't be in the right place at the right time?

Beside us, another of his fraternity brothers had been reciting his lines.

I kicked at what I hoped were his shins as I applied some more spirit gum to Griff's mustache.

"Ow! What'd you do that for?"

"You have the emphasis on the wrong word. Put it on the last one, not the first one."

He repeated it. "Like that?"

"Right."

I glanced up at Griff. He seemed so stiff all of a sudden. His face had gone red. Had he been holding his breath that whole time?

"I didn't mean for you to go all purple. Just . . . don't exhale quite so strongly."

He let out his pent-up breath with a whoosh of licorice-scented air.

I sighed as his mustache lifted up and flapped free.

"Just . . ." I took his hand and lifted it to his lip. "Just hold it there for a while. It should set before you have to go on."

As I'd been gluing Griff's mustache, Irene had peeked out around the edge of the curtain. Now she turned to me, eyes wide. "I have to go."

"Not yet. You don't go on until midway through the scene." I recited her cue.

She'd put the crepe-papered whisk she was using as a scepter down on the props table and shrugged out of her fur-tipped cloak. "I mean I have to leave."

"Leave? *Now*? But—but you can't!"

She'd found her cloche hat and pocketbook and was touching up her lipstick by the illumination of the flashlight. She regarded herself in the mirror, rubbing her lips together and smiling into her compact mirror. Then she snapped it shut. "It can't be helped. You'll have to do without me."

"You can't just leave!" But apparently, she could. I watched as, out behind the audience, she joined a tall beanpole of a man dressed in black tie. She sent one last look over her shoulder toward the stage as he grabbed at her hand and pulled her away.

"Where'd Irene go?" The props girl was standing there holding Irene's scepter.

"She's . . . gone."

"Gone where?"

"I don't know." It didn't matter. We still had half the play left, and I had to figure out how to make the show go on without her.

It didn't take long to realize I was the only one who could fill in for Irene. In the first place, my role as jester wasn't a very big one. In the second place, I was the only other person who knew her lines. The costume girl helped me don the fur-tipped cloak. I drew it tight around my throat so no one would be able to see the jester costume underneath, but there was really nothing I could do about my hair. Irene's was black and mine was blond. If I did a good enough job of acting, then I hoped I could make everyone forget I wasn't her.

I made it through act two by throwing the cloak on and off behind the tree, hunching when I played the jester and standing regally tall when I was the queen. As I said my lines, I scanned the audience for my parents, but I didn't see them.

Act three started with a boom. Quite literally. A tympani drum filled in for cannon fire during the epic battle with the trolls. Though the king handily won the war, the queen, doubting his ability to triumph, had previously betrayed him. She'd gone behind his back with an offer of peace, which the troll prince had accepted. For all intents and purposes, she had turned the king into a dastardly, ruthless murderer, ruining his good name forever.

The climax of the play occurred as the king confronted the queen, asking her why she'd done it.

Griff clasped my hand in his. "Did you doubt my strength? Or my courage? I would have fought a thousand battles, I would have died a thousand deaths, knowing you believed in me . . . that you believed in us. Just tell me that you love me still." And my goodness, but didn't he draw me close and then dip me right over backward as if he were Rudolph Valentino!

The play was a tragedy, so the queen was supposed to re-fuse the king's love. She was supposed to be mean and evil and wicked, just like Irene had turned out to be. But as he took me into his arms, my knees melted, and I threw an arm around his neck so I wouldn't dissolve into a puddle right there on the floor.

His arm tightened around my waist.

As I looked into his eyes, I wanted to believe every word he said. And I wanted to be forgiven, even though I'd done all the wrong things. Even though I was no good for him and had ruined his reputation, I wanted to believe he loved me still. And so I said, "Yes—I do! I *do* love you!" before I could remember I wasn't supposed to.

He pulled me closer and bent toward my ear. "You're supposed to say, 'No.'"

" . . . what?" How come I'd never realized before what a truly tragic thing the queen had done?

"Ellis!" He said it with a hiss. "You're supposed to say 'No'!"

"No?" But . . . I didn't want to. I'd never immersed myself so fully in a role before. It was so strange and . . . and wonderful. How was it I'd imagined the queen could so glibly refuse his love? Why hadn't I realized she would have second thoughts? And then third ones after that? Why didn't I know how much she'd crave forgiveness and that the worst of it was, she couldn't manage to forgive herself? It was all so much . . . *more* . . . so much more complicated, so much more emotional, so much more complex than I'd thought.

"Ellis?"

"What?"

"My back's really starting to hurt."

"Oh!" I put a hand to his chest, straightened, and then

turned away from him toward the audience, my other hand at my brow as if I couldn't bear to look at him any longer. And it was true: I couldn't. There was too much love shining from his eyes, and I couldn't figure out why because I didn't deserve him. I mean, *she* didn't deserve him.

"No!" I was supposed to add, "Not for a hundred thousand victories. Not even for one hundred thousand eternities." But it just seemed a little too cruel. So with that final word ringing through the air, the curtain fell for the last time.

My parents had never shown up, so Griff offered to walk me back to the dormitory. I'd played two roles. I'd made the audience laugh, and then I'd turned right around and made them cry. I'd become my part so completely I'd all but melted in Griff's arms and thrown away any chance I had of leaving Boston with no regrets. It was the best work I'd ever done . . . and my parents hadn't been there to see any of it.

"Want one?" Griff held his open palm out to me.

"What?"

"Licorice. Want one?"

"No. Thanks."

He closed up his fist and jammed it into his trouser pocket. "I'm sure glad that's over!" He sounded suspiciously happy as he spoke the words.

"Didn't you like the play?"

"I liked it fine—and I still can't believe you actually wrote it—but acting is a lot of work. I've never been good at that sort of thing. I'm not like you."

"You wouldn't want to be me."

"No." He smiled agreeably. "Then I wouldn't be able to play football."

Football! There it was again. Why did everything always have to be about football?

"So, why *do* it? Acting in all those plays? Is it for the applause?"

I felt a blush rise on my cheeks, and it didn't have anything to do with the way Griff was looking at me. Applause wasn't why I liked acting. I'd act even if no one was watching. In fact, I did it all the time. "I just—I like being other people." I liked it much more than being myself. Truth be told, I did a better job at being almost anyone other than myself. "I don't do it for the applause. I do it because I'm good at it. Do you play football for the applause?"

He slowed his pace and glanced over at me. "Naw. When I'm playing football, I decide what happens. I call the plays. And when I'm out there on the field, nothing else matters. I don't have to worry about all those things people say about my being governor someday. I don't have to worry I'll maybe end up disappointing them. . . ." His gaze dropped from mine. He shrugged. "I can just . . . throw the ball. And I'm really good at throwing the ball."

I knew all about disappointing people. I put my hand on his arm.

He stopped walking and held it up, pressing our palms together, examining them the same way he'd studied a starfish that had stranded itself on the shore at Buzzards Bay back when we'd been little.

I'm sure he didn't mean to make my insides melt away, but

as I looked at my hand lying there in his, I honestly couldn't think of any good reason to pull it away. Except for the fact he'd just said something that wasn't right. I pulled my hand from his and socked him in the arm. "You shouldn't worry about those people, Griff."

"No?"

"Do you even want to do all those things everyone wants you to?"

"I don't know. I guess . . . maybe . . . I don't know." He sighed. "They call me *Prince*, did you know that? Like I'm some kind of royalty or something."

"You are." He was! "You're something really special, Griffin Phillips."

"But I'm not *that*."

"I know you're not."

He sent me a sidelong glance. "Sometimes I think you're about the only one who does."

That blush started creeping up my cheeks again. If I was any kind of decent actress, you'd think I would have figured out how to stop myself from blushing, but I never had.

"I think we're the same, you and I. And I just want you to know, all those things I said at the end, as the king, I really meant them."

"Oh, Griff . . ." I was supposed to be stopping him from saying things like that, not giving him opportunities. Panic fluttered in my chest. I needed to keep him from saying something he'd regret. Something I'd have to deny. Why couldn't life be fair? Why couldn't I be a girl he could be proud of instead of just dumb old Ellis Eton?

"I mean, I know it was just supposed to be acting and

all, but I need to tell you—if it weren't for you being here, Ellis—"

I couldn't let him finish because it wasn't fair. I wasn't going to be in Boston very much longer, and if he knew I was leaving, he wouldn't be saying things like that. So I kissed him on the cheek and made a dash for the dormitory.

Friday was moving-out day. We were supposed to pack up everything in the morning so we could move it back home for the summer. And we were to do a thorough cleaning besides. Just the thought of it made me tired, so I lay in bed after waking for a few minutes, repeating the phrase, "Every day, in every way, I'm getting better and better." One of Louise's aunts had gone to France for psychoanalysis the summer before and came back with that phrase as her cure. It was supposed to work as long as you repeated it each day and really meant it each time you said it. I always repeated it ten times for good measure, and I always put a lot of feeling into it.

Every day, in every way, I'm getting better and better.

I'd been saying it every day for so long you might have thought it would have started working by now, but I didn't seem to be getting any better. At much of anything.

When I couldn't ignore the banging about of trunks anymore, I got up and started packing, though it seemed like it shouldn't have taken as long as it did. My shoes were at the bottom of my trunk. I'd found my stack of dance cards from the year, and I was trying to figure out what to do with them. I thought I might tie them up with a ribbon, but a search through my drawers hadn't turned any up. A chain of bobby pins didn't really do the trick, so I set them aside and picked up my mah-jongg set instead. It was missing three tiles, so I started a search for them—which led me back to the drawer my dance cards had been sitting in, where I found the most darling rhinestone hair bandeau I hadn't even remembered I owned. Which was a real shame since I could have used it for a play back in January—I'd had the starring role as a princess, and it would have made a much better garland for my hair than the ratty old ribbon I'd been given to wear. I was trying to remember how I'd come by it when one of the freshmen knocked at the door and poked her head around the doorframe.

"Your sister's here to see you."

"Julia?"

She shrugged.

What was Julia doing here? It was an awfully long way from Brookline early on a Friday morning, and she wasn't one for visiting. After she'd come back from Europe, she mainly just stayed at home. What if—? Fear gripped my heart. The only reason she'd be here at school was if something bad had happened!

I dropped the bandeau and sprinted out the door, straight into—"Janie? Where's Julia?"

She tottered, reaching out toward me, and then toppled to the floor. "Julia . . . your sister?"

"Someone said she was here."

Janie shrugged, and that's when I remembered she looked like me. That is, I looked like her. Or . . . we looked like each other. She was our cook's daughter, and when we were little, people were always mistaking Janie for me. Once, we traded places for a whole day. Nobody missed me, but I got Janie in trouble with all the staff, dirtying up the house behind them and terrorizing the horses in the stable. Not that I meant to do any of that. But for a month afterward, boy, did I hear about it! *"Why can't you just be good, Ellis, like you were that one day?"* That was the last time I ever traded anything with Janie and the last time anyone ever accused me of being good at anything.

She was staring up at me from the floor.

"I'm sorry." I gave her a hand up. We were both blondes with brown eyebrows, although hers were very nearly black. We shared the same wavy hair, although hers always seemed to stay exactly in place while mine did whatever it pleased, which generally meant it formed a sort of fuzzy halo around my head. We were about the same height: short. If someone took all the oomph out of me, Janie is exactly what they would get. And as I peered at her, I realized she looked rather more pale than normal and . . . had she been *crying*? "Is everything all right?"

"No . . . it's—"

"Wait. Wait just a second. Let me get you a handkerchief." I had some. I knew I had some somewhere. The trick of it was to remember exactly where I'd put them. I rummaged through my trunk for a few moments before I realized I hadn't put them anywhere at all. They were right where they'd been all year: in one of my hatboxes. I found one and handed it to her, then sat her down on my bed. "Oops. Wait." I took her hand and yanked her up to standing and pulled my coverlet up over the pillow. "There."

She sat and put the handkerchief to the corner of an eye.

"Now, what is it? Can you tell me?"

"It's my mother. Hadn't you heard?"

"Heard what?"

She wrapped her arms about herself as if she were cold. "She died."

"She's *dead*?" Mrs. Winslow couldn't be dead. I would have known if she were dead. Someone would have told me. "She can't be dead. I know she can't be dead."

Janie's shoulders collapsed, and she began to wail.

"Oh! I'm so, *so* sorry." It must be true if Janie was that upset about it. I sat down beside her, put an arm about her, and let her have a good cry on my shoulder.

Eventually she stopped crying and dabbed at her eyes instead. I went to get her a glass of water and, when I came back, she told me there was to be a funeral up in Maine, where Mrs. Winslow had been born.

While she was telling me about it, I spied a lid on my dresser and tried to remember what it belonged to. It was broad and flat, so it had to be from a jar of cream, didn't it? It looked like it was from a jar of cream. But then you'd think there ought to be a jar of cream without a lid around somewhere if that were the case, but I hadn't come across one in my packing.

" . . . so what do you think, Ellis? I know it's a lot to ask, but would you do it? For me?"

"What? I'm sorry. I was just . . ."

She looked at me for one long moment, then her face crumpled and her shoulders folded. "I shouldn't have come." She was shaking her head as tears streaked down her cheeks once more. "And I'm sorry to have asked. Never mind." She got up and started toward the door.

"Wait. I'm sorry. I'm truly terribly sorry. Here you are, you've lost your mother, and of course I'll do it." I went to her and took up her hand between both of mine, clasping it to my bosom and looking her in the eyes. "I will. I'll do it. I promise."

"Really?"

I nodded. "Truly."

"Oh, Ellis, thank you so much." She embraced me before having another good cry for rather a long while as I looked around for my hats before realizing I didn't have any—which was a big relief because it was one thing less to pack. Or three things, actually. I'd brought three hats to school with me in the fall. That first one I'd left behind at some fraternity dance. The second had blown right off my head in a storm we'd had in February, and the third one . . . the third one had been snatched away by that goose at the beginning of the week. But I hadn't really liked that one anyway. It had been a wide-brimmed straw with a bunch of cream-colored bows, and I'd always thought it made my head look as if it were topped by a big pastry puff.

Janie sniffed a good, long sniff. "Are you sure, Ellis?"

I patted her on the shoulder. "Of course I'm sure."

"It would only be for two weeks."

"That's fine. I want to do whatever I can to help." Janie had always been nice to me, and Mrs. Winslow had worked for us for practically forever. Helping her daughter was the least I could do. I surveyed the room once more as I stood there. It seemed like there should be more things to put into the trunk. Hadn't I come to school with more things?

"I'll have to tell you how it all works. Maybe I could come over this weekend . . ."

"Come over anytime. I'll be back at the house this afternoon."

"How about seven tomorrow morning?"

"*Seven!*"

"It might take a while to tell you everything."

"Let's at least be reasonable about it then. Come at ten."

"Ten. Tomorrow. And you'll be there?"

"I'll be there. I promise I will. And then you'll tell me how I can help?" Because she hadn't really said, had she? I didn't think she had. At least . . . it didn't seem like she had.

I was late to lunch. All the rolls were gone by the time I arrived and most of the slaw as well. Louise left her place at one of the other tables and came to sit beside me.

I glanced up toward her. "You're already finished?"

She shrugged. "My hips are too big, and all those new dress styles might as well have been made for boys, so I'm on a diet."

"Which one? That Hay diet?" I could never remember how it went, whether you were supposed to eat meat with potatoes or without and whether or not you could eat cheese. It was beyond me how anyone could starve themselves to death on purpose.

"That one didn't work. I'm on the grapefruit one now. You can eat anything you want as long as you eat grapefruit with it." Louise glanced up as Mary joined us. "Only . . . I don't really care for grapefruit."

"Shouldn't take long to start working, then."

Mary elbowed Louise. "Did you hear Irene telling us girls about the cigarette diet?"

I nearly retched. "Cigarette diet! People eat cigarettes?"

Irene must have heard her name, for she sat down at the table as if gracing us with her presence. "No. You smoke them instead of eating dessert."

I stabbed at my fish with a fork. "Sounds like a bunch of nonsense to me."

"Only because you can't stand the smoke. Bet you wish you could."

She already knew I wished I could. We'd talked about it when we'd roomed together, how our fondest daydreams included walking around in a glamorous, smoke-colored haze. Only now she was the one actually doing it.

"Don't worry." Irene bent close as she got up. "There's a new tapeworm diet. All you'd have to do is swallow a pill that has a tapeworm egg in it and before you know it, all your unstylish curves will be gone!" She smiled as she left.

Mary scowled at her. "With friends like that . . . ! What'd you ever do to her?"

"Nothing." I'd done nothing at all. I put my fork down. I wasn't hungry anymore.

Louise inched her chair closer. "So, I never had the chance to ask you. Did he?"

"Did who what?" I was still thinking about Irene. We'd been the best of friends at the beginning of the year, and now all of a sudden, she was . . . *mean*.

"Did Prince ever pin you?"

"First of all, his name is *Griffin*. Second of all, *no*. And third of all, *he's not going to*. He's never even asked me on a date."

"He might as well have. You're the only girl he ever talks to."

I was? Really? "Well . . ." Well. That was something I hadn't really noticed before.

Louise patted my hand. "Don't worry. He's going to. I promise you he's going to."

"But I don't—"

"What you need to do is take your mind off it. Why don't we go to Billings & Stover for a soda in an hour, after we've finished packing."

An hour wasn't quite enough time for me to finish. I'd thrown the contents of my desk drawers into the trunk and found that jar of cream that belonged to the lid, but I hadn't even started emptying my closet. I figured I could do it once I got back. As I took one last look over the room, I realized there were some big puffy dirt-colored balls of goodness-knew-what in the corners. I used the toe of my shoe to scrape them out and hurry them along into the hallway where Mrs. Smith was going to have someone come along later and sweep up behind us. I took one last look again and noticed a whole bunch of dust on the windowsill. I'd already packed my handkerchiefs and didn't have anything to wipe it off with anymore, so I picked up the hem of my skirt to do it and found it wouldn't reach. No one was around to do any looking, so I just sat down on the sill and wiggled along the length of it. As I left the room brushing my bottom off,

I realized I'd marked up the tips of my shoes with the dust balls and wasn't that just perfect because it was one more thing my mother would be able to scold me about.

I was debating whether to try to find something to wipe them off with or hope that I could just sneak up the back stairs once I got home when I saw Irene come out of her room balancing a stack of hatboxes with one hand as she tried to close her door with the other.

I almost turned around and went back into my room, but she'd already seen me by then.

"Ellis! Could you—would you mind helping me?"

Well, yes, in fact, I did mind! "Are you planning on insulting me again? Or abandoning me in expectation that I'll just fill in for you?" My goodness! When I was mad I sounded just like my mother.

Her face flushed. "Listen, Ellis. I'm really sorry for the other night at your play. I told Floyd not to come for me until after it was over, but he forgot and then, once he was there . . . well . . . he hates waiting for me, and it put him in a bad mood." She looked over at me. "Trust me, you don't want to be around him when he's in a bad mood!"

I took two of the boxes off the top of her stack. "Is he the one who gave you the black eye?"

Her eyes darted from mine. "He didn't mean it. He really didn't. I'd made him mad, but he was so apologetic. He promised it would never happen again." She tried hard to smile, but her lips were wobbling.

"Isn't he . . . I mean . . . I've never actually met him, I've only seen him from a very long way off, but isn't he a little old for you?"

"We can't all date the captain of the Harvard football team, can we?" She grabbed the boxes from me and tried to put them on top of hers, only she lost her grip and the stack of them cascaded to the floor.

"Oh! I'm sorry." I stooped to retrieve them. "Let me help. I didn't really mean to—"

"You never mean anything, and you're always so nice about it. But not everything can be fixed by being sorry!"

"I never said it could be."

"I'm not like you and I never will be. No matter how hard I try, it just won't work. And I want to be somebody someday, don't you understand?"

Of course I understood. I wanted to be someone too. Someone different than I already was. "Irene, I—"

"And sometimes you have to take risks and—and overcome your inhibitions in order to make things happen!"

"If you say so."

She took a deep breath and tried on a smile, but I could tell she wasn't really happy. "Anyway, I have to go now. Floyd's waiting for me."

Louise and Mary were waiting for me, but I let Irene go on down the stairs by herself before I followed her.

Mary, Louise, and I were halfway to Billings & Stover when I realized what day it was. "It's Friday!"

Mary was looking at me as if I'd gone mad. "Sure. And yesterday was Thursday."

"No! It's *Friday*." Good grief! "The Chilton Club. Symphony! I have to go." Last time I'd completely forgotten about

something really important, I'd asked my father to get me one
of those clever little books he always carried around in his coat
pocket so that I could transcribe everything I was supposed to
remember into it, things like symphony. But I suppose it only
worked if I actually remembered to take it out of my desk and
look at it once in a while. And now it was probably buried
at the bottom of my trunk. I ran down the sidewalk, shoes
flapping beneath me. As I rounded the corner to the dormitory, I saw the car already waiting. Oysters and clambakes!

I rapped on the window. The driver got out. Bowed.

"Just—five minutes."

"Yes, Miss Eton, but—"

"Five."

I bolted up the stairs and down the hall. Martha was standing outside my door, wringing her hands. "Something's happened."

Something was always happening to Martha. There was
always some strange noise in the hall or some odd shadow
in her room. "Where?"

She nodded toward my door as she chewed on her lip. "In
there."

"In . . . *my* room?"

She nodded again.

"Are you sure?"

"There was . . . well, there was a . . . it sounded like . . .
a boom."

"A *boom*! When?"

"About . . ." She consulted the watch that was pinned to
the bosom of her blouse, turning it nearly upside down and
twisting the material in the process. "Four minutes ago."

In *my* room? I put the key in the lock and turned it. Opened the door slowly. Stuck my head inside. My room wasn't very big, and most of my things were already packed, so it didn't take long to determine there was no one there inside.

I pushed the door wide and stepped in. "There's nothing—" But . . . there *was* something. There was a smell. A very strong, very yeasty, stench. Like . . . a moldy loaf of bread. Or . . . overripe grape juice.

Irene!

I pulled my closet door open and nearly gagged. Or cried. I couldn't decide which to do. Irene's jug of grape juice had exploded, spewing the wine all over my clothes. Most of my dresses and all of my skirts were dripping with it. And now I had . . . "What time is it?"

She cocked her head and screwed her blouse around again. "One thirteen."

I only had two minutes to figure it all out.

Her nose was twitching like a rabbit's. "What's that smell? It's revolting!"

"Irene's wine."

"Wine!" Martha's brows rose alarmingly. "But you can't have wine in your room. It's against the—"

"Yes, I know! But what am I supposed to do about it now?" And what was I supposed to wear to symphony?

I rifled through my dresses and found all of them soaked but for one. And even that had been stained along the hem, but since it was already red, maybe no one would notice. I'd seen the dress back in October and knew I had to have it for the Christmas ball, so I'd used up the allowance money I'd been saving for Hollywood to buy it. But I'd come down with a head cold, and not even a teakettle's worth of lemon and honey water had been able to cure me in time for the dance.

I had never worn it, but I was going to now. There was no help for it. I couldn't go to symphony in my vest blouse, and the red dress was the only thing left.

Martha stood there blinking as I shed my blouse and skirt and pulled the dress on over my head.

"Isn't that a bit . . . formal? I don't know if you want to—"

"Just . . . don't say anything." I pulled my squirrel-collared coat from the back of my closet and pulled it on, fastening it tight around the dress.

"You can't wear *that*! It must be eighty degrees outside."

But I couldn't wear a red satin evening dress with beaded trim to symphony by itself, either. "Do you have a hat I can borrow?"

5

Of course Martha's hat was an old-style toque, but beggars couldn't be choosers. At some point the driver came up to my room in the dormitory. I suppose it was all right since most of the other girls had gone home. I threw the rest of my closet into the trunk, and he latched the lid, lifted it to his shoulder, and started off down the hall.

By the time we reached the colonnaded symphony hall, I was truly and officially late. Though the orchestra was not yet playing, everyone had already abandoned the lobby for the concert hall. I slipped into the seat next to Mother's. She was reading the program, but she glanced up as I sat down. "Why on earth are you wearing—?" She studied me with a worried frown and then put out a hand to touch my forehead. "Are you ill?"

I dodged her hand. "I'll be fine."

The orchestra struck up the beginning strains of an opus from Brahms' *Academic Overture*. I settled into my seat, determined not to fidget, not to start humming, not to do any of the things I normally did.

Mother glanced in my direction, her nose wrinkling. "*What* is that smell?"

I dipped my chin and sniffed at the dress beneath my coat. Oh crumb!

"Ellis? Have you been *drinking*?"

Before I knew it, she'd grabbed hold of me by the ear and was dragging me through the hall, out into the lobby.

"I don't have the words—! I've known you to disobey me and disregard me and to—to—be an utter disaster! But I've never known you to break the law!" She stepped closer as an usher came out from the hall. "You're an Eton. You have a reputation to uphold. You have *our* reputation to uphold! And that doesn't have anything to do with becoming mixed up in . . . in . . . illegal alcohol!"

"I didn't—"

"This is unbelievable."

"It wasn't—"

"This really is the last straw!"

"It wasn't my fault!"

"Oh? Someone dragged you into one of those . . . those . . . what do they call them?"

"Speakeasies?"

"Speakeasies!" Mother threw up her hands. "And forced you to take a drink? Is that what happened? Really, Ellis, I just don't know what to do with you anymore."

"It wasn't like that at all! Someone put a jug of grape juice in my closet and—"

"And now you're making *bathtub gin*?"

"In my *closet*, not my bathtub. I don't have a bathtub. At

least not one of my own. Not at the dormitory. And I'm not making anything at all. *It wasn't mine.*"

Her eyes had grown round in horror. "The dormitory? You did this at the dormitory?"

"I didn't do it. It wasn't me." It was Irene.

She pressed her lips into a firm, straight line. "This really is the end. With your inattention to basic proprieties and your propensity to scandalize the entire city, you've left me with no choice. I'm going to have to send you to Granny."

I heard myself gasp. Granny lived way out in the woods, miles from nowhere. She was a hundred years old, and the only reason her heart kept beating was because she was too stubborn to let it stop. She was a bent, sour-mouthed widow who didn't have time for foolishness and had never liked me at all. If my mother made me go to Granny's, all hope of Hollywood, all hope of life in general, was gone. "Please don't. I promise . . . anything! I'll promise you anything! Please don't make me go!"

She looked at me, her eyes swimming in pools of sudden tears. "I just don't know how I failed you, but I must have. If I'd done the right things, then you wouldn't be this way . . . would you?"

So now I was all her fault?

"Just . . . go wait over there in that chair."

When we got home, my mother told me I'd have to speak to my father about the wine after supper and that my sister was there for the weekend with my nephews. At least she'd warned me. It's not that I minded the boys, but I did resent how quick Julia always was to assume I'd watch them for her.

"I'll expect you to be on your best behavior. It's time you learned how to set a proper example for the younger generation."

I put a foot to the stairs.

"And we're having that poor Phillips boy over for supper tonight."

Poor Phillips boy. I couldn't help rolling my eyes. My mother must be the only person in the world to think Griff might be poor in any sense of the word. The Phillipses had plenty of money, and Griff was rich as Midas in the adulation of the entire population of the city. The only thing he lacked was a mother. She'd died in the influenza epidemic during the war. "Do we have to?"

"Ellis! You really ought to start treating him like the man he is. You're not a child any longer and—"

I ran on up to the landing, held on to the newel post, and spun myself around the corner and headed up to my room.

"Honestly, Ellis! . . . Don't be late for supper."

I hadn't meant to be.

It's just that I found an old copy of *Movie Weekly* as I was unpacking my trunk. It had a full-color spread of Antonio Moreno's new mansion, which was exactly the kind I was going to buy when I became a movie star. It was one of those Mediterranean-style houses with a sun-splashed courtyard, rounded, red-tile roofed towers, and balconies outlined with iron grillwork. It had a bathroom *inside* the master bedroom, plenty of space, and lots of light. In fact, it was the exact opposite of our old red brick Bulfinch with its boring wood-paneled walls, long dark halls, and wavy glass windowpanes. The magazines said it never got cold in Hollywood and it never rained! I'd be able to leave all my coats and sweaters behind, which would make it that much easier to go. There wasn't anything at all I would miss about Boston.

Except . . . except for Griff.

No matter how much I told myself I wouldn't, I knew that I would. I wished I were different. I wish God had made me better or smarter or *something* that would make me deserving of Griff's attention. Something that would let me feel right about accepting his pin. Sometimes, though it wasn't too terribly often, I almost wondered what it might be like to be married to him, even though I knew I couldn't. Shouldn't. I mean, I could marry him; it would be as easy as accepting his fraternity pin, and then accepting his marriage proposal, and then actually getting married . . . but the point of it all was that I shouldn't because I wouldn't be any good for him. My, but it was hard to do the right thing!

I was halfway through an article on Nita Naldi's latest movie when I realized the house had gone silent. There was no creaking from my sister's old room and there was no thumping up in the attic where Mother still kept the nursery for my nephews. I pushed away from my pillow and tiptoed to the door. As I opened it, I heard a murmur of voices from downstairs amidst the clatter of silverware scraping against plates.

Oysters and clambakes!

What to do? I chewed on a fingernail. I could go downstairs and endure the scowls of my mother, the reprimand of my father, and the smirks of my brother and sister or . . . I could stay in my room and starve to death.

It wasn't much of a choice, so I determined to make the best of it. At least Griff was down there. They wouldn't yell at me in front of him.

I slipped from my skirt and blouse and into a flounced orange georgette dress and then exchanged my old T-straps for my satin pumps. Taking up a hand mirror for a peek at my hair, I pulled a face at myself.

Although I wore my pumps down the Oriental-carpeted hall, I pulled them off when I reached the front stair. Holding them in one hand, I sat on the banister and slid to the landing. Touching down with one foot, I slipped past the newel post and then slid down the final flight. I froze mid-slide as one of my nephews glanced over.

His brows rose, and his mouth fell open.

Griff reached over and stuffed a piece of roll into it.

After slipping my shoes on, I took a deep breath and walked into the dining room as if I expected everyone to be delighted to see me. In my experience, it never hurt to hope. But Mother followed my progress to the empty chair beside Griff with narrowed eyes.

At least Father waited until I was seated before he spoke. His mustache was twitching and his eyes were glaring at me from behind his old-fashioned wire-rimmed eyeglasses. "So glad you decided to join us, Ellis. Are we to feel honored?"

Across from me, my little brother, Lawrence, snickered. I kicked him—hard—under the table. He choked on his lamb chop.

"Whatever are they teaching at Radcliffe that they've neglected manners and common courtesy?" My sister, Julia, could always be counted on to be snide.

"Latin and mathematics. Along with English literature. And the dissection of frogs."

She tried to smile and failed.

Griffin was hiding a smile of his own beneath his napkin.

"Are they green *inside* too?" My nephew Marshall looked as if he really wanted to know, but he was only five years old, so it was hard to tell.

His younger brother, Henry, tried to talk around a mouthful of food. "I like frogs."

Mother cut in on him. "Griffin was just telling us about his plans for the summer."

Well, thank goodness, because I had no idea what the inside of a frog looked like! I'd fainted dead away the moment Louise had slit it open. I glanced over at Griff as I cut into my lamb chop. "What are you doing?"

"I've agreed to intern for the Governor's Finance Commission."

At least he sounded excited about it; it sounded rather boring to me. I gave him another glance.

Mother was smiling. "The governor requested him. *By name.*"

He waved a hand as if to dismiss my mother's compliment. "It's only because he's my uncle."

Father was shaking his head. "Doesn't mean he had to. He wouldn't have requested you if he didn't think you'd do a good job of it."

Mother was rapping Marshall on the elbow with the handle of her knife.

Ow! I knew how that felt, and I couldn't help but sympathize as I saw tears spring to his eyes.

"If I wanted to see your elbows at the table, I would have set a place for them."

His chin trembled as he cradled his elbow in his hand.

Griff leaned around behind me toward him. "Hey. Maybe after supper we could throw around the football. See if you've got what it takes to play for Harvard."

Marshall's eyes brightened.

"Can I come too? We could show them what a real play looks like." Lawrence might have thought he sounded indifferent, and at the age of eighteen he was definitely practicing, but here he had misjudged. He was practically begging.

"*May* I come too." My mother pounced on the mistake like a cat.

Marshall turned to her with a frown. "I don't think you'd like it, Grandmother. You might get your dress dirty. Can Auntie Ellis come, though?"

"No." My mother answered before I could. "There are some things your grandfather and I need to discuss with her."

"You're not going to yell at her, are you?"

"I never raise my voice at anyone."

Griff gave my neck a squeeze at the back where no one else could see it.

"How are your grades, Ellis? Got your finals back yet?" Lawrence was smirking.

I shouldn't have kicked him. I knew I shouldn't have. "They're fine." Fine enough, considering I wasn't planning to return to college in the fall.

"And how are the plans for Cosmopolitan Club coming?" Now my sister was ganging up on me too!

I shrugged. Mary had been sick the day I was supposed to put the announcement in the *Radcliffe News,* and I'd forgotten all about it while I'd walked with her over to the doctor's and then waited with her while she'd been examined. I'd missed an economics exam that day, too, while I'd gone down to the pharmacy for her medicine—which was the reason my grade was so bad. I'd tried to explain my absence, but Professor Whitmore accused me of offering excuses and wouldn't even listen. "How about you, Julia? How are *your* clubs coming?"

She refused to answer, just like I knew she would. Since she'd gotten married, unlike the rest of her old college friends, she hadn't gotten involved in anything at all. It was almost like she was trying to avoid everyone.

Griff leaned in toward the table as he addressed my mother. "Ellis is always busy, every time I see her."

Mother put down her fork and gestured for the butler to collect the plates as she eyed me. "Yes. Ellis is very prolific. For every project she completes and cause she takes on, she seems to leave two unfinished."

She made it seem as if I didn't even try! I wish she could be me for just one day so she'd see what a lot of trouble I went to in order to keep everything from turning out even worse. How would she like to wake up each morning knowing that as hard as she tried, no matter what she did, everything was likely doomed to failure before she even started? Sometimes I wondered if it was worth it to even get out of bed.

"Why don't we have dessert?" Father smiled as if everyone

was in agreement, no one had taken offense, and everything was fine.

As the sherry was poured, Griff asked after the telephone company. Telephones were my father's favorite project. Though he was chairman of the board of the telephone company, his interest went well beyond the proprietary. He was enamored of receivers and handsets and ringing tones of all sorts. And he was always talking about the modern lunchrooms and bathrooms and working hours the hello girls down at the switchboards had been given.

"Business is splendid! There are forty thousand telephones in the city and more being added every day. Next year I suppose we'll have to put in an automatic dialer—just no other way around it."

Griff found my hand under the table and gave it a squeeze. "I've heard about those. You just pick up the handset and dial straight through. But . . . do you think people can really be depended on to dial by themselves, without an operator? I'd think it would be too confusing trying to remember a four-digit number."

"That's what I told him." Mother was looking at Griff with an approving eye. "How can anyone be expected to memorize a telephone number? And then dial it without making a mistake? If you let people do it for themselves, it's just asking for trouble. Leave it to the professionals, that's what I say."

After dessert had been cleared away, after Lawrence and Marshall had dragged Griff out the back, Mother sighed a long, heavy sigh as she glared at me from the foot of the table. "Would you like to explain yourself?"

What was the use of an explanation? Wouldn't it be better just to get to the point? "I'm sorry, I really am, but it wasn't my fault."

"Nothing is ever your fault and still things keep happening! What you need, Ellis, is to focus and stop wasting all the chances life is giving you. You need to start . . ." She shook her head, but I knew what she wanted to say. I needed to start buckling down and applying myself. "You're not just anybody. You're an Eton. And if Etons just went around doing whatever they wanted, shirking their responsibilities, then what on earth would this world come to? Somebody, somewhere, has to step up and do for those who can't. *We* are those somebodies, Ellis. And you are one of us."

Be somebody.

That's what I wanted. That's exactly what I wanted. I wanted to be somebody different. I wanted to be somebody famous. The leading lady. The one people would gaze at in the darkness of a movie palace and dream of becoming. For once in my life, I wanted to be the one everyone else wanted to be.

And being somebody is exactly what my mother wanted for me too. Although her Somebody wasn't my Somebody, given enough time, I was sure I could make her proud of me. Who wouldn't be proud of me when my name was up on a marquee, surrounded by blinking lights?

My father was looking at us with a mystified expression. "But . . . you said you were sorry, Ellis." He glanced up at my mother. "Didn't she say she was sorry?"

Mother nodded.

"For . . . what? Exactly?"

My mother told him about the wine.

"But—! I don't understand how—!"

Mother's lips had folded into a grim line. "Go on, Ellis. Explain yourself."

"I told one of the girls she could keep some grape juice in my closet. And being in the dark like that, I guess it started to . . . well . . ." It had done exactly what the label had warned it would do.

My father sighed. "I can guess what happened. But I don't understand why she would ask something like that of you. You do understand if anyone had found out about this, they might have thought the worst of you. Prohibition is the law in this land."

I didn't see why they were so upset about it. It wasn't mine; I hadn't drunk any of it. And even if I had, I don't know why they would have cared. "We still drink sherry here. And you still drink sherry at the club. . . ."

"That's different."

"But how?"

"Well . . . you see, the law isn't meant for people like us. It was meant for the poor, and all those immigrants, people who aren't able to handle their alcohol like we are."

"So then why does it have to apply to me?" Not that I ever would drink alcohol myself. I couldn't stand the smell. It reminded me too much of Granny's cough tonic.

"It applies to you because you're an Eton. You have to set a good example. You might think we're old-fashioned, but your mother and I know about college hijinks, so we've allowed for some latitude in our expectations. But I know I speak for both of us when I say we consider this incident beyond the pale. Do you understand what I'm saying?"

"You're saying . . . I should do as you say."

"Exactly."

"And not as you do."

Mother and Father exchanged a glance. Father cleared his throat. "You've grown up living a sheltered life, so we know this can be difficult to understand. It's a bit complicated, the way Prohibition works, but trust us when we say that as reasonable adults who practice self-discipline, we understand what we're doing."

"But I don't? Is that what you're saying?" I didn't mean to be testy, and honestly, I didn't care, but it didn't seem quite fair. I folded my napkin and put it on the table beside my plate. Then I stood.

Mother held out her hand as I walked by.

I put mine into it, and she drew me toward her, putting her other hand to my cheek. As I bent, she kissed me, squeezing my hand before letting it drop. "We just don't want you to fall in with the wrong element."

"I won't." At least I didn't plan on it, and I don't think anyone would quite consider Irene the wrong element, and even if she was, I wasn't falling in with her. I ought to have just left without saying anything else, but considering the circumstances, I didn't have much choice. "About the closet . . . ?"

That warm, rather maternal look in my mother's eyes sharpened with suspicion. "Yes?"

"When the grape juice exploded, you might say it got on most everything."

Her brow rose. "And by that you mean?"

"The grape juice was really quite dark colored, and most of my spring and summer clothes were rather light colored and . . ." I'd done it again. I'd managed to extinguish every bit of lingering affection and replace it with disappointment and despair.

"Oh, Ellis."

I started my summer off the next day at church, helping the Missionary Aid Society prepare some barrels to be shipped to a church in Manchuria. Mostly it involved sorting through huge piles of clothing that had been collected in spring and separating out girls' clothing from boys' and men's from women's.

It made me wish I had some money of my own to donate, but I'd used it all on dresses and movies and ice cream sodas. And even if I hadn't, I would have been saving it for a train ticket to Hollywood.

Much of the clothing appeared to have been pulled from trunks in which they'd been stored for ten or twenty years along with camphor and tobacco snuff. It made me want to pinch my nose. I held up a dress. "Don't you think . . . ?" It was so old-fashioned.

My mother looked over at me. "What did you say, Ellis?"

"It's just that . . . I wondered . . . are these clothes for the missionaries or the Manchurians?"

"I don't know. Why? Does it matter?"

I turned the dress round so she could see the high-collared, ruffled front yoke of it. "It might if those missionaries read *Ladies' Home Journal*."

"I should think people who don't have very much would be happy with whatever they're given."

Maybe. I folded it up and placed it on the pile waiting to be put into a barrel marked *For Ladies*. "Maybe someone can make something from it. Like . . . some sort of cushion." Or something. "Do you think any of them even have one of those old corsets to go with it?" Granny still wore those sorts of contraptions, and I had often wondered if they weren't partly to blame for her chronic ill-temper.

"It's not how you look on the outside that's important."

I knew that. I'd known that since forever. But wouldn't you tend to behave better if your outsides looked nice as well? "But no one's going to fit in any of these dresses if they don't have a corset."

Mother was frowning. "You might be right. . . ."

I took the dress from the pile and walked over to Mrs. Cooper, who'd been bossing everyone around all morning. As I was explaining about how the dress was so old-fashioned and how it probably needed a corset and wondering whether anyone in Manchuria would be able to wear it at all, I was struck with inspiration. "If you want to give them away, then we could use them down at Radcliffe."

"Radcliffe? For what?"

"For the theater."

"The *theater*!" Her chins were quivering.

"Sure. That coat over there would be terrific for a dastardly villain, and this dress could maybe be used for some consumptive old granny and the dress over there could be a costume for a medieval lady, maybe, if we do Shakespeare next year—"

"These are meant for the missionaries!"

"But that's what I mean. Just because you send them doesn't mean they'll like them or even ever wear them, especially if they don't have any place to stage theatrical events."

"What are you trying to say?"

My mother had come to stand beside us. "Ellis, I think that—"

"I'm just saying if *I* were sent all of these . . . I just wonder if they're really going to be very useful, that's all."

"People who are destitute aren't in a position to be choosy."

"Then maybe that's why we ought to be careful what we send them."

"Are you saying our charity isn't appreciated?"

Was I? I guess . . . maybe . . . "Yes. I suppose I am."

Her mouth fell open.

"We ought to collect money next autumn and send it to them so they can buy the kind of clothes they're used to wearing. They'd be new then . . . or at least not quite so old."

She gasped. "But do you know what they wear over there?"

"No." But it had to be something more fashionable than all of these discarded clothes. "Do you know?"

"Well . . . no. But I'm sure we wouldn't be sending barrels of clothes to them if their own clothing were adequate and appropriate."

"I really think I should pack up all of these and have someone take them down to Radcliffe, and we could store them at the theater until next term when we can . . ." But *we* wouldn't be doing anything with them. I wouldn't be there next year.

Mother was tugging on my arm. "I think what would be nice is if you could sit down in this chair, Ellis." She swung one away from the table and pushed me down into it. "And you can read to us from the Scriptures as we finish packing these barrels."

"But I only wanted to—"

She handed me a Bible. "Why don't you read Romans?"

I made a face before I could stop myself. Reading Romans was like taking cod-liver oil. It was the kind of thing people always said to do because it would be good for you, but it was never any fun while you did it. All it talked about was sin, sin, and more sin. If I had talked about sin that much at home when I was younger, I would have gotten my mouth washed out with a bar of Ivory soap. But Mrs. Cooper was nodding and all the other women seemed to be in agreement, so I took the Bible and opened it. At least it would be better than sorting through all those old clothes. The inside of my nose was still tingling from all that camphor.

I read about the apostle Paul wanting to visit Rome and the wrath of God and then about some things that made the ladies hurry me along to the second chapter. After that there were lots of verses about the law followed by another passage I was kindly asked to skip, which made me wonder why all those verses were there in the first place if they weren't meant to be read. I started to despair of ever getting to the end of it all when the words suddenly started to make sense. "'So the trouble is not with the law, for it is spiritual and good. The trouble is with me, for I am all too human, a slave to sin. I don't really understand myself, for I want to do what is right, but I don't do it.'"

I did that kind of thing all the time! I read that part aloud twice, hoping Mother was listening.

"'And I know that nothing good lives in me, that is, in my sinful nature. I want to do what is right, but I can't. I want to do what is good, but I don't. I don't want to do what is wrong, but I do it anyway.'"

That's all I ever seemed to do: the wrong thing, all the time.

"'Oh, what a miserable person I am!'"

Was that ever the truth.

I kept on reading and got through most of the rest of Romans before the barrels were pronounced packed. We didn't reach home until after eleven, and as we walked into the front hall, the maid bobbed a curtsy. "There's a Miss Winslow to see you, Miss Eton."

Mother was eyeing me. "Would that be Janie?"

"Janie? . . . Janie!" And all at once I remembered. I'd promised to meet her at ten for some reason so important I knew I couldn't possibly ever forget it, but then I had. Why did I always have to be so stupid? "Where is she?"

"Downstairs. In the kitchen."

Oysters and clambakes! In the kitchen? Where her mother used to work? "For goodness' sake, don't leave her there!" She was probably crying her eyes out by now. And it was very nearly noon. "Bring her up to my room along with some tea and something to go with. Sandwiches, maybe?"

"There's a lovely brown bread just come from the oven."

"Just as long as it has something on top of it. Or in between it." I was famished and goodness knew Janie probably was too.

I had just enough time to pull the covers up over my bed and take off the hat I'd borrowed from Mother when the maid knocked on the open door, set a tea tray down on my desk, and then left.

I drew Janie into the room. "I'm so sorry I forgot, but I'm here now."

She just stood there in the doorway, wringing a handkerchief between her hands.

I poured a cup of tea and held it out to her. "So . . . what did you need to see me about?"

A frown settled between her eyes. "You—you promised to help me. Don't you remember?"

"Yes. Of course. Of *course* I remember doing that! It's just—I don't quite remember what it was I promised to help you *with*."

"Ellis!"

"But I'll still do it. Don't worry. I can do it."

"If you can't remember to meet me at your own house, then how are you going to remember to fill in for me at work?"

"Do what?"

"Fill in for me. Down at the switchboard. For two weeks."

"Two *weeks*! You want me to work for you for two weeks?"

"Yes!" She said it with no little exasperation.

"Doing what?"

"Replacing me. Pretending to *be* me. I already told you all this, don't you remember? I need to take my mother back to Maine to be buried and find my father to let him know what's happened."

"You have a father?" There was a Mr. Winslow? "How long have you had a father?" And why hadn't I known about it?

"Of course I have a father. Where do you think we went all those summers when you were down at the shore?" Now she was looking as if she were mad. As mad as a person like Janie could look. Her mouth was pinched in at the corners and her neck had gone red in splotches.

I'd never seen anyone look like that, so I tried to make my mouth do the same thing, but I don't think I succeeded. I'd have to practice in front of a mirror. It might come in handy to be able to pull a face like that.

"He's a fisherman up in Maine. And this time of year, he's probably already gone—"

"Gone where?"

"*Fishing!* Which is why I need some time."

Time? "In order to . . . ?"

Throwing up her hands, she stalked to the door. I'd never seen her so mad! "Never mind. Forget the whole thing. I need someone I can count on, and I can see you're not that person."

"Wait. I know I'm not the most . . . I know I mess things up, but I can do this. I want to do this. I feel terrible about your mother, and I want to help you, I really do. Please. Let me try."

It was fascinating, watching suspicion and desperate need war in her eyes. As soon as she was gone, I'd practice that look too. Finally she sighed. "I don't know who else I'd get to do it. You're the only one I know who doesn't already have a job or isn't married, and you're the only one I know who could even pretend to be me."

I threw my arms around her and gave her a hug. "I won't let you down!" This was a perfect opportunity. The role I'd had in my own play had been make-believe, but this was real. And I was going to make sure I succeeded!

llis?" Janie was frowning as she disentangled me from her neck.

I blinked. "What?"

"Stop looking like that. Every time you look that way, something bad happens."

"Nothing bad is going to happen. I promise. Only . . . you'll be away two weeks, and I'll be working your job . . . do you think . . . could I keep the money I'll be earning for you?"

"All of it?" Her voice wavered. "I guess . . . I suppose that's only fair. . . ."

This was perfect! It would solve all my problems. I'd work for two weeks, I'd earn some money I *would not spend*—no matter how badly I wanted to—and then I'd leave for Hollywood! I'd be gone before we even left for the summer house at the shore. I could have laughed out loud, I was that excited, but I didn't think it would be proper. I had a job to do, and judging by Janie's face, it was no laughing matter. People with jobs had to be serious, reliable, and dependable. In short, I would need to be the very opposite of me. Everything would depend on how well I played this role. I couldn't have asked for a better opportunity. "Talk to me for a minute."

" . . . why?"

"So I can get your accent down. I'll have to be able to do it if you want me to pretend to be you."

"You'll have to do more than talk like me."

You'll have to do more than talk like me. You'll have to do more than talk like me. "You'll have to do more than talk like me." No. That wasn't it. It didn't sound like she sent her words through her nose the way I did. I reached out my hand and cupped her nose. "Say that again."

She batted my hand away. "Pay attention!"

Pay attention. Pay attention. "Pay attention." I had it! "How was that?"

"Ellis, how are you going to keep my job for me if you sit down at the switchboard and don't even know how to work it?"

Oh. Well, I hadn't gotten round to thinking about that part of it yet. "What do I have to do?"

She opened up her pocketbook and took a sheet of paper from it. Unfolding it, she walked over to my bed and spread it out across the blanket. "This is what my position board looks like."

I went over and took a look. "What's a position board?"

"It's my switchboard at the Tremont Exchange, down by Washington Street. It's where I patch through calls. I'm a B operator at position board number 10."

"Maybe I should take some notes." I rifled through my desk to find a bit of paper and a pencil. "Position board 10. And how will I know where it is?"

"It has a 10 at the top. See?" She pointed toward her drawing. "And my shift starts at seven."

I felt my hopes sink. "In the morning?"

"In the morning. And you can't be late, or you'll get me fired."

"Don't be late." I wrote it in big letters on my paper.

"When you come in, you'll sit on the stool in front of the board. It's a high one and it spins, but you're not supposed to turn around. And you can't wrap your legs around it either."

"Fine. I'll just sit there."

"I mean it."

I wrote down about the stool in big letters too.

"Just in front of you will be a headset looped over a hook. It's connected to the board. You'll put it on over your ears and adjust the mouthpiece to sit about right here"—she pointed to her collarbone—"so you'll be able to speak into it. It's like a receiver."

"So I come in, I sit on the stool, and I put on the headset."

Janie nodded. "Are you sure you're getting all this?"

"What could be simpler?"

She eyed me with doubt, but then she turned back to her drawing. "The A operator receives the telephone call, asks for the number, and then passes it to you. Since you're the B operator, all you have to do is connect that caller to the number they're calling."

"How?"

"Do you see this switchboard? Right here, along the bottom, close to the board, are pairs of jacks."

"On that part that looks like a little desk?"

"Yes. If the A operator is passing you a call, a white light will flicker somewhere up on the board in front of you. You'll take up a jack from the bottom of the board—any one you want—and you'll plug it in beneath the light. It will have a long cord attached to it."

"And what do I do with that?"

"Nothing. Just ignore it. So after you plug the jack in, you'll flip the switch beneath the pair of cords."

"But . . . it's not a pair anymore if one of them is plugged into the board."

"Right. But the switch is located beneath where they both were, on that desk in front of you."

I nodded.

"That switch connects you to operator A. You'll say, 'Number, please' and she'll respond with the number you need to call. All you have to do is pick up the second jack and plug it into the right number. Don't forget: You always have to work with pairs in order to complete the circuit. Plugging in that second jack connects the call."

"And how will I know if it's the right number?"

"My board only has a hundred and twenty telephone numbers. They're all marked. If a call comes to you, then it has to be to one of them."

"Right."

"So you connect that second jack and you listen for the other end to pick up. If someone picks up, then you flip the switch again to pass the call. If it's busy, then you tell the caller. And when they hang up, you unplug both jacks and put them back."

There seemed to be an awful lot of jacks involved in this.

"Just remember, you always work with *pairs* of jacks. You

can't connect just one and expect anything to happen. Understand?"

I nodded. I thought I did. I hoped so.

"But you still have to know how to talk to the callers."

"That's what I was practicing!" Although I still wasn't sure I'd gotten her accent right.

"You have to talk with a smile in your voice."

"A smile *in* my voice? Should I write that down?"

"Yes! No matter what a caller says to you, under no circumstances can you reply with anything but 'I'm sorry, sir.' Or 'ma'am.' You have to be polite."

"Of course I'll be polite."

"'A soft answer turneth away wrath.'"

"I'll be good. I promise."

She gave me a long look. Then she sighed. "I wouldn't ask you to do this if I didn't have to."

"Of course you have to. Everything will be fine."

She took a deep breath as if she needed extra courage. "Let's talk about these jacks here." She was pointing to a row that was at the very bottom of the board, just above the desk. "This far one is for the chief operator. If a caller has an emergency, then just connect the call there and flip the switch to pass it through. She'll know what to do. And the rest of that line is for operators passing calls out of the exchange. The first three are for long-distance calls and the rest are for other exchanges in the city."

Oh dear. I hoped I would remember all of that.

"But don't worry. You shouldn't have to use them because you're a B operator. You really should only have to patch calls through to the numbers on your board."

Good.

"Just . . . pass through the calls like you're supposed to and avoid the chief operator and the supervisor."

"How will I know who they are?"

"The chief, Miss Hastings, sits at a desk behind the bank of switchboards, and the supervisor spends the shift walking up and down the boards. If you keep your head down and don't talk too loudly, then neither of them should notice you're not me. *Please* try not to be noticed!"

"I will. I mean . . . I won't. I won't be noticed."

"Sometimes Miss Hastings listens in on the calls. Just . . . try to talk like me, with a smile in your voice. That's the most important thing."

Smile in my voice. I drew a line underneath that on my paper. She held up her drawing and told me to explain to her how to patch a telephone call through, and then she coached me in talking with a smile in my voice.

"It helps if you actually smile."

I smiled. "Is this better?"

"Ye-es . . . but . . . could you not sound quite so much like your mother?"

I tried again. And again.

"Could you do it one more time?"

I did it one more time, and then she asked me to explain again about patching calls through. I traced the steps on the drawing as I explained and then she asked me to close my eyes while I explained. And then she asked me questions and I explained. And still she didn't seem quite satisfied. "If you could only—"

"I think I patched through about a day's worth of telephone calls just now."

Janie was standing there, biting her lip as she looked at me. "I warned the girl who sits next to me on the shift about you. Doris is her name. I've been living at her place until I can find somewhere else. She knows to expect you and said she'd try to help you if she could."

"*If?*"

"You're not supposed to turn around, remember?"

"Right."

"Or talk to anyone except for your callers. And the A operator."

"But . . . what if I have to use the bathroom?"

"Raise your hand and ask the supervisor before you go. Oh—and the lunch room is one floor up. And I have to warn you—"

"I'll be fine."

"But—"

"Really. I'll do it all perfectly. I won't get into any trouble at all."

"But Miss Hastings is—"

I grabbed her hand and put my other atop it. "Trust me."

"I guess . . . I guess I have to. Just promise me you won't be late."

"I won't be late."

"And you won't forget: two weeks. Starting on Monday."

"*This* Monday?"

"Ellis!"

"It's fine. I'll be fine!"

"I'll return on Sunday. I'll meet you here when I get back into the city in case there's anything you need to tell me before I go back to work."

Monday was rather short notice, but I couldn't go back on my word now.

"So . . . are you going to be ready, Ellis?" Mother was staring at me from the end of the table as we ate supper that night. My father, my brother, my sister, and my nephews were staring at me too.

" . . . for?"

"For summer at the shore." Julia was wearing the expression of long-suffering superiority that had only gotten worse since she'd been married.

"Of course I'm ready for summer at the shore." July and August on Buzzards Bay, mucking up clams, playing tennis, walking miles and miles around sandy inlets, doing a whole lot of nothing at all, just like always. Only, this year, I'd be in Hollywood!

"But have you packed yet?"

My goodness, but Mother was putting a fine point on it. "I will."

"Yes, but when? Haven't you been listening? We're leaving Monday morning."

"*This* Monday morning?"

Lawrence sneered. "I don't know why God bothered to give you two ears since you don't even use one of them."

I would have stuck my tongue out at him, but I didn't want to be a bad example for the boys. "We go to the shore in July and August."

Mother sighed. "Yes. And this year we're also going in June."

"But—"

"You always say you wish you could stay there forever."
Mother was speaking at me the way she spoke to Henry when
he was being unreasonable.

"I know, but—"

"Really, Ellis, you need to pack your things tonight."

"But I can't go!" What was wrong with everybody? Why
hadn't they bothered to tell me? And what about tradition!

"Of course you can go."

"Of course I can't because I have to work for—" Oysters
and clambakes! I'd almost gone and ruined everything. Or . . .
maybe I actually *had* ruined everything. Everyone was staring at me. Still.

"You have to *work*?" Lawrence was trying hard not to laugh
as he said it.

"I do." I busied myself with my ham steak, hoping everyone
would just leave it at that.

"You have a *job*?" Lawrence hooted the words as if he
couldn't quite believe them.

"Of sorts. And it's very important, so I can't go to the
shore just now."

"But it's all been planned. I'm taking the boys. You have
to go!" In Julia's mind, at least, it was all settled.

Mother tapped a spoon against her glass, and immediately,
silence descended. "You'll just have to quit. You can't stay
here in the city by yourself."

Father held up a hand. "Now wait just a minute. If Ellis
has got herself a job, perhaps she should keep it."

I weighed the risk of saying something against the risk of
saying nothing. Janie really needed her job, especially since
Mrs. Winslow had died, and if I went to the shore, then I

wouldn't be there to work it for her and she'd get fired. I had to say something. "It's only for two weeks."

Mother had put down her spoon and pushed back her plate as she met my father's eyes. "What two-week job could possibly be worth giving up extra time at the shore? I've already made our plans."

Father lifted his brow. "I don't know." He directed his gaze toward me. "What sort of job is it?"

I couldn't really say, could I? Because they'd wonder why I was filling in for Janie, and Father was likely to know the chief or the supervisor and if he mentioned Janie just needed a couple weeks off and they gave it to her then I'd have no other way to earn the money I needed. At least, not so quickly. I was doing her a favor and she was doing me a favor and, really, that's all that mattered, wasn't it? "It's a . . . well . . . it's . . . I'll be . . ."

"She just wants to stay since Griffin is staying." Julia screwed up her mouth in a scowl.

"I do not!"

Father looked from her toward me. "Ellis? What sort of job is it?"

"It's . . . helping the less fortunate."

Julia huffed and puffed. "None of the less fortunate expect to be helped in the summer. They can wait until autumn."

Mother gasped. "Really, Julia!"

"Well, they can. I promised the boys Buzzards Bay."

The boys didn't really seem to care as far as I could see. One of them was shoving olives onto his fingertips, and the other was trying to insert the stem of a spoon up his . . . I reached over and tugged it down before Mother could spot him.

"Which less fortunate?" Father asked the question as if he really wanted to know.

"It's, um . . . well . . . it's an orphan." Kind of. I mean, before she'd told me there was a Mr. Winslow, I'd thought Janie was one.

Mother brightened. "Oh! Then you must be helping down at the Orphan Asylum with the pageant for their benefit."

"It's not actually those—"

"Since your father has to stay in the city I suppose . . ."

What on earth pageant was she speaking of? "It's only *one* orphan I'm helping. It's not the asylum. What I meant was—" What on earth was *I* thinking of! Telling them would only get Janie in trouble and cost me a train ticket to Hollywood.

"I think it's wonderful you're choosing to spend your time so charitably." Mother actually smiled at me! "I'm quite proud of you, Ellis."

She was *proud* of me?

"You can come out to the shore once the pageant's over."

"But, Mother—!"

Mother shushed Julia. "Ellis has taken up a cause. We all need to be supportive."

Sunday morning was spent in church, and after a dinner of cold roast, Mother and Lawrence readied for the annual migration to the shore with a great clatter, banging trunks and bags and hatboxes about.

"Have you seen my tennis racket, El?" Lawrence poked his head around my bedroom door.

I looked up from my magazine. "Your what?"

"My racket."

"Um . . . no." Not since I'd borrowed it to use in a play back at the beginning of the term.

"Have you seen yours, then?"

"Sure. It's in my closet."

"Can I take it?"

"Are you taking your blanket robe with you?" It was so much cozier than my silk kimono.

"No."

"Mind if I use it?"

"Go ahead." His muffled answer came from my closet, where he was rooting around.

Which got me to thinking: What did a hello girl wear when she worked at the switchboard? I spent some time that evening going through the few dresses I had that weren't stained with grape juice as I tried to decide. They were all several seasons out of date, but it wasn't as if anyone was going to see me. Still, that didn't mean I had to make a bad impression. I oughtn't be too formal, but at the same time, it wouldn't do to be too casual either. I needed to . . . well, I needed to look like Janie, that's what I needed to do! But what did Janie wear? What had she worn when I'd seen her last? I closed my eyes and tried to conjure her, but I couldn't. All I kept seeing was a gray, shapeless sort of form.

Gray and shapeless.

I didn't have anything gray and shapeless. I had yellow and shapeless. Or white and shapeless. Or lilac or green. I chewed on a nail. Costuming was critical. In order to be the character, I had to look like the character. The important thing was not to be noticed for who I was; I had to be accepted for who I was pretending to be. And in this case, since I was going to be Janie, it was better that I not be noticed at all.

White would have to do.

And I'd wear flesh-colored stockings and my . . . which shoes? Not my old T-straps. But I couldn't wear my silk pumps or my galoshes . . . could I?

No.

At least . . . not the galoshes. Too conspicuous.

I rummaged through my jewelry chest and pulled out a string of beads. Just because I was pretending to be someone else didn't mean I had to look ugly while I was doing it. Now I just needed a hat. I'd darken my brows a bit. I wouldn't wear any lipstick, and I'd hold myself with an air of timidity. I practiced in the mirror for a while, then closed my eyes and imagined myself as Janie and started to walk with that rolled-shoulder way she had.

"Ellis."

My eyes flew open.

Mother was stepping into my room, a sweater draped over her arm and a hatbox dangling from her hand. "What time do you need to wake up in the morning?"

"For . . . ?"

"For the orphans."

"Oh. Oh!" Early. "I need to be there at seven."

"Better make it five thirty, then. That's what I'll tell the maid. And I'll let the kitchen know to have breakfast ready for you at six o'clock sharp. And the driver to be ready for you at six forty-five."

Five thirty! Six! Six forty-five!

She came over to kiss my cheek. "Kiss me now. I won't be up that early in the morning."

I pecked her on the cheek.

"Don't look like that. There are many people who get up far earlier every day. This will be good for you."

Five thirty was dreadfully early in the morning! I wandered around my room for a few minutes trying to remember why it was that I was up and then, once I remembered about the job, I threw on my kimono, washed my face and—where had I put my kohl pencil? And how was I supposed to darken my brows when I couldn't find it? I might have used shoe polish if I'd had some.

I could ask Lawrence.

No. If I woke him, he'd wonder what I was doing and I'd have to explain and then he'd have something else to hold over my head.

What to use? Maybe . . . what was black? Soot? Ashes?

A fountain pen!

Using the mirror, I marked in my brows with the pen. My, but they were dark! Although Janie *was* one of those blondes with very dark brows. I put the pen down and took an entirely objective look at myself. If I narrowed my eyes and didn't look too closely, I was relatively certain I could pass for her.

I combed a bit of Lawrence's petroleum jelly through my

hair and tried to adjust the waves to look like Janie's, praying they would stay. After rolling up my stockings and fastening my dress, I draped the beads around my neck. I practiced talking like Janie for a few minutes, then tiptoed down the stairs and into the dining room.

It had been so long since I'd been up for breakfast at home I'd forgotten what was served. It was toasted brown bread and tea, which made me remember why I'd always thought breakfast not worth having.

"Is there any coffee?"

The maid's brows rose as she shook her head.

That was a shame. I'd gotten used to coffee at Radcliffe.

I dunked my toast into the tea and drank up what was left.

At quarter to seven, the driver helped me into the car, and by five minutes to seven, he was stopping in front of the Female Orphan Asylum.

I leaned forward. "You don't happen to know where the central switchboard is around here . . . ?"

He pointed down the street where several girls were entering a building. I slid across the seat as he opened the door, then stepped down onto the street.

"When shall I pick you up, miss?"

"Oh. At . . . um . . ." I hadn't thought to ask Janie when work ended. "How about five o'clock?"

Janie Winslow. Janie Winslow. I needed to become Janie Winslow. I took a deep breath and reminded myself that being Janie would be as difficult a role to play as I'd ever had. Usually I played characters people paid attention to, but

Janie had never been very remarkable. She was never noticed because she really wasn't very noticeable. So as long as no one noticed me, then they wouldn't notice I wasn't her, and I'd succeed at playing the toughest role I'd ever had! As I walked up the steps toward the building, I turned my shoulders in and looked at the ground as I followed two girls inside. I was hoping they were hello girls, although if they were, then they were much more fashionable than I had thought. Much more fashionable, on the whole, than I was.

I sped my pace to keep up, and when they opened a door, I slipped inside behind them. It turned out to be a bathroom with two long benches and several rows of shelving nailed up along the wall. As the girls unpinned their hats and pushed them up onto a shelf, I did the same. They left their pocketbooks as well.

I did that too.

As they turned to leave, one of them stopped beside me. "I thought you were going to find someone to work for you, Janie!"

"I was." This must be Doris. I felt myself grinning. I couldn't help it. "I did."

"You're not—" She took a step closer. "You're not Janie!"

I'd done it! I'd passed the first and most important of tests!

"You're tall enough and you look enough like her but . . ." She cast an appraising glance at my dress before her gaze dropped to linger on my shoes. "I thought she said she was going to get some girl from that big house her mother had worked in."

"I am. I mean, that's me."

She frowned at me for a moment, then stuck out her hand. "I'm Doris. Pleased to meet you."

I shook it.

She pulled two cards from the wall, handing one to me. "Here." She stuck it into a machine that had a clock face on it. When she drew it out, a hole had been punched into it. "Do yours."

I did the same.

"Follow me, and I'll show you where your board is." She linked her arm through mine as she pulled me toward the door. We approached a room that buzzed with voices. "Stick close."

Three sides of the large room were lined with what had to have been switchboards, but they didn't look at all like Janie's drawing. They were big, and they sprouted all kinds of cords.

Doris elbowed me toward an empty stool. It was so tall I had to climb it just to sit down.

My switchboard friend glanced pointedly at the board toward . . . Ah! *There* was the headset. I put it on, adjusting it at the top of my head so it fit over my ears but as I bent my head forward, I whacked my chin on the mouthpiece.

Ow!

Rubbing my chin, I looked my board over, trying to remember everything Janie had told me. There was the little desk . . . and the pairs of jacks . . . and looming atop it was the switchboard with all kinds of gaping round holes. And—oh! There was a blinking light.

What was it she'd said about blinking lights?

I was . . . I was supposed to . . . work with pairs of jacks. And cords. But . . . what was I supposed to do with them?

Don't turn around.

Speak with a smile in your voice.

Avoid the supervisor.

But what was I supposed to do with the cords?

I snuck a look at Doris but she was just . . . sitting there. I took a peek at the girl who sat on my other side. As I watched, she took up a jack with one of those cords and plugged it— oh! I remembered.

I took a jack just like she had and plugged it in beneath the blinking light. "Number, please."

"Tremont-4624."

"Thank you."

I looked at all the empty holes in the board in front of me. Which one was Tremont-4624? Janie said they'd be marked, but I didn't see any numbers. There had to be some system to it, didn't there? There were two, four . . . ten rows of jacks with two, four, six, eight . . . fifteen columns in each row. And on the sides, the rows were marked off with numbers and . . . oh! I saw it now. They were marked off in groups of fifteen. All right so . . . I made a calculation, counting off numbers, then picked up the second jack and plugged it in.

In my headset I heard a ringing and then the sound of someone picking up on the other end. Thank goodness!

"Hello? Hello?" A male voice.

"Pete? This is Larry. I was wondering, did you want . . ."

I wasn't supposed to be able to hear conversations, was I? It didn't seem like I ought to be able to, but how was I supposed to make the talking go away? I glanced over and saw Doris gesturing toward my shelf.

I looked down, but I couldn't see anything.

Her arm shot past me as she flicked at a switch beneath the pair of cords I'd used and the conversation was cut off.

I remembered now! I was supposed to plug the cords into

95

the jack and flip the switch. I'd forgotten about that switch. But I didn't have time to thank her, I didn't have time to do anything, because another light was already blinking on the board.

I reached down for another jack, then plugged it in beneath the light. "Number, please."

"Tremont-4571."

I found the corresponding number on the board and plugged the other jack into it. The line returned a busy signal. What was I supposed to do with a busy signal?

I closed my eyes and tried to remember the notes I'd written on the back of that old envelope. I was supposed to . . . I was supposed to . . . tell the caller the line was busy.

I told the caller.

There. I'd done it. But *two* more lights were flickering now. I wondered . . . what was I supposed to do when I had two calls come through at once? I picked up a jack and plugged it in. "Number, please."

"Tremont-4649."

I was starting to patch the call through when that other blinking light caught my eye. I might as well patch them both at once. Wouldn't it be more efficient that way? "Number, please."

"Tremont-4569."

I took the first cord and found Tremont-4569. The call rang through and I flipped the switch. Then I took the second cord and found Tremont-4649. The line was busy, so I . . . huh. One of the old cords was still plugged in to where I'd gotten the busy signal before. I supposed . . . I should unplug it, shouldn't I?

Sneaking a look at the girls on either side of me, I unplugged it, quickly plugged the new call in to Tremont-4649, *and* I flipped the switch.

There.

I leaned against the back of my stool, exhausted by my efforts. But then two new lights started blinking at me. Good gracious, was there nothing else people had to do in the city but make telephone calls? "Number, please."

"Tremont-4649. And could you transfer it correctly this time?"

"I just—I did—"

"No, you didn't. Just *take the call*." The A operator didn't have to be so mean about it, did she?

I patched the call through to Tremont-4649, just like I had before. Then I plugged a jack in beneath the second light. "Number, please."

"Tremont-4569. And I'll thank you to do it correctly this time!"

I plugged the jack into 4569. It rang through, so I flipped the switch. But . . . had I flipped the switch on the other call? Had I even patched the other one through?

I couldn't remember.

I chewed on a nail. Had I or hadn't I?

Another light flickered, so I grabbed a jack from a third pair in order to plug it in, only it wouldn't stretch far enough. I tried again, more forcefully, but only succeeded in yanking my neck forward.

Ow!

Why was my neck . . . ? I looked down and realized my long strands of beads had become tangled in a cord. In several cords, in fact. How was I supposed to . . . ?

I looked over at Doris, but she was speaking into her mouth-piece, patching calls through on her board. I looked in the other direction, but that girl was busy as well.

I tried to pull the beads off over my head, but they got hung up on my headset and that blasted light was still blinking at me.

Oysters and clambakes!

I leaned forward, as close to the board as I could, and plugged the cord in. I was so close to the board now the jacks were pressing in to my cheek. I could hardly even move my mouth to speak. "Number, please."

"Tremont-4582."

Well that was nice, but I couldn't back up far enough now to even find it!

What I really needed was to—I gave my beads a tug. Nothing happened. Maybe if I unplugged the cords and then plugged them all back in quickly, no one would notice. I grabbed my beads with one hand and then put the other hand up to the cords that dangled from the jacks.

One, two . . . !

I yanked the cords out, tugged my beads free, and then . . . oh. Now I didn't know which jacks they all belonged to. I put them all back where I thought they'd been and then prayed for another light to flicker.

Flicker.

Soon.

Anytime now.

Hadn't Doris been wearing a necklace? I wondered how she kept hers from getting caught up in all the cords. I snuck a look. That was clever! She'd drawn it up at her throat in front, letting it dangle down her back.

I made the adjustment and then four lights lit up at once. I patched through the first two calls, then realized I didn't have enough cords for the last two. I checked again. They were all in use.

As I was trying to decide what to do, Doris reached over and pulled a handful of cords from the board, placing them back onto the shelf. She removed one side of her headset. "When the lights go off, pull the cords out!"

It was going to be a long day. I could tell.

8

The supervisor finally tapped me on the shoulder and excused me for lunch. I nearly fell off my stool in relief. She walked past me and then tapped Doris as well, who proceeded to thread an arm through mine and pull me down the hall. As we walked, she reached a finger behind her ear, pulled something out, and popped it into her mouth.

"Is that . . . ?"

She blew a bubble and sucked it back in, popping it. "Chewing gum. Can't chew it while I work, and it's a shame to let a good piece go to waste." She led us back to the bathroom, where she pulled a sack from the shelf. "Aren't you going to get yours?"

"Isn't there a lunchroom?"

She wrinkled her nose. "Sure. But why would you want to eat that slop?"

"I didn't bring anything else to eat."

She shrugged. "So you'll know better tomorrow. Might not taste good, but it won't kill you." I followed her out the hall and up a flight of stairs.

"I thought . . . isn't the lunchroom supposed to serve lunch to everyone?" That was something Father was so proud of, that everyone had the chance to eat a hot lunch every day.

"They do. But that doesn't mean we have to eat it."

"But . . . maybe people think the food is just fine." My father sure did. "You should tell someone about it."

"Who's going to listen to us complain? With that strike a few years ago, everyone figures we already got what we were after."

"But that's not fair!"

She smiled as she slapped me on the arm. "Fair? You're funny! Only people that got nothing else to do worry about what's fair."

But it still didn't seem right, and I didn't understand why Father hadn't heard about the food being so bad.

As we walked on, I heard music playing. It was a lively song that sounded like a rendition of "Yes! We Have No Bananas." Doris threw open a door. "See? It's not so bad if you don't count the food. We even got a piano."

She was right. It wasn't so bad, although it was unfortunate it smelled of cabbage. But the room was large and bright. At one end was a kitchen fronted by a long counter, which was staffed by several women wearing large white aprons and hairnets. There were round tables scattered about the center of the room, and a bulletin board at the back was plastered with a multitude of papers.

"We've even got a phonograph. And crossword books and a stack of magazines."

"Crosswords?"

"You like them too? You should talk to Ethel. She's a real brain. Did one last week in fifteen minutes."

"Fifteen minutes!" That was impossible. Even Martha at the dormitory took at least half an hour.

"We got a dictionary too. Word is, they're all sold out in the city. But we pooled our money, and Dottie knows someone who works at Brattle Book Shop. It's an old one, but it's got all the words in it."

"You pooled your money for a *dictionary*?" At school we pooled our money for mah-jongg sets or magazines. Some of the girls pooled theirs for cigarettes.

"Oh sure." She snapped her gum. "Lots of the girls take correspondence courses. Although they're talking about buying their own dictionary. On account of the girls doing crossword puzzles keep taking it."

I liked crossword puzzles, although I wasn't crazy about them the way some people were. But had she mentioned magazines? "Do you think there's a *Photoplay*? Or a *Movie Weekly*?"

"Don't know. But there's a *True Confessions* and a *True Stories* and a *True Romance*!" She winked at me. "I know because I bring them in." She walked over to a pile sitting at one end of a table. "Oh. And look: *Real Confessions*." She turned the pile over. "And *Real Stories* and *Real Romance* too." But she turned up her nose at them and fished *True Confessions* out of the jumble. "Read this one. It has 'Kidnapped by a Gypsy Lover' and 'Confession of a Chinese Slave Girl.'" She fanned her face with it as she recited the articles.

"I'm not sure I . . ." A flush of horror swept my face. I

wasn't supposed to be me—I was supposed to be Janie! How could I have forgotten so easily? "Does *Janie* read these?"

She thrust it at me. "*Everyone* reads these."

I tried to see past her to the table. "Are you sure there aren't any *Photoplays*?"

"*Photoplay*! Movies are pretend. These—" she waved the magazine beneath my nose—"these are *real life*." She pointed to the kitchen behind me. "Better go get your lunch. It's all right if it's still hot, but if you let it get cold . . ." She shuddered.

I tucked the magazine under my arm. Janie. I was supposed to be Janie. Weaving around the tables, I rolled my shoulders forward and kept my eyes on the floor as I approached the counter.

"Your ma ain't cooking for you today, huh?"

Startled, I glanced up at the woman serving up lunch.

She looked at me through narrowed eyes. "You're looking peaked."

Peaked? Then I must be doing something right. Janie never wore rouge. At least not that I had ever noticed. I took the plate the woman offered me and turned around, working my way back to Doris's table. There were several other girls sitting there by the time I'd returned.

"So she's *not* Janie?" They were speaking to Doris though they were looking at me.

Doris was beaming. "No. But she's doing good, isn't she?"

One of them peered up at me as I sat.

I glanced over at her.

The girl addressed me. "You got a name?"

"Janie."

"You got a other name?"

"Janie *is* my other name." At least for the time being.

"Oh! That's funny. Imagine there being two of you and looking just the same."

I ate. It wasn't too bad considering I couldn't really tell what it was. Only . . . "Doris, how come so many of us are eating now? Isn't anyone patching through calls?"

"There aren't that many that come in. It's lunchtime. Everyone's eating. It'll start to get busy again after one. Don't worry."

Worry! I hadn't worked this hard since I'd tried to study for my economics test.

One of the girls got up and went over to the piano. Her fingers took a walk up and down the keyboard and then launched into "Ma! He's Making Eyes at Me." As some of the girls finished lunch, they went over and sat down or stood beside her and started singing. Someone began a game of Old Maid, and over at a table in the corner, a cluster of girls sat poring over some books.

"Don't know why they bother." Doris saw me looking in their direction.

"What are they studying for?"

"Couple of them want to be secretaries and work in one of those fancy offices, but how can you practice without one of those typewriters or Dictaphones? The only way to be a secretary is to . . . be one, you know? And they got to work here, so they can't just quit, but if they don't quit, then how are they ever going to be secretaries?"

Very good questions.

"Couple of them even want to go to school."

"High school?"

"College."

"Then why don't they?"

"You really *are* funny! They don't have the money. They got to work in order to save up money for school, but even once they save up the money, they can't quit working to go to school because they got to have money in order to keep paying the bills. See? You got to have money in order to do something."

"But . . . you all get paid. You must have *some* money."

"Well, sure we do. But then there's rent and food and clothes. And after that, there's not much left."

"But . . . what about amusement parks, and movies, and . . . and everything else?" That's what was so glamorous about working. Working girls were liberated and independent. They were thoroughly modern. "Working girls are supposed to be the ones having all the fun."

She looked at me askance. "Fun! You think working is *fun*? I only work because I have to. That's the only reason any of us are here. Being a hello girl is better than most jobs, I guess, but I'd rather not have to work at all. I'd almost rather get married. Any of us would."

I just assumed they were living the life I'd always dreamed of. That's what it seemed like from the movies anyway.

"Here." Doris pushed her magazine back in my direction. I took it up and started on the gypsy kidnapping story, but I kept imagining Rudolph Valentino as the gypsy and couldn't really understand why anyone would want to try to escape from him. Even Agnes Ayres in *The Sheik* had eventually succumbed to his charms.

"Ready?"

I looked up to find Doris staring down at me, hand on her hip. At some point the girl at the piano had stopped playing and the room had emptied. "Oh!" Was it time to go back to work already? "I suppose so . . ."

"You suppose!" She laughed. "You'd *better* be ready. You got Janie's job to keep for her."

"Do we get a break later?" Maybe then I could finish the rest of the magazine article.

"Sure we do. When we go home after our shift, we can have all the break we want!"

I stopped by the bathroom as we passed and pulled an old receipt from my pocketbook and begged a pencil from Doris. If I wrote down each number as it was given me, then maybe I wouldn't make so many mistakes. As long as I didn't let the supervisor see what I was doing, then it might just work. I turned it over and folded it into a small square so I could hide it in my palm.

Lights started blinking on my board just as soon as I wiggled my way back up onto the stool. I pulled the headset down, chose a cord, and plugged it in. "Number, please."

I wrote it down, remembering to throw my beads over my shoulder before I reached for the second cord. And I remembered to flip the switch on that first call too . . . and the second, and pretty soon I got into a good routine.

But then the calls started coming in too quickly.

That's when I forgot to flip the switch. I was reaching to plug in another cord when I was startled by a voice in my headset.

"Hello?"

"Hi."

"That you, Paddy?"

"Sure it's me. You sounded worried last night so I thought I should call. What's eating you?"

I was reaching to flip the switch when a third light started blinking. Should I . . . ?

"I don't think that Phillips kid is going to play along."

"Don't worry. You got all summer to take care of it."

"But I get the feeling he could cause a lot of trouble. That Prince has turned out to be a royal pain."

The man had a distinct way of speaking, saying *rile* instead of *royal*. I mouthed it once before I realized he was talking about a prince. *And* he'd mentioned "that Phillips kid." Were they . . . were they talking about Griff?!

"Don't worry. King's already got a plan to take care of everything."

What did they mean, *take care of everything*?

"What do you mean, take care of everything?"

"He's ready to do what he has to."

"Do you mean . . . is he planning on taking the kid out of the picture?"

That was funny. He'd said *pitcher* instead of *picture*. I tried the phrase out too before the meaning of the words hit me. Out of the picture? I felt my mouth drop open. *Out of the picture* meant—!

"That kid don't know what's good for him. King's just gonna knock him off that throne, that's all. In plain sight of everybody so there's no mistake about it. But if what you say is true, he's got to do it soon. In order to send a message. If you're not going to play along, then you're not going to get to play, see? It's the principle of the thing."

I heard myself gasp. "What are you saying? You can't just go around threatening—"

"Hey! Who's that on the phone?"

I clapped a hand to my mouth.

"Who's there?"

I flipped the switch with a trembling hand and the voices went away.

Who were those people? And what were they planning to do to Griff?

By the time my shift was finished, I'd misconnected a dozen calls and failed to pick up a few others entirely. What was it Griff had gotten himself into? And how were those men planning on stopping him? They said they were going to put him out of the picture. When people said that in the movies, it meant they were planning to *kill* someone!

If I hadn't opened my mouth, I could have listened in longer, but I had. So now I had to figure it all out from what I'd overheard. It was like a crossword puzzle. The kind where you didn't know the word going down, but you hoped if you could fill in the word going across, it would give you enough to get by on.

I ran straight up the stairs to my room once I got home. I had to think.

Griff was doing something someone didn't like.

But that wasn't possible, was it? School had just gotten out, and he'd said he was working on some commission all summer.

And who were those people anyway? They'd talked about

someone they called the king and their accents were definitely Irish.

Maybe . . . would the operator who'd passed the call to me remember the telephone number? If only I could just apply myself and buckle down and think! There had to be some way to work it all out. I nibbled a fingernail to the quick as I paced across my bedroom floor. I didn't know where the call had come from, but I *had* patched it through. That had to mean something.

But what!

"Ellis?" I heard my father's call float up from downstairs.

Oysters and clambakes! It must be time for supper.

"Rather quiet with just the two of us," Father said as he looked around at the empty chairs.

There was something niggling at the back of my mind. Something about that telephone call.

"How was your day?"

"Hard."

His brows rose.

"Hard. It was hard because . . ." I took a drink of water. "It's very sad to be an orphan."

He nodded. "Quite. I think it's quite admirable, what you're doing."

Admirable? Was he talking about me?

"You have a gift, Ellis, and it's gratifying to see you put it to good use for a change."

Gratifying? Admirable? For once, I was doing something

right! Except . . . I wasn't, was I? I mean, I *was* doing something right. I was helping Janie out. And I was going to try to help Griff out as well. So I was doing something right even though Father was talking about the wrong thing and didn't really know it. But why should the particulars matter? What my parents didn't know couldn't hurt them. They'd never find out I wasn't really working at the orphan asylum, and it was rather nice to think my father thought I was admirable. I liked the feeling. "Do you think . . . could I go over to the Phillipses' after supper?" Maybe I'd be able to figure out what Griff had gotten mixed up in.

"Tonight?" My father was frowning. "I don't know . . ."

"Griff said he was working in the city this summer too. Since I don't think he'll be going to the shore, I thought I'd just . . ." I shrugged.

"I suppose. Sure. Why not?"

That's why I liked my father. Mother would have asked "Why?" instead.

I only had to wait a few minutes in the parlor before Griff came down. Their parlor looked like ours, with a large bay window framed by black shutters. But theirs was painted in the mustardy yellow Griff's mother had preferred, while ours was decorated in the burgundy and dark green colors my grandmother Eton had liked. I walked past a table. They had a collection of spoons in a cabinet on the far wall. I was looking at one done in gold with a strange triangular shape to its bowl when Griff came up behind me. "Ellis?"

I turned around, spoon in my hand.

He caught it as it dropped from my fingers, then put it back in the cabinet. "It's from Siam." Dressed in a white shirt with the sleeves rolled up and a pair of white flannel trousers, he didn't look at all the way he did on the Yard: like some football hero or campus royalty. He looked . . . tired.

"How's your job?"

"Hard."

Then that made two of our jobs. I glanced up into his eyes. How was I supposed to ask if he was doing anything that might be making some king mad? Or if he knew any Irish? "Well . . . how?"

"How what?"

"How is it hard?"

"Oh. I don't know . . ." He shrugged. "It's a lot of numbers."

Numbers? How could numbers get him into trouble with Irish people? "Are you sure?"

"Of course I'm sure. That's all I did all day. Sit in the commission's office and add up a bunch of numbers that didn't seem to want to be added up."

They sounded like the numbers in my mathematics class.

He sighed as he sat in an armchair and stretched out those long legs of his. "How's *your* job?"

"My what?" How did he know what I was doing?

"Your job. Your mother said you were working down at the orphan asylum."

"My mother said that?" I went back to the spoon collection. I really didn't see how a triangular spoon worked. Did people in Siam have different-shaped mouths than we did?

"I think it's really terrific, what you're doing."

SIRI MITCHELL

"You do?"

He rose and came to stand beside me, resting his arm on the top of the cabinet. "I do."

His eyes were truly blue. You couldn't really say they were gray or hazel or anything else but a clear, strong, deep blue.

He leaned toward me.

The evening light touched his hair, sparking it into a golden fire. He reached out and pried the spoon from my hand.

I hadn't realized I was holding it again.

After he set it back on the shelf, he kept hold of my hand.

"Do you know any Irish, Griff?"

He blinked. "What?"

Oysters and clambakes! This figuring things out might be trickier than I thought it would be. Should I just tell him what I'd heard?

He was looking at me, puzzlement clouding his eyes.

No, I shouldn't. I *couldn't* tell him. He was the one person who never despaired of me, and I didn't want him to start now. If I told him I suspected he was about to be murdered, I just knew I'd hear him say, "Oh, Ellis!" He'd wonder how I'd managed to hear it, and I'd have to tell him about my real job, and then he wouldn't think I was terrific anymore . . . even though I didn't really need him to think I was more terrific than he already did because that's why I was leaving in the first place. The truth was I'd never been as terrific as he seemed to think I was.

No, I'd figure it all out by myself and then I'd save him . . . and maybe I wouldn't even ever have to tell him about the telephone call and he'd be able to go on thinking I really was terrific. I wouldn't feel so bad about ducking off to go to

115

Hollywood, then. Saving his life would be like . . . a going-away present. My gift to him.

"What were you saying about Irish people?"

Irish people? Oh! "Do you know any?"

"I don't—I don't think so." He rocked back onto his heels, leaning against the wall. "Although, now that I think about it, the cook is Irish. And the driver."

"Have you ever done anything to make them mad at you?"

"When I was little . . ." He looked away and then looked back. Was he blushing?

"You remember, Ellis! We used to sneak cookies from the kitchen all the time. But I don't think Mrs. O'Malley ever got *mad* at us."

No. She hadn't. In fact, I suspected she used to leave those plates in a place where we didn't have to stretch too far to reach them.

"Why are you worried about Irish people?"

"Um . . . well . . . don't you ever worry about people?"

"I worry about you. About us. I was thinking . . ." He put a hand down into his pocket.

Oh dear. This was headed toward dangerous territory. I could tell by the look in his eyes. He had the pin there in his trousers, didn't he? "What's to worry about?" I turned and walked over toward the divan, running a hand across that nice, scrumptious, glossy wood framing on its camel back.

"Why do you do that?"

"Do what?" I walked on, putting a chair, as well as the divan, between us.

"You're running away again."

I was. But not in the way he thought. Or maybe I was running away *in addition* to the way he thought I was. I was running away from him and his fraternity pin, and I was also running away from Boston. Just two more weeks.

He brought his hand out, fist closed around something.

It seemed far more important to hurry up and leave than to figure out if he knew anyone else who was Irish. "Well . . ." I made a dash toward the entry hall. "Good luck tomorrow. I hope the numbers add up. Bye."

"Ellis, wait!"

Waiting is what I'd been doing for far too long. I'd save Griff—with or without his help—and then I was finally going to leave.

Saving someone is far easier said than done. Especially when you don't quite know what it is you're saving him from. I found a pack of cards in my desk drawer and sat down to shuffle them. Griff wasn't going to be any help, that was clear. He couldn't even remember which Irish he knew!

I arched the cards and watched as they fell into place when the arch collapsed.

But he'd made someone mad, that's for sure!

I struck the edge of the cards against the desk to align them, then shuffled the pack again.

He'd just started his job, so it's not like he had time to do much else but work with numbers on that commission.

I hated numbers.

But how could numbers get a person into trouble? Besides not being the right ones on a test?

Beats me.

Putting the cards aside, I got up and dug around the chest I'd brought from school, pulling out my phonograph. Now, where had I put all my records? I pawed around through piles of sweaters and stacks of skirts, most of them marked by wine stains. Why hadn't Irene just obeyed the rules? If she'd done what she was supposed to do, then my clothes wouldn't all be ruined. Which made me wonder about her clothes again and where she was getting the money for them. When I'd shared the room with her, she'd been worse than I had at begging money from people. Which reminded me about the money I owed Mary and Louise. Maybe I could use some of the money I got from working Janie's job to repay them.

There was my little book! A lot of good it had done me. I turned around and dropped it into the wastepaper basket.

Oh! I was doing it again. If I was going to keep Griff from getting murdered before I left, then I had to concentrate on figuring out what those men on the telephone were talking about. They'd mentioned a king, hadn't they? Which didn't make any sense at all. We didn't have kings anymore in America.

I pulled a sweater from the trunk, set it aside, and plunged my hand to the bottom. There were the records. I pulled them out and set them in a pile on the floor. Then I sat down right beside them to think.

What was it they'd said again about that king?

Banana oil! Why did I have to be so stupid? The king was going to . . . something about a throne. *Knock Griff off his throne.* That was it! And *take him out of the picture.*

That's why I had to do something.

But what?

That was the problem. What was I supposed to do? I could go to the police, but then what would I say? That I'd heard someone say something about a prince, and I'd decided they were talking about Griff? Even to me, it sounded like nonsense. They'd ask me who it was I'd heard, and I'd tell them the men were Irish.

Well, there were thousands of Irish in Boston, so that didn't help any.

And when they asked me where the call had come from . . . I didn't know. And where had the call gone to? I didn't know that either. And even if I knew, what would it tell me?

At least I knew one thing for certain: Whatever they were planning on doing, it would be out in the open so everyone could see it. That sounded awfully ominous, but at least I wouldn't have to worry about Griff during the day when he was at work. Or at night when he was home. So that meant . . . what did it mean? When *did* I have to worry about him?

Something wasn't making any sense.

I listened to my records for a while as I shuffled my cards, but when I went to bed, I still didn't have any answers.

"Janie or . . . whoever you are!" Doris hissed at me when I walked into the bathroom and gestured me over with a waving of her hands. "What did you do yesterday?"

I shrugged. "I worked. Right alongside you."

"But some of the girls are complaining to Miss Hastings that they couldn't pass their telephone calls to you. And when they did, they were disconnected or connected to the wrong numbers."

"I only did it once." Or twice. Although there *was* that incident with my beads. "Today I'll get it right. I promise."

"You'd better. The chief is going to listen in on you!"

Miss Hastings? The one I'd promised Janie wouldn't notice me? "What should I do?"

"You do it right. You have to. Janie really needs this job."

Janie needed it? I needed it! I still had to figure out what was supposed to happen to Griff, and I still had to earn the money.

I put my pocketbook up on the shelf and turned to follow Doris, but then I remembered that old receipt and pencil from the day before. I grabbed them and pushed them into my pocket before leaving. Once I got settled on my stool, I pulled them out and set them on the shelf before me. My goodness but I'd taken a lot of calls the day before. One, two . . . I counted them all up and there were sixty-three of them. I turned the paper over.

Sixty-three calls yesterday. That was more than I remembered, but it had to be right because I'd written down all of those numbers. At least the ones from the afternoon. I shuddered when I thought about those Irish voices on the other end of the telephone line.

Wait a minute. Wait just a minute!

I'd written all of those numbers down. That meant . . . that meant one of them belonged to the call I'd overheard. But which one was it? I'd folded and refolded the paper so many different times I didn't know where I'd started.

Someone tapped me on the shoulder. I turned, expecting to see Doris, but it wasn't her. It was Miss Hastings. She was staring over the top of her glasses at me. "Janie Winslow."

Janie. I had to be Janie. I lowered my gaze and smiled at the floor.

"I need you to come with me."

"But I—I have telephone calls to patch through."

"Not right now, you don't. And not yesterday, apparently, either! I had a lot of complaints about you." She marched me down the hall and up the stairs.

If she were going to fire me, wouldn't she be marching me toward the door instead? "May I ask where we're going?"

"There's a policeman here who wants to talk to you."

A policeman? Was she going to have me arrested? Just for transferring calls to a wrong number or two?

She flung the door open and pushed me through.

"I—" I forgot everything I was going to say because standing right there in front of me was Rod La Rocque in the flesh—with a squared-off cleft chin and dark, brooding eyes—or at least a very close approximation of him.

He winked at me.

"This is Janie Winslow. As I told you, she's usually very reliable. There have been no complaints at all in her service." She turned toward me. "Until yesterday."

He put out a hand. "Pleased to meet you, Miss Winslow."

As Miss Hastings left us, I put my hand into his, feeling like I'd just walked into a real live movie. And the best of it was, I actually felt like I imagined Janie always did: good and smart and capable.

He drew me off to one of the round tables in the center of the room and we sat down.

"Pleased to meet you, Officer . . . ?"

"Officer Jack Feeney. If it's all right with you, I need to ask you some questions."

I nodded.

"Can you state your full name and your address?"

"El . . . I mean, Janie . . . Winslow?" Did she have a middle name? Probably. Didn't everyone have a middle name? But . . . what was I supposed to give as my address? "I've just moved in with a girlfriend, but I'm only staying with her until I find a place of my own, so I don't really have an address right now, at least not one I'd want to give you, but if you need to find me, you know where I work, so why don't you just use this one?"

"Can you give me the address of your parents, then? They'd always know where to find you, wouldn't they?"

"They would, I suppose, if they were alive, but my mother died just this past weekend and I don't have any brothers and sisters." At least I didn't think Janie had any brothers and sisters, but then again, I hadn't thought she had a father either. "Maybe the best thing to do is just not try to contact me for a while. At least, not until I get settled somewhere."

As I'd been talking, he'd started to look as if his collar was too tight. Now his face had gone flush. "I'm sorry. I didn't mean to bring up . . . that. You have my sympathies. So . . . er . . . how long have you been working here?"

"Just—" Oops. *Not* just since yesterday. I had, but Janie hadn't. "I . . ." didn't know. How long had Janie been here? I kicked myself in the shin to get my brain to start working again. Ow! Of all the times to be stupid, this was *not* one of them. Janie. I was supposed to be Janie. "It seems like forever, but I suppose it's only been a few years now."

"I have great admiration for people like you."

"You—you do?"

"Of course I do. Do you know how many emergency calls you hello girls have taken in the past year?"

124

"Well . . . no, I don't. How many?"

He smiled. "I don't know either. Not exactly, anyway. But quite a few. I can tell you must be very dedicated to your work."

"You can?"

"Aren't you?"

For the next two weeks I was. I nodded, smiling a Janie smile.

"But it must get a little boring sometimes."

"Boring?" Boring was the one thing it was not. The switchboard had been so busy yesterday I'd hardly had a chance to breathe. "I don't think boring is the right word."

"Dull? Dreary? Unexciting? What would you call it?"

"Hard."

"Hard?" His brows peaked in surprise.

"Hard."

"Even after all those years you've worked here? I'd think you'd be able to almost transfer a telephone call in your sleep."

"I did last night. In my dreams." I'd patched through endless telephone calls from one Irish man to another.

Officer Feeney laughed outright. "I think I like you, Miss Winslow." He crossed his arms, putting his elbows on the tabletop, and leaned toward me. "I'm a policeman, Miss Winslow, so you can trust me."

I found myself nodding, even though he hadn't asked me a question.

"Don't you ever listen in on a telephone call or two just to pass the time?"

"Only when I—" I put a hand to my mouth as I felt a blush color my cheeks.

"Only when . . . ?"

Why couldn't I just keep my mouth shut? "Only when I don't mean to."

"You only listen in when you don't mean to?" He leaned back and scratched at his ear. "How does that work?"

"When you patch through a call you have to . . . well . . . there are two cords you have to plug in. I'm a B operator, so I take a call from the A operator. She passes it to me through one cord and then I plug in the second cord and patch the call through. Only I have to flip a switch when I do it. And sometimes I forget to."

"But the chief operator said normally you're—"

"I know, I know." Normally Janie really was Janie. "But . . . yesterday was . . . hard. So many calls came in all at the same time I just . . . I just . . . forgot."

"And so you listened in?"

"I didn't mean to. And it was only until I could flip the switch, and once I did, I didn't hear anything else."

The officer drummed his fingertips on the table as he looked at me. Then he looked away. "You didn't hear anything surprising, did you?" His gaze swung back.

I kept my eyes down the way Janie would have. My shoulders were already rolled forward. "Surprising? Of course I was surprised! I thought I'd remembered to flip the switch. But then I heard the voices . . ."

"You didn't happen to say anything to them, did you?"

"To whom?"

"To whoever it was that was talking."

"I don't know." I said the words in Janie's careful way, as if I were truly trying to remember. There was something

important about all those questions he was asking! I wished
I could work out what it was.

"You don't know?" He seemed puzzled.

"What?" What was it I wasn't supposed to know?

"What?"

"*What* don't I know?" I wished he'd make more sense.

"You said *you* didn't know."

"Didn't know what?"

"What you didn't know."

Did he have to be so mean about it? Now I was confused.

He threw up his hands. "I don't know what you don't
know!" He muttered something to himself. Then he leveled
a look at me. "It's not right to listen in on other people's
telephone calls, Miss Winslow."

"I didn't mean to."

"I know you didn't. But the thing is, you might hear something you're not supposed to. And in that case . . ."

I held my breath.

"In that case, things might get a little dangerous for you."

For me? Dangerous for Griff, more like!

"*If* you happened to mention what you heard to anyone."

"It would be hard to mention something to anyone if
I couldn't remember what I wasn't supposed to mention,
wouldn't it?"

He looked at me through narrowed eyes, as if he were
trying to make out what I'd said. "True enough. But if you
do remember, and you do want to mention it to someone,
you know where to find me." He rose and put a finger to his
forehead in salute. Then he walked toward the door.

"I don't, actually."

He paused in his step. "Don't what?"

"Don't know where to find you."

A smile hovered at his lips as if he thought I was telling a joke. "Down at the precinct."

"Which one?"

He turned around with a sigh. "Can't a guy make a decent exit? I haven't gotten a third-degree like yours since I was in the army." He jammed his hat on his head. "At the station on Harrison. Any more questions, miss?"

"No. I think you've answered them all."

He burst into laughter. "You know, you're a real goof. You want to go somewhere tomorrow night?"

Did I? "I . . . don't know."

"You don't know. Is there anything you *do* know?"

"It's just that I don't know you very well. At all. I don't know you at all." And there was something about him . . . something I just couldn't quite lay a finger on. But it bothered me.

"Well, how about this: What time is your shift over tomorrow night?"

"Tomorrow?" Tomorrow was Wednesday. Was my shift over at the same time every night? "Five?"

"Is this another thing you don't know?"

"No. Yes."

He walked over and chucked me on the chin. "I think I'll call you the I-don't-know girl instead of the hello girl." He winked. "I'll meet you out on the sidewalk, and we'll go somewhere."

"Where?"

He raised a finger as if to preclude more comments. "No more questions. It's for me to know and you to find out."

128

I worked the rest of my shift in a state of nerves. I tried to get rid of them by being Janie. She would never have listened in on a telephone call in the first place! But being Janie didn't help much, and it didn't keep my thoughts from straying toward Griff.

If I couldn't figure out who those people on the telephone were and how they planned to murder him, then I was just going to have to stick as close to him as I could. That was the best plan I could come up with. At least then I might be able to foil *their* plans.

As I ate supper with Father, I tried to think of a way to get out of spending the next evening with him. I didn't want to lie about it; I already felt bad he assumed I was helping out down at the orphan asylum.

My father took a drink from his glass and pushed back his plate. "I was thinking, with everyone else at the shore, we ought to take advantage of it and have some fun. How about seeing *Girl Shy* at the Exeter tomorrow night? You can be my best girl."

"No!"

He looked a bit taken aback. "But you can't have seen the movie. I had my secretary call this morning, and they've just got it in. They assured her I would like it, and that you would as well."

I probably *would* like it! If it weren't for Griff and his sticking his nose into other people's business, then I'd be able to go. Honestly! People shouldn't go around doing things that could get them murdered. It was very inconvenient.

"Ellis?"

"I wish I could but . . . I can't. I already made a promise to a friend." At least, I hoped the policeman, Jack, would turn out to be my friend.

He held up a hand. "Say no more. I understand. Why would you want to go out with dear old dad when you could be with your girlfriends instead?"

"It's not that. It's just—"

"No need to explain. Maybe some other time."

I liked my father. I really did. And once I left for Hollywood, I didn't know when I'd make it back to Boston. I'd probably be contracted for movies, which would tie me up for . . . for years. "I wish I—"

He leaned forward and brushed my nose with the tip of his newspaper. "Not to worry, Buttercup. Some other time."

But . . . there wasn't going to be another time.

I stalked over to the Phillipses' house. Of all the lousy timing. Why did Griff have to pick *this* summer to get murdered? I could just about . . . bean him on the head with something.

Something really hard! Why did it have to be *me* patching through that telephone call? Why did he have to go and make someone want to kill him? And why did he have to look at me with such delight as he greeted me?

That was the worst.

But if having my intentions misunderstood is what it took to save his life, then . . . I'd just have to suffer. I needed to figure out where he was going to go that would be in plain sight of everybody.

"Ellis!"

"Hi . . . Griff. I just . . . came over." There wasn't much of a social season in summer. At least not in the city. If it were any time of year but this, I could almost guarantee I'd be able to keep an eye on him by going to dinner parties or the theater or symphony, and it wouldn't look quite so much as if I were trying to throw myself at his feet.

"I'm glad. Do you want . . . do you want some tea? Or something else maybe?"

"No thanks." I strayed from him over to the fireplace. There was a ship in a bottle sitting up there on the mantel. I wondered how people put ships in bottles. It seemed like such an impossible thing to do.

"Is there something you wanted?" He'd come to stand beside me.

I stood on my toes to look at the neck of the bottle. It was awfully narrow. I didn't see how to get a ship inside there.

"Ellis?"

"What?" Oh. "No. There's nothing I wanted." Except to keep him from getting murdered. That was the main thing.

"Then . . ."

I turned to him. "Don't mind me. Just pretend I'm not here."

He smiled a slow smile, which started at one corner of his mouth and worked its way toward the other. "That's pretty hard to do."

"Maybe . . . do you mind if I close the curtains?" Twilight hadn't yet fallen, and there were still people about on the street. I walked over and freed the curtains, letting them fall together. Now no one could see in.

"I guess not . . . but it sure is dark."

That's what lights were for. I walked over to the light switch and flipped it. "There. Perfect." I noticed books spread out all over the table. Was he working? "How are your numbers?"

"My what?"

"Your numbers. Did you get them figured out?"

"Maybe. I don't know. In a way."

"How many ways can there be?" I'd tried different ways of figuring numbers out too, but my professor didn't acknowledge there was any other way to answer a test question than his own.

"Quite a few, apparently. Especially when you're trying to hide things."

Hide things? "What things?"

"Well . . ." He walked over to the table and turned the book toward me. "Come over here and take a look."

I walked over to his end of the table.

He pulled out the chair so I could sit, then squatted beside me, an arm around the back of the chair. He was so close I could smell that scent that was uniquely Griff: dusty sandalwood, pungent leather, and the licorice he was always eating

132

when he thought no one was looking. Those scents always reminded me of him. And of home. Maybe I'd pack a bunch of licorice in my bag when I went to Hollywood.

"See right here, in this first column?"

I looked where he was pointing.

"That number represents the full amount in this account. And over here . . ." His finger skipped to the next column. "These are all the things that were bought with the money. And down here . . ." His finger slid to the bottom of both columns. "Those numbers are the same, right?"

"Yes."

"That's because all the money for that account was spent."

"So there's no money left." I knew how that felt.

"Right. And back here . . ." He flipped through some of the pages. "All of those expenses ought to be written here somewhere as goods that were acquired or services that were enlisted. If you spend money, you ought to get something in return."

"What about a movie?"

He blinked as he looked over at me. "What about it?"

"What do you get if you spend money on a movie? Or a magazine? Or a . . . newspaper?"

"Well . . . I suppose you get . . . entertainment. But that's not what I'm talking about. In an office, you ought to be accumulating pencils or carbon paper or . . . sewer services. The money never disappears, it just shows up in different places."

"But what if it doesn't? What if you never see it again?"

"If it doesn't, then where did it go? Sometimes it's just a matter of it being improperly recorded."

"But . . . what if it wasn't recorded at all?"

"Exactly." He seemed to take great satisfaction from closing the book with a thump.

"Exactly . . . what?"

"If it wasn't recorded at all, then why? That's the question you have to ask yourself."

"Maybe . . . someone forgot."

"Maybe. But what if there's a pattern of someone forgetting?"

"Then maybe that person ought to be fired." It seemed simple enough to me. I got up and wandered over toward that ship in the bottle again.

"That's what I'm trying to do."

I turned. "You're trying to fire someone?"

"I'm trying to get someone fired."

"Who?"

"The mayor."

The *mayor*? "You can't—you can't just fire the mayor!" Mayor Curley might not be the most honest man in the city, but he'd been voted into office by a majority of someone. Irish, mostly. And Italians.

"Someone needs to."

"But—why does it have to be you?"

"It's not me. It's the Finance Commission. That's what we're trying to do. We have someone in the mayor's office copying records for us so we can find proof of Curley's corruption."

"So . . . you're not really working with numbers this summer?"

"The numbers are just clues. It's justice we're really working for."

And the mayor was *Irish*! I stuck a finger in the bottle

just to make sure it was really as narrow as it seemed. Griff might not know anyone who was Irish, but the mayor sure did. And if he knew Griff and the commission were out to fire him, then . . . he might be willing to do just about anything to stop them. He might even want to put Griff *out of the picture*!

The bottle's neck really was that narrow. I pulled my finger out. "Griff, I—" I turned, meaning to talk to him, but he was so close I ended up practically walking into his arms instead.

"There's something I've been meaning to ask you, Ellis. . . ."

"I don't think—"

"I really want to talk to you. . . ."

As he looked down into my eyes, something queer started happening with my knees.

He put his hands on my shoulders, cupping them as if I were something precious or fragile, which might break. "I need to ask you something, Ellis."

"No."

"No?" He dropped his hands, shoving them into his pockets. "You don't even know what I was going to say."

"Not 'no' to your question." Although no is actually what I wanted to say, I'd planned to write it all down in a letter before I left. "'No' to . . . your wanting to talk. I'm . . . late. I'm late. I have to be going. *Now*."

"Late to what?"

"Late. I'm late at getting going. I should have been gone by now." Long gone. And here I was, still in Boston. "Don't . . . go anywhere tonight." I wouldn't be able to sleep if I thought he might be wandering around the city, followed by whoever it was that wanted to shove him off his throne. "And don't talk to anybody. In fact, do you think you can do your work at home for the next few days?"

"Ellis?"

"I would strongly consider it. In fact, I really think you should. Bye." I left before he could say anything else. Honestly, I needed to think, and I couldn't while Griff threatened to stick me with that fraternity pin every time I turned around.

I hurried home and ran up the back stairs to my room, turned on my phonograph, and put on a Marion Harris record. Then I pushed my window up higher to catch the breeze. Although . . . there wasn't much of one I could feel, so I sat in the open window and stuck an arm out just to see. Ah. There it was! Ever so slight but still refreshing.

I took a long look outside to make sure no one was lurking around Griff's house, and then I sat there for a while listening to "It Had to Be You," counting the cats that lay in the square soaking up the warmth the sun had baked into the paving stones earlier in the day. Once the record ended, I ducked back inside, ready to buckle down and concentrate.

Griff was hoping to fire the mayor. The mayor was Irish. I'd overheard Irish people threatening to do something to Griff. That was a nice, tidy circle. The only thing I didn't know was who the people on the telephone were and what exactly they were planning to do. But I *did* have the telephone number they'd used. I just didn't know which one it was. There had to be some way to find out, because if I could hear them talk, then I would recognize their voices. I was sure I would. One of them had sounded as if he had something stuck in his throat. And the other . . . there had been something distinctive about the way he pronounced his words.

Since I had all the telephone numbers I'd transferred calls to that first afternoon, I ought to be able to do something with them, shouldn't I? Maybe . . . what if I called each one? I could do it in between transferring telephone calls!

No.

That would take forever; there was rarely a moment when I wasn't transferring a telephone call. And besides, operators like me only patched calls through. If there was a way to initiate one, I didn't know how.

I took out the receipt I'd written the numbers on and flattened it out on my desk. I was in this circle too now. The two men had heard my voice and a policeman knew I'd overheard the call. In fact, he'd come to warn me not to talk about it. I was definitely part of this circle. And the policeman was too, wasn't he?

I rummaged in my desk drawer for a piece of paper. Pulling one out, I put my name at the top of it. Then I drew a curving line to a spot halfway down. I wrote *Irish Man 1*. I drew another curving line to the bottom of the paper. There I wrote *Irish Man 2*. From there I drew a curving line halfway up the page and wrote *Jack*. And then I closed the circle with one last curving line and connected me to everyone else.

At one end of the telephone conversation was me and at the other end was Jack. If Jack had known I'd listened in on the telephone call, then one of those two Irish men must have told him. So at least one of them knew him. That meant . . . I chewed on my fingernail as I thought about what it all meant. And when I figured it out, a chill crept up my spine. Jack was one of the bad guys! And I'd agreed to meet him the next evening for a date.

My hands started shaking, and it felt like everything I'd eaten for supper no longer liked it so much down there in my stomach.

I took a deep breath. Everything was going to be all right. This was good. Because . . . because if I knew Jack and he knew the men from the telephone call, then—?

Then?

I wished I were smarter. I hit my head with the palm of my hand to bang some sense into it, and then I turned my record over. I felt better once I heard Marion Harris singing "Jealous." I could figure this out. I knew I could.

I had to.

Jack thought I didn't know anything. Or that if I did, I couldn't remember it. So all I had to do was keep him thinking I didn't know anything. And while he was thinking that, I'd get him to tell me everything *he* knew.

That was it!

I did a quick little dance, twisting on the balls of my feet, stepping forward and then taking a step backward.

Jack had been sent to find out what I knew.

Forward and back. Forward and back. Bah-bah-de-be-*bah-bah*.

But what he didn't know was I could use him to figure out what he knew. And he knew what was going on . . . didn't he?

I bent and placed my hands on my knees, crossing and then re-crossing them as I brought my knees together and then pulled them apart.

Had I worked that out right?

Swinging my arms, I stepped forward with a kick and then stepped back and kicked again.

Griff. Mayor. Irish. Telephone men. Jack. Me.

Griff was working to fire the mayor who was Irish. The telephone men who had heard me had been Irish. Jack had been sent to find the person who had heard them . . . who was me. Jack was connected with the men on the telephone, who must be connected to the mayor, who was connected to Griff's work. That had to be it.

I danced around the room. It couldn't be anything else. I spun around, waving my hands in the air above my head. Then I bowed to all the imaginary onlookers as I blew kisses. I took off my dress and pulled Lawrence's old blanket robe on, and I walked down the hall to brush my teeth.

It took a while to pin up my hair, but I hummed "I Won't Say I Will, but I Won't Say I Won't" as I did it. Afterward, as I crawled into bed and closed my eyes, I imagined going back to campus next autumn and telling everyone how I'd worked out Griff was going to be murdered. But then I realized I wasn't going to be there.

I would still know, though.

Sitting up, I punched my pillow into shape. I would know just how hard I'd had to apply myself to work it all out. I'd know I had finally buckled down, I'd focused all my concentration, and I'd done it. That was the important thing.

I closed my eyes again, took a deep breath, rolled onto my side, and prepared to sleep.

But then I realized there was something I'd forgotten.

The king. I'd forgotten all about that king.

Oysters and clambakes!

And I still had a date to go on with Jack.

I didn't sleep very well.

And I managed to chew all of my fingernails to the quick while I wasn't doing it, which meant I had a hard time pulling the pins out of my hair. And plugging in all those cords down at Central.

Ow!

By lunchtime I was sucking on my fingers as I climbed the stairs to the cafeteria.

I hadn't dropped any telephone calls. I hadn't forgotten to flip any switches. And I hadn't transferred any calls to a wrong number—that I knew of, anyway. But I also hadn't thought much about Jack. He would be waiting out on the sidewalk for me at the end of the day and . . . I didn't know what to do. I couldn't sneak past him. I mean . . . I could, but I wouldn't because he could help me figure out how to keep Griff alive. So I had to meet him. Even though . . . I wondered if it was safe.

No one knew I worked here, and no one knew where I was going with him. Even *I* didn't know where I was going with him! I could disappear from the face of the earth, and no one would ever know where I'd gone.

I tore a corner from the page of a magazine and asked to borrow a pencil from a girl who was working a crossword puzzle.

She handed it to me with a wordless frown.

I scrawled Jack's name and precinct on it and then I took it to Doris. "I am going to place my life in your hands."

She looked at me with a blank gaze for a moment. And then her eyes widened. "Oh! You're good. It's Mary Pickford, right? In—oh! What was the name of her last movie?"

It was. But that wasn't important. What was important was that someone knew who I was seeing. "I'm going out tonight after work."

"With who?" She fluttered her lashes. "See? Mildred Harris. How'd I do?"

Not very well. Mildred Harris fluttered hers with much more grace. But that's why I was such a good actress: I noticed those kinds of things. "It's with someone I don't know very well. And if anything happens to me, if I don't show up at work tomorrow . . ." I held the scrap up in front of her. "This is his name."

She took it, turning it so she could read it. "Jack Feeney. Harrison Avenue?"

"That's the station where he works. He's a policeman."

"Are you sure he's a policeman?"

"Of course I'm sure!" He had to be a policeman, didn't he? He'd been wearing a uniform.

"Because what if he's just pretending? Oh! What if he's one of those fellows like in *True Confessions*? Maybe he wants to kidnap you and make you his gypsy queen!"

"I don't think—"

"And what if . . . golly! I hope everything will be all right. Maybe you shouldn't go."

"I have to go. So if anything happens to me, just . . . take that to the police station. Only . . . maybe not his station. Maybe you should take it to a different one."

She nodded. "Right."

As I sat in front of my board that afternoon, I had even more to worry about. What if Jack wasn't who he said he was? What if he was a *truly bad*, bad guy?

Then that would be *really* very bad.

And where was he planning on taking me? I wished I knew. I would have chewed on a fingernail—indeed, I tried to—but I had bitten them all off. One thing, at least, was good. Jack didn't know me as Ellis. So the most important thing was to keep being Janie. And then I had to figure out what was going on just as quickly as I could.

W here are we going?" I threw a glance up at Jack as
we walked along the sidewalk. He sure didn't look
like a bad guy, but looks could be deceiving.

He smiled. "Curiosity killed the cat, baby. Didn't you know
that?" He put his hand to my waist and guided me around
a newsstand.

"Are we going to walk there?" Because if we were, that
meant we'd be staying in the city, around people. He couldn't
do anything bad to me if we stayed in the city.

"Whad'you expect? I'm a policeman, not a prince."

"I hadn't meant to imply—"

"But don't worry. I can still show you a good time."

He *seemed* like a policeman. He looked like one. And he
hadn't bundled me into some dark, sinister-looking car. But
still . . . Doris was right. He could be anyone at all. I stopped
walking.

It took him a moment to realize it. Then he turned around
and headed back toward me.

"I don't know you very well, Jack. . . ."

"You want a formal introduction? Now?"

"I think I'd like to know *something* about you if we're going to be spending the evening together."

"Maybe I'd like to know something about you too, Miss I Don't Know." He winked as he said it. "So, where you from?"

"Here."

"Here. As in right here?"

"Very nearly." Twenty blocks north and several over, up on Beacon Hill. "And where are you from?"

"Here and there. Here more than anywhere."

That wasn't very helpful. "And you've been a policeman for . . . ?"

"More than long enough." He clamped his lips together after he'd answered.

"And before that . . . ?"

"Before that I was holed up in a trench filled with mud and guts in the fields of Flanders fighting the Boche. And before you ask 'before that,' I'll tell you straight: There's nothing worth remembering in my past. So . . . shall we?" He gestured to the train station across the street. "Anyway, it's not important where you came from. What's important is where you're going."

I could agree with that. "I'm going to Hollywood."

The corners of his eyes crinkled as he smiled at me. "That's the way, sister! No point in dreaming if you don't dream big."

"Where are you going?"

"Somewhere. I'm going from nowhere to somewhere just as soon as I can."

"Somewhere no one has it in for you, where you can just be . . . free. Somewhere different. Somewhere exciting."

He looked down at me. "Exactly."

I smiled, and he smiled back. As long as he didn't try anything, I thought—I hoped—I'd be fine.

Jack bought two tickets for the elevated railway, and twenty minutes later we got off and walked into a neighborhood that looked . . . well, frankly, it looked unsavory. Garbage erupted from the alleyways, and swarms of children raced through the streets between automobiles. There was a distinct smell of garlic and coffee. And there were flies. Lots and lots of flies. We stepped onto the street to pass a group of old women who were sitting in chairs arranged on the sidewalk. They glared at us as if we were walking through their front parlor.

I must have shrunk back because Jack put an arm around me, letting his hand flap free from my shoulder as we walked. "Don't worry, baby. I saw worse in the war and I survived. We're just here for a good time."

"Where are we?"

"The North End. Haven't you been here before?"

The north end of what? I shook my head.

"Well, buck up. We're only passing through."

Did people really live here? Like *this*? The fluttering of laundry hanging on lines strung between buildings caught my eye. Apparently they did.

We walked through alleys and shabby narrow streets that didn't belong to the Boston I knew. As we turned a corner, we passed by a quaint little grocery. Zanfini's, it was called.

Jack tugged on my arm and pulled me away down into a stairway that led to a basement-level door.

He rapped on it with a knuckle.

A little window set into the door slid open.

He shot a look over his shoulder up the stairs and then stepped closer to the door. "Joe sent me."

The door cracked open. He started through, but I hung back. I knew what this was. I'd heard about them before from some of the girls. It was a *speakeasy*! "I don't think I should go in there. And I don't think you should either."

"Relax, baby. This place isn't on the list for tonight."

"What list?"

Sighing, he held up a finger to the man tending the door and stepped back out, bending to talk into my ear. "It's not going to be raided . . . at least not tonight. So we're safe, see?" He put an arm around my shoulders and turned me toward the door.

Raided! I hadn't been worried about being caught in a raid. I was worried about being there at all. And so should he. "But—but—you're a policeman!"

"That's right. And you're a hello girl. And we both deserve a drink after a hard day's work, right?" Eyeing the man at the door, he pushed me through it and we were enveloped by a blanket of hot, stale air and the blue haze of cigarette smoke.

My nose wrinkled. It smelled all yeasty, like the insides of Lawrence's smelly old shoes.

There was a band playing on a stage at the back of the long narrow room. A bar along one of the side walls looked very much like the one at the country club, only this one had both men *and* women lounging along it. And cigarette smoke drifted from everyone's lips.

At least they were only drinking coffee.

I tapped Jack's arm. "This . . . isn't right."

He took a look around the room. "You said it. There ought

to be a free table at this hour." He gestured a waiter over and said something to him I couldn't hear for all the noise in the place.

The man turned and bent toward a table.

The people sitting at it looked up at the waiter, looked over at Jack, and then they gathered their things and left. The waiter pulled out a chair, gesturing us over. "Here you are, Mr. Feeney. Anything you need, just tell me."

Jack winked at me as the waiter left. "That's better."

"What did you say to him?"

"I do people favors, they do me favors." He shrugged as he sat, then gestured toward one of the empty chairs. "Go on. Have a seat."

Favors? I didn't want to be too obvious about things but . . . "Do you ever do favors for Irish people?"

"Sure. And Italians too."

"What kind of favors?"

"Oh . . . I don't know." He grimaced. "I'm starting to sound like you."

I tried to be the most Ellis-like Janie I could, opening my eyes wide and fluttering my lashes as if I were the dumb Dora I felt like most of the time. "You must know a lot of important people, being a policeman and all."

"I know some."

"Do you know the governor?"

He put an elbow on the table as he looked around the room. "Naw. Never met him. Seems like a flat tire."

"Do you know . . ." Who was that baseball player Lawrence was always going on about? " . . . the Babe?"

"Wouldn't I like to!"

147

"How about the mayor?"

"Mayor Curley? Sure. Everyone knows him."

I felt my heart pause in its beating. "Did you ever do any favors for him?"

He stopped looking at the crowd and fixed his gaze on me. "This is starting to sound like the third degree." He looked past me and then summoned someone with the crook of his finger.

The waiter soon appeared.

Jack looked up at him. "What have you got to eat?"

The waiter rattled off the choices. Jack ordered for both of us. With people drinking coffee and Jack ordering food, maybe my fears had been ill-founded. Maybe this was just a restaurant after all. I felt myself begin to relax. Maybe everything was going to be fine. Except Jack had said he knew the mayor. "Have you ever . . . shaken his hand?"

"Whose hand? The mayor's?" He looked at me through narrowed eyes. "Don't tell me you're one of those dames who's crazy about him."

"No, I—"

"I guess I could introduce you sometime if you really want to meet him."

"No!"

He cocked his head and gave me a knowing look. "So you're one of those who thinks he's not good enough to *be* mayor? Are you one of those lace-curtain Irish who got something against him?"

"I just think a mayor ought to follow the laws he makes like everyone else has to."

"Baby, let me tell you something." As he leaned close, I

couldn't keep myself from doing the same. "*Nobody* follows the laws."

"I do."

"And I'll bet that's only because you don't know any better. But I'll tell you something else: You'll never get anywhere by just following along, doing what people tell you to."

"But I—"

"Take me, for instance. I could just keep my head down and mind my own business and never be anything but a policeman. But I looked around and decided, what's the use in that?" He reached into his pocket and pulled out a pack of cigarettes. "Nobody likes a stool pigeon. There's people getting rich in this city, making money on the side, just by being friendly. And what's that cost me? Nothing. But it sure makes me an awful lot."

"But those favors you do . . . are they . . . wrong?"

"Wrong doesn't matter anymore. I was in the war with a bunch of fellows who worried about what was right and what was wrong, and guess what? They're not here anymore. You do what you have to, you know what I mean? And what's the harm in looking the other way? In letting people have a little fun once in a while?"

Plenty, if it meant making plans to murder Griff! "But you never . . . you've never actually *hurt* anyone, have you?"

"Naw. Seen enough blood and guts when I was in the trenches."

So if he was telling the truth, he wasn't in on the plot. He was just . . . what *was* he doing? I wished I could think faster! Clearly the telephone men were part of the plan, but that didn't mean Jack was, did it? I gave up trying to figure it out right then, but there was still one thing that bothered me. "Why do people keep voting for the mayor if he doesn't follow his own rules?"

"He buys their votes."

"Buys them? But—that's illegal!"

"Are you sure you're from around here? He doesn't pay them in money. He pays them in jobs and paved roads and playgrounds for their kids. They vote for him because he tells them what they want to hear, and he gives them what they want. Nobody votes for someone who's going to sit there in city hall and shake his finger at them. The mayor's just like everybody else. That's why they vote for him."

"But . . . he's very unfair, favoring his friends and buying votes."

"A person'd think you didn't have any friends yourself! Who do you want him to favor? His enemies? What's the good in being mayor if you can't reward the people who vote for you?"

"Well . . . I never actually thought—"

"You sound like you're one of those bluebloods who live up on Beacon Hill."

I shrugged.

"They had their turn; they made their pile. Now it's time for the rest of us."

"You make him sound like Robin Hood."

"Exactly! Bury the rich and help the poor. Or at least, don't worry so much about the rich and help the poor. Who wouldn't like a guy like that?"

Me. And Griff. And—and nearly everyone I knew! Why should we be despised for making money? What was wrong with that? Why should they hate us for it when they wanted the chance to make some too? "But can't you see? He isn't Robin Hood anymore. He's become that awful king who stole all the power in the first place."

"You have a funny way of looking at things, baby. Do me a favor—stop thinking. Start eating." He pointed to the plates the waiter was setting down in front of us.

I did. And I have to say, it was much better than the cafeteria food down at Central. But I wasn't here to eat. I was here to figure out what Jack knew. "So . . . what are you working on now? At work?"

"Work."

"Aren't you . . . arresting anyone? Or catching any thieves?"

"I'm trying to keep out of trouble, that's what I'm doing. You haven't remembered anything, have you? From that telephone call?"

I shook my head.

"Good. Then let's just forget about it."

"But what if I did?"

"What if you did." He looked at me the same way my father did when he found out I'd done something I shouldn't have. "If you did, you'd come and tell me. And then you'd forget about it again."

"But what if I couldn't forget?"

"What if you couldn't forget." He put down his fork and folded his hands behind his plate. "If you couldn't forget . . . then I suppose, it wouldn't really matter, would it? Unless you recognized the voices of the people who were talking. And even then it probably wouldn't matter, because how could you know what they were talking about? And even if you did know, what could you do about it? Because if it were something you felt you had to tell the police, well . . ." He opened his arms wide. "Here I am. So you'd end up telling me."

"So if I told you . . . then what would you do?"

He gave me a long, hard look. And then he dropped his gaze. "I don't know."

The hairs at the back of my neck stood on end.

"Thing is, I think you're a peach, baby. And you weren't trying to listen in on any telephone calls. So do me a favor—forget what you heard—and I'll do you a favor."

He'd do me a favor? "So are you saying . . . we're friends?"

"Yeah. That's right. We're friends."

"But what if—"

"Listen to me. Just let it go. Forget about it. Forget about the whole thing."

"But what if someone was going to get hurt because I didn't say something?"

"Who could get hurt? There's this kid, this—prince, they call him. He lives up on that hill, thinks he's above all the rest of us, and he won't do anyone any favors. All that's going to happen is someone's going to get him to reconsider. Get it? That's all."

"But what if he doesn't want to . . . or won't?"

"He's a smart kid. He'll know what side the toast is buttered on."

"But what—"

"Don't make me have to do something I don't want to do, baby. I can be Jack or I can be Officer Feeney. Which do you want me to be?"

"Jack . . . ? I—"

"Good choice. Now. I didn't bring you here to talk about

things we're not going to talk about. I brought you here because I thought we could have a good time."

A good time? With someone who was threatening me!
Because that's what he was doing, wasn't it? Trying to keep
me from telling him the truth? Not that I would because it
would be much too dangerous and then I wouldn't find out
anything about what those people planned to do to Griff. I
still hadn't really found out anything I hadn't already known,
but at least now I knew I hadn't made it all up. I tried out
a Marion Mack smile. Everything was going to be fine. I
couldn't admit to being Ellis, and right now I might not be
doing that great a job of being Janie, but I could be a dumb
Dora all right!

"Anything you say, Jack."

13

I don't know why girls insisted they had heaps of fun at places like this. An hour later, the heat and cigarette smoke had made my body numb, and the buzz and hum of the jazz the band was playing was making my mind numb too. It was a funny sort of feeling . . . as if everything had gone hazy. And crazy. As if I wasn't myself at all.

I didn't like it.

The waiter had asked if another couple could join our table. He was very apologetic about it, but Jack hadn't seemed to mind. So now we were sitting arm-to-arm, pressed against each other, and I didn't like that either.

"Ellis!"

My head snapped up before I could remind myself I wasn't Ellis. I was supposed to be Janie.

But unfortunately, Irene Bennett didn't know that. "Ellis! Over here!"

Jack leaned back and looked over my shoulder. "Who's that dame shouting at?"

I tried to look as if I had no idea, but when I turned, I saw

Irene crawling across the tops of tables toward ours. When she stood up on one and leaped toward us, Jack popped up and caught her hand, helping her clear the gap. She jumped down, planting herself between us. "Who'd have ever thought I'd see you here?"

"A friend of yours?" Jack was watching us, a bemused smile on his face.

"Jack, this is Irene. Irene . . ."

She decided to commandeer half my chair and then threw her arm about my neck. Now she was whispering in my ear. "Where'd you find him? He's delicious!" She pressed her temple against mine as if we were best of friends again.

It was my turn to whisper into her ear. "I'm pretending not to be Ellis right now. Can you call me Janie?"

"Janie! Sure, why not? Have you got a cigarette?"

"Cigarette?"

"Sure, baby. Here you go." Jack pulled two from a pack, stuck them into his mouth, and then he pulled a lighter from his shirt pocket. He lit them both and took a big puff. Once the tips were glowing, he took one from his mouth and handed it to me.

Irene intercepted it and took it from him instead. "Ellis doesn't smoke." She had to raise her voice to be heard.

"Who's this Ellis you keep talking about?" He was signalling madly for a waiter.

I jammed Irene in the ribs with my elbow.

She bobbled the cigarette, nearly dropping it. "What?"

I pulled it from her lips and crushed it out in an ashtray.

"Why'd you go and do that for?"

Jack had propped an elbow on the table. "No: *who*."

156

Jack fairly shouted the word. "That's what I want to know. I haven't been so confused since I was at Belleau Wood, back in the war."

"Who, what?" Irene was pouting.

I almost wished I'd let her keep the awful thing. "Irene and I were in a—a—play a week ago. And I was playing this jester and she was—"

Irene wasn't listening anymore; she was staring intently into the cloud of cigarette smoke that swirled around her head.

"She was the queen."

Jack didn't look any less confused, but he'd finally succeeded in getting a waiter's attention. The man leaned close. Jack nodded to me. "What are you drinking?"

"A . . . coffee?" That's what everyone else seemed to be drinking.

"Coffee! What do you think this place is, baby? A diner?" He glanced up at the waiter. "Get me a whiskey. Old-fashioned. And two sidecars for the ladies."

I stopped the waiter with a hand to his arm. "Make that one. I don't really feel like anything."

Irene had stopped him too. "Make mine a French 75 instead."

Jack whistled, brow raised. "That's not for the faint of heart."

Irene gave him a smoldering look. "And neither am I."

Honestly! I elbowed her again.

After several minutes, the waiter deposited two coffee cups on the table. Irene snatched one up and downed it.

I gasped. "Careful—hot!"

She put it down with a raucous laugh. "What do you think was in there? Thanks, Jack!" With a wink and a kiss on his lips, she pushed off through the tables on her way back to wherever it was she had come from.

Jack asked me to dance, so we left our table and worked our way toward the band at the end of the room.

I saw Irene had stopped at someone's table and was sitting on the lap of a man I hoped she knew. It looked like . . . was it that man from the theater? The one she'd gone off with that night?

As we passed, Irene shot up, grabbed me around the arm, and pulled me close, eyeing Jack as she did so. "You've always been a nice girl, Ellis, so I'm going to tell you something. Don't ever let a man buy you a drink. They buy you a drink, and they think you owe them something." Her grip on my arm was making my fingers grow numb.

"I won't." I hadn't. Jack had wanted to, but I'd told him no.

"They say you just have to get over your inhibitions. So I did." She laughed as she threw her arms up and did a shimmy, making the beads around her neck sway. It was a strange kind of hollow-sounding laugh that didn't match the look in her eyes.

The man she'd been with stood and planted a kiss on her neck, then snaked an arm around her waist.

She swatted his hand away with another of those odd laughs. "The modern girl isn't supposed to believe in romance . . . or love."

Not believe in love? That was like not believing in happy endings! "But if you don't believe in love, what is there to believe in?"

The man reached out from behind her with a lighted cigarette. She took his hand in hers and guided it to her mouth,
taking a greedy drag. Then she blew out the smoke in a ring.
"What is there to believe in? You don't have to believe in
anything anymore. Don't you know that? There's nothing
left *to* believe in." She took another drag before turning to
kiss the man on the mouth.

He pulled her close, pressing another kiss to her neck.

She pulled away, putting a hand to his chest. "What do
you believe in, Floyd?"

"I believe I'll have another drink!"

The table cheered as they all picked up their coffee cups
and waved them in the air.

Though he went on kissing her neck, she grabbed my arm
again. "You don't have to believe in anything, Ellis. That's
the trouble with you. You just have to be happy."

"Are you happy, Irene?"

"Delirious! Can't you tell?"

Jack tugged at my hand. "Let's go dance." I didn't mind
when he pulled me toward the stage. Maybe after we danced
we could leave.

The band was playing a lively tune, and we broke out into
a Charleston. Jack somehow always managed to stay close
despite our twisting legs and flying arms. As the band segued
into another song, Jack cleared a table, grabbed me around
the waist, and set me down atop it. At least there was more
room to dance up there, so I did—my beads flying and my
hair spilling down into my eyes.

After the song was done, Jack gave me his hand and helped
me down. Another girl took my place. We worked our way

back toward the table we'd left, but our chairs had already been claimed.

"That friend of yours. Seems like she knows how to have some fun. Sure I can't buy you a drink? Look what it did for her."

I followed his gaze and then gasped. Irene was shimmying up on stage with some musician who was playing a saxophone. As we watched, the song ended. She turned her back to us, bent at the waist and flipped up her—oh my goodness!

"Get hot! Get hot!" Jack and most of the rest of the men in the room gave her a wolf whistle. Several of the girls were . . . clapping?! Why?

Poor Irene! She must either be ill or overcome by the heat to make such a display of herself. Someone really ought to go and cover her up. I made my way around the tables toward the stage. She was still doing it. Bending over and flipping up her skirt. Again and again and again. I put a hand over my eyes to block the view. What was wrong with her?

When I got to the stage, I reached up, grabbed hold of her hand, and pulled her down.

Or tried to.

She didn't want to come.

I dropped her arm and climbed up on the stage, and then I practically had to wrestle with her to get her to stop. When that didn't work, I reached out and grabbed her by the ear.

Someone started booing. "Aw, come on! Don't be such a wet blanket."

She was laughing that strange laugh again. "Did you see me?"

"Everyone saw you, Irene."

SIRI MITCHELL

"Do you think so? I hope so!"

I gave her a none-too-gentle push toward the stairs. "What on earth possessed you—!"

"Oh, it's all in good fun."

Good fun was spitting watermelon seeds off the back porch at the shore . . . or changing pepper shakers for the salt shakers. "I don't even know what to say to you. What would the dean think?"

"You should pay attention to your own potatoes! What's it to you what I do?"

"I don't even think you *know* what you're doing . . . do you?"

"People like it. Men like it. Didn't you hear them whistling?"

"Some men would whistle at any girl. And a decent man would have turned away. Some things just shouldn't be done. By anybody!"

"I'm not a Lowell or an Eton or a Cabot. And I don't have a Prince Phillips either. I don't have the luxury of knowing my family's already got my future taken care of. Girls like me have to do for themselves. We have to take what we can get."

"And you're hoping to find someone worth having here?" I turned her so she could look out on all those drunken faces with their red-rimmed eyes.

"Just—" She pushed me. "Go away. You're being a party pooper."

As I stumbled, she disappeared into the crowd. The band started on another song, and then everyone went back to drinking and talking and laughing. Suddenly I was tired of it all. Was I the only one not having a good time?

161

Up ahead, at the far end of the room, I could just about make out the door. Inching past tables, slipping between all the people, I finally reached it.

When we'd first come in the sun had been out; it had long since set. But at least it was quieter outside, and I wasn't standing shoulder to shoulder with people I didn't know.

I climbed the stairs and turned into the alley, then sat down on a curb.

Every day, in every way, I'm getting better and better. Tears started to slip down my cheeks. *Every day, in every way, I'm getting better and better.* I was supposed to be getting better! Why wasn't I getting any smarter? Or at least a little less stupid? And what was I doing here with a man who was connected to killers? Maybe I'd already gotten as better as I was ever going to get.

A wave of despair swept up from the pit of my stomach and rolled right over the top of my head. For the first time, the thought occurred to me that perhaps I'd chosen too big a part for myself to play. Who was I trying to kid? Sometimes I couldn't even remember to pretend to be Janie. The suspicion I wasn't even good at the one thing I'd always thought I was good at began to grow. And if I wasn't good at acting, how could I expect anyone to put me in a movie? But I *had* to be good at acting! I had to keep Jack thinking I was just some dumb Dora. He was my best chance at keeping Griff alive.

I covered my face with my hands and sobbed. I couldn't do anything right. I shouldn't be here; I should be at the Exeter with my father.

Why did I have to be me?

Mother and Father wanted me to be good. Griff wanted

me to be his girl. Jack wanted me to keep my mouth shut and forget about what I'd heard, and Irene wanted me to go away. But I couldn't do any of those things. I couldn't be the person everyone wanted me to be. It was like that chapter I'd read from Romans at the Missionary Aid Society: I'd tried, over and over again, to be the person I knew I ought to be, and I'd only ever ended up making everything worse. If I tried any harder, they'd just all end up hating me even more.

So that's why I was going to Hollywood just as soon as I could get away from here. I'd leave today, right now, only I'd promised Janie I'd keep her job for her. And there was Griff to worry about, and Jack. And now there was Irene too. There were too many people who needed too many things.

It would be easy if I were the film actress Colleen Moore. Then I could just tell Mother and Father I wasn't a good student and I never would be, and they'd just smile and say they knew and they loved me anyway. If I were Colleen Moore, I could tell Griff I wasn't any good for him and why couldn't he just see that, and then he'd embrace me and say, *"I guess there was no harm in trying."*

How could I ever be myself when they were certain I was somebody different? How could I look them in the eyes and say something I just knew was going to disappoint them?

I nearly laughed aloud. Why was I worrying about disappointing everyone? It was the only thing I seemed to be good at doing. I disappointed someone nearly every day. *Every day, in every way, I'm getting worse and worse.* That's the phrase I ought to be repeating.

"Janie?" Jack's call floated toward me from around the corner. He must be looking for me.

I dabbed at my eyes with the heels of my hands, trying to hide the traces of my tears.

"Janie . . ." Jack appeared around the corner. "There you are! You shouldn't be alone out here by yourself. Come back inside."

If I had to go back inside that smelly old place, I'd just about scream! I tried on a pout. "Do we have to? It's so noisy. And stuffy. And besides, I couldn't even hear you talk in there." I rose and linked my arm through his.

"I suppose we don't have to. But then . . . what would we do?"

"Why . . . we'd . . . we'd walk."

"Walk?"

"What's wrong with walking?"

"Nothing." He glanced down at me. "But you sure are an odd bird. Most girls like to drink. And dance."

"I'm not most girls."

Jack laughed. "You can say that again! So . . . where do I drop you?"

"Drop me?"

"Where do you live?"

"Where do I live?" I hadn't given one thought yet to how I was supposed to get home. I'd told the driver not to pick me up at Central, only I hadn't realized he wouldn't be picking me up at all. I needed to be escorted home, only the problem was, I couldn't be. I was Janie, and Janie lived . . . who knew where. With Doris! But . . . where did Doris live? I was used to a driver taking me where I needed to go and picking me up again. What did people do who didn't have drivers? I'd just have to go back home by myself. "Don't worry about it.

I'll just walk." Jack had said we were in the north end of the city. If that were true, then I just had to go south. And then go west. Only . . . I'd gotten so turned around coming to the speakeasy, I didn't know which way south was.

"I'll walk along with you."

"You don't have to." Although . . . it was a bit of a way back up to Beacon Hill and, really, was it safe to walk there all by myself?

"I might be just a cop, but that doesn't mean I don't know how to treat a girl. So where to?"

Maybe I could talk him into leaving me at the bottom of the hill. "Beacon Hill."

He whistled. "Beacon Hill!"

"It's not just rich people up there. Servants live in those houses too, you know. People like my mother." I hadn't lied. Janie's mother had lived there, and my mother did too, in the same house even, which just went to show how much truth I was telling!

He scoffed as we started off through the night.

14

Jack insisted on riding with me on the elevated railway and walking me *all* the way home, and then he wouldn't leave until I went inside. Since I was pretending to be Janie, I took him round to the back entrance and gave a wave as I slipped inside. And after that, I still had to creep upstairs. Once I'd made it to my room, I glanced out the window and saw a light still blazing at the Phillipses' house. I yanked the curtains shut. This was all Griff's fault! Him and his dumb numbers.

I hung up my dress and then went down the hall to brush my teeth. When I came back it smelled as if I'd brought the speakeasy home with me. I sniffed at the dress.

Gracious, but it stank!

Pushing aside the curtains, I opened the window and hooked the dress over the frame. But the smell still seemed to follow me wherever I went.

Pulling at the strap of my slip, I sniffed the material and nearly choked, coughing. The smell was *me*! There was nothing for it but a bath. And by the time I'd put up my hair in pins, it was long past midnight. I tried to go to sleep, but I just couldn't. I hadn't lost so much sleep over anything since my end-of-term final exams.

So I got up, pulled out a deck of cards, and sat at my desk, shuffling them.

Griff didn't know anything about the plot against him, and he didn't know any Irish people, so there was nothing more to be found out from that side of things. If I wanted to figure out who that king was, I needed to talk to Jack again. I'd just have to go see him down at the precinct station and make him ask me on another date.

The next day, instead of taking me directly home, I asked the chauffeur to take me to the police instead.

"To the station, miss? Are you sure?"

I was. Although I became quite a bit less certain once I set foot inside. Two men were having a fistfight right in the front hall. A policeman was dragging a youth down a corridor, and standing against the wall were three women wearing quite a bit less clothing than Theda Bara ever had in her movies.

I resisted the urge to cover my eyes with my pocketbook as I walked to the front desk.

"I'd like to see Jack Feeney, please."

He raised a brow. "Are you sure you want Jack? Because if you're not, then you could have me."

I let my gaze drop to my toes, just like Janie did whenever anyone teased her. "I'm sure."

"Just a minute, then."

It took about ten minutes. And during that time, I managed to almost have my pocketbook stolen right from underneath my arm, and then I was very nearly knocked over by a man who reeked of liquor.

"Miss Winslow." Jack hailed me with a smile, but as he approached, it dropped from his face. "Don't tell me you're here because you remembered something."

"No. I'm here because—"

He leaned forward. "*Don't tell me.*"

I leaned toward him. "Don't tell you what?"

"Anything."

He pulled up the counter and walked through. And then he took me by the elbow and hustled me right out of the station.

When we reached the sidewalk, he finally dropped my arm as he turned to face me. "Don't tell me your conscience got the better of you."

"My conscience rarely ever does that . . . even though it probably should. At least . . . that's what my mother keeps telling me."

He laughed. "So . . . what is it, then?"

"I just wanted to thank you for last night."

"You're welcome." He was looking up the street with some interest as he answered. And then he turned and looked in the other direction.

I turned to look too, only it didn't seem like there was anything to see. "Is there something—"

"Listen, can we go somewhere and talk?"

"Now?"

"Now. Only I just . . . just give me a minute. I'll be right back."

When he disappeared into the station, I told the driver to

let my father know I'd had to work late and that someone would give me a ride home.

Jack came out just as the car was driving off. "I don't suppose you'd want to go back to the North End, would you?"

"No." I had no desire to see the inside of a speakeasy ever again.

"Then I'm at the end of good ideas." He was glancing up and down the street again.

"Let's go . . ." Someplace out in the open, where everyone could see us. "Let's go to the Public Garden."

He shrugged and put his hand to the small of my back, gesturing forward with his other hand. "Fine by me."

We walked over to Tremont Street and up to the Public Garden, where we traded asphalt streets for paths and grass and flowers.

He took a deep breath as he pushed his hat up his forehead. "I haven't been to the Garden in years."

A string of giggling girls ran past us chasing a duck.

"And I've forgotten what it was like to be that happy."

I glanced over at him.

His mouth was set in a firm, straight line. "Never thought I'd even get out of Europe alive. Lots of the fellows didn't."

"That ought to make you happy, then."

"It should. But it doesn't because it makes a person wonder, Why me? Why was I the lucky one? Why wasn't it my head got blown off instead of his? And then it makes you ask if you deserved it."

"Deserved what?"

"Deserved living. Maybe the other guy was a better guy

than you were. Maybe he was the one who should have lived. Maybe you're the one who should have died."

"That's a morbid way of looking at things." Maybe that's why he'd forgotten how to be happy.

"War is a morbid way of dealing with things, don't you think?"

I shrugged. "I guess." I hadn't thought much about the war. All of my friends had been too young to go and all of our fathers had been too old. One of our servants had gone to fight. He hadn't come back, but by the time we were told he'd died, he'd already been replaced.

Jack swept a hand over his face, and when he was done, he looked like his normal self again. "Do you want to go on a swan boat?"

I looked at the boats plying their way around the lagoon, seats filled with couples or children. "I don't think so."

"Then can I buy you an ice cream?"

He bought us both a cone. We found a bench fronting the lagoon and sat down to eat. I finished mine before he did, so I decided I might as well ask him my question. "Do you know any kings, Jack?"

"Sure. The king of hearts, the king of spades, the king of clubs, and the king of diamonds."

"I'm serious."

"So am I, baby."

He didn't seem like a bad guy so much as he seemed rather . . . sad.

Janie would not have approved of this. At all. She wouldn't be sitting here if she were me, which was quite funny if you thought about it because I *was* her. And if I hadn't done such a poor job of being her, if I hadn't botched that telephone transfer, then I wouldn't be here either. But I was and I had a feeling, even if she'd made the same mistake I had, she never would have agreed to go with Jack anywhere.

"Are you asking about that telephone call again?"

I nodded.

"I'm a gambling man, so what I'm about to say is based on experience with all kinds of fellows you wouldn't want your mother to meet. Stop asking around about kings and things you don't know anything about. It won't do you any good, and it might just get you into trouble. Some people get nervous when other people start asking questions."

So there *was* a king!

"Understand?"

"Sure, Jack."

"And don't come down to the station again. You seem like a nice girl, and you don't deserve to be involved in any of this. I'm trying to keep you out of trouble."

And I was trying to keep Griff out of trouble.

He pulled a pack of cigarettes from his pocket. "Want one?"

"No. It's a dirty habit, and you shouldn't smoke." I made a swipe at the packet, but he pulled it out of reach.

"No kidding—picked it up in the trenches. But it's good for the nerves."

"What have you got to be nervous about?" He was a policeman for goodness' sake.

"You'd be surprised."

"Then tell me. How did you . . . how did you start with all of this? Doing favors for people? And making friends?"

He sent a sideways look over at me as he took a drag on his cigarette. He exhaled with a long sigh. "You don't want to hear my sob story."

"But I do."

He waved his hand, which only had the effect of sending his cigarette smoke in my direction.

I coughed.

"Sorry." He waved his hand in the other direction, trying to send the smoke away, but it only made it worse.

"See there? I always make a mess of things."

I could have smiled, hearing my own thoughts repeated by him. "Tell me."

"You owe people one favor and then you owe them two favors and then pretty soon you owe them everything you have. See?"

Frankly? "No."

He sighed. "You really . . . ?" The look he sent me was one of pure frustration, but then he took another look. "You really don't, do you? Maybe living up on that hill really does make people see things differently."

"I'm not so different from you." Only he was a boy and I was a girl. And he was a policeman and I was a co-ed, although I wasn't planning to be one for much longer, and he'd been in the war and I hadn't . . . so maybe we didn't have so much in common after all. Except making a mess of everything. From what he'd said, we were both good at that.

"They say confession is good for the soul. I suppose . . . maybe it is. See, most of the fellows I grew up with got drafted, just like me. But some of them didn't. And a couple of them got into trouble while I was gone."

"What did they—"

"Doesn't matter." He said it so firmly, I didn't dare to pursue it. "When I came back, I didn't know any of that. And besides, I'd gotten a job right off the bat with the police department. Kept me away from my old neighborhood. But I ran into them one day down at a bar. We had a drink. They said they had to meet someone and wanted to know, would I drive?"

He sounded so miserable, I wanted to make him feel better about it, whatever it turned out to be. "That doesn't sound like anything terrible. It sounds like you were just trying to be friendly."

"Just being friendly. That's right. I used to know my way around the city, figured it hadn't changed much since I'd been gone. I didn't have anything better to do, and I wasn't on duty that day. Why not, I said. One thing led to another." He broke off. "I'm not going to tell you what they did."

"I won't tell anyone."

He turned to look at me. "You wouldn't want to. But you'd probably feel like you ought to and that's no way to live."

"But—"

"You asked for the story. I'm trying to oblige. Now. You going to listen or do I stop talking?"

"I'll listen."

"So they did something bad and there I am, driving the getaway car."

"Did you know they had—"

"Wasn't any way I couldn't have known."

"So you were—?" What did that make him? Not one of the bad guys. At least, not exactly.

"An accessory to the crime. That's what it's called. You didn't commit the crime, but you helped someone else in the doing of it. Doesn't look very good, does it? A cop who's an accessory to the crime?"

"I guess it wouldn't."

"They thanked me, said they'd never bother me about anything again, and they didn't. Not for over a year."

"But . . . ?"

"But one day after work, they asked me if I couldn't do them another favor." He shrugged. "What could I say?"

"But . . . they aren't your real friends. Real friends wouldn't ask you to do whatever it is they asked you to do. You know that, don't you?"

"Sure I know that. But like I said, you try to do the right thing by someone. Over there, in the trenches, I traded places with a buddy one night. Let him sleep in my spot instead. There was less mud in mine, and he was fighting a . . ." He paused to scratch at his ear. He swallowed. "He was fighting a cold. I thought I was doing the right thing, just trying to be nice, only a mortar came in the middle of the night and landed right on top of him. Never could find any trace of him. I looked all over. Dog tags . . . something. Didn't find nothing. That mortar was meant for me, don't you see? Only it got him instead."

"So . . . what are you saying? That you somehow deserve this?" Even I was smart enough to see the foolishness in that.

"Naw. I'm saying it doesn't really matter."

"Doesn't really—! Of course it matters. You can't just— you can't just let them boss you around like that!"

"What choice have I got?"

"You can tell them to do their own dirty work." That's what they called it in the movies: dirty work.

As he looked at me his mouth stretched with amusement. "Sure. Just like that. And then they'll turn me over to my boss for all those favors I've been doing for them. I have thought about refusing, once or twice. But the only thing I can figure is I'd find myself in jail. And can you guess how they treat cops in there?"

"But it's blackmail!"

"That's what they call it."

"And you're not doing something about it?"

"What would you like me to do?"

Something. Anything! Anything but sit beside me on a bench smoking a cigarette, telling me there was nothing he could do.

"There's nothing I can do. I just have to keep on doing favors and hope that if I can save up enough money, someday I can leave this all behind. Skip town. You know?"

He *was* just like me. "Skip town and go to Hollywood."

Jack smiled. "That's right. Maybe I should go to Hollywood too. I could look you up when I get there."

"But don't you think—"

"No. I don't think, not anymore. Nothing to be gained by thinking. Most of the cops I know are doing favors on the side for somebody. City Hall. Rumrunners. Bootleggers. So in the end, who really cares?"

"Who really—!"

He held up a finger as he cut me off. "But listen now to what I tell you: You've got to keep clear of all of this. A nice girl like you shouldn't even be seen with me. People might start to get the wrong idea."

"But . . . what about that kid you were talking about? The one they mentioned on the telephone." Kid? Listen to me! Griff was ten months older than I was.

"What about him?"

"What's going to happen to him?"

"You can't worry about what's going to happen to other people. I figured that out during the war. The only person who matters is you."

"But—but what if I know him or something?"

"You don't know him. Might have seen him since you live up on that hill. Or heard of him, maybe. Most people have heard of him. But you don't know him."

"How do you know?"

"Because people like him don't have time to say hello to people like you and me. Anyway, they're not going to do anything to him if he starts doing what he's told. He's a smart kid. He probably will."

Griff most definitely would not! "But what if he doesn't?"

Jack narrowed his eyes as if my question had caused him physical pain. "He will. No use thinking too far ahead."

"But the men on the telephone seemed to think he wouldn't. And they were planning what to—" I clapped a hand over my mouth. I wasn't supposed to be remembering the conversation. I was supposed to let him think I'd forgotten about it. Or hadn't really heard it in the first place.

"I kind of figured that's the way it is. You're too smart not to have remembered what they said."

Too *smart*? Oh sure! The one time someone thought I was actually smart was the one time I truly didn't want to be. "I guess I—"

"Don't worry. I already told them you don't remember anything. But you've got to stop asking questions. *Now*."

I must have spent an hour pacing in my room that night. I wasn't supposed to see Jack again, and he didn't want me asking any more questions, so I wasn't going to get any information from him.

But there *did* seem to be a king involved. So that was one thing.

And Griff truly did seem to be in some kind of danger, didn't he? I mean, Jack hadn't actually said so, but he didn't *not* say so either. So . . . from what he hadn't said, I could assume Griff truly was in trouble and that was very bad.

At first the bad guys were just voices on the other end of the telephone lines. But now they were people Jack knew. They seemed to be getting closer and closer. Which just meant that I had to be on guard. And no matter what, I had to keep Griff alive and *that* meant I had to figure it all out before I left for Hollywood in just a week and a half.

I was so close! If only I could figure out who the king was.

But Griff didn't know anything, and Jack wasn't going to tell me anything. If I needed information, it looked like I'd just have to find it somewhere else.

Griff. Mayor. Irish. Telephone men. Jack. Me.

Griff was out. The mayor seemed to be the problem. I didn't know any Irish, and Jack wouldn't tell me anything. That just left the men from the telephone call. I supposed . . . I'd just have to ask *them* who the king was.

15

I thought about it the next day at work as I patched through
telephone calls. I still had the list of numbers I'd recorded
that first afternoon, and that telephone number had to be
among them. I just didn't know which one it was. If only I
could hear one of the voices again! If I couldn't call all those
numbers from work, I had to find a different telephone to
use. I'd have to do it from home.

But . . . what if I called the right number and someone
else answered? I'd never know it was the right number then,
would I?

I chewed on a nail as I thought about it.

What if someone else *did* answer the telephone?

I could always ask for the man of the house. That's what
I'd do. I'd just start calling the telephone numbers. And then,
once I'd found the right one I'd . . . well . . . what *would* I do?

A light blinked on the board in front of me. I plugged a
jack in and flipped the switch. "Number, please."

"Tremont-4613."

I plugged in the other jack and flipped the switch again.

179

Even if I was able to match the telephone number to one of the voices, I couldn't take that information to the police. Jack had told me not to talk to him anymore. And even if I discovered the right telephone number, it still wouldn't tell me anything else about those men. It was just a number, not a name, not an address—and Griff would still be in danger. I still wouldn't be any closer to solving the puzzle.

I hated puzzles.

Janie would probably be really good at this. She was smart that way.

Another light flickered. I plugged a jack in and flipped the switch. "Number, please."

Why couldn't I be good at anything? Well . . . I was good at some things, but why couldn't I be good at something that was worth being good at!

I tromped up the stairs behind Doris at noon. The lunch wasn't half bad. I'm pretty sure it was chipped beef.

She leaned close as I finished. "Why the long face?"

"I'm trying to figure something out."

"Doing one of those crossword puzzles?"

"No. That would be easy compared to this."

"So tell me what it is. Maybe I can help."

Maybe she could. "Say you want to find out who someone is, but you only have his telephone number . . . could you do it?"

"Well, sure!"

"But how?"

"Call the telephone operator."

"Call the . . . ?" But the telephone operator was *me*. "How would I—I mean *she*. How would *she* know?"

"What kind of dumb Dora are you? You call Central, tell them the number, they transfer you to the station, the station transfers you to the right board, and then you ask whatever hello girl answers."

Which would *still* be me. "I don't understand how she'd know something like that."

"She'd look it up in the file box. She'd be a B operator just like you. So she'd pull out the card with that number on it, and she'd tell you what address it's assigned to."

"Just like that?"

"Well, sure! I mean . . . wait—did Janie not tell you?"

"Tell me what?!" The whole conversation reminded me of my economics tests. I was pretty sure I was supposed to know everything on them, but somehow none of it ever made any sense.

"When we go back down to work, I'll show you."

"See?" Doris was pointing to a box that was sitting underneath the desk part of my board.

I hadn't noticed it before.

She leaned over, pulled it out, and lifted the lid. "There's a card for every number on your board." She pulled one out and handed it to me.

I read *Tremont-4627* and then eyed the address underneath it. "So each one of my numbers has a card?"

She nodded as she stowed her gum behind her ear. "There's one hundred and fifty of them, one for every number, in case someone calls with an emergency. That way, you can tell the police or fire department where to go, only you'll never have to because you're a B operator . . . but you could. If you had to. So . . . now you know."

Lights were already blinking on my board, so I sat down, put my headset on, and went to work with growing excitement. All I had to do was make those telephone calls. Once I recognized the voice and could check the telephone number against the card in the box, I'd know where the call had gone!

I got through my shift without any trouble. I got home without any trouble. I almost made it up the stairs without trouble, but then I heard someone call my name. I slowly turned around. " . . . Griff?"

"Hi." He stuck his hands in his pockets. "My father's away in Washington for a few days, and your father and I were thinking, well . . . we had kind of thought that . . ."

While he'd been talking, my father had joined him down at the foot of the staircase. "Why don't we all go down to Union Oyster House for dinner this evening?"

"Tonight? Right *now*?"

He shrugged, which is something he never would have done if Mother had been there. "Why not?"

Why not? Because—because I had something important to do. And Griff couldn't just go out traipsing around the city. He was supposed to be lying low. And staying out of sight. He could be murdered at any time! "I'm not really feeling very well." In fact, I hadn't been feeling very well since I'd overheard that telephone conversation.

Both their faces fell.

"Are you sick?" My father was looking at me with worry

etched into his forehead above his eyeglasses. "Maybe I should send a telegram to your mother."

"No! No. I'm not sick. Not exactly. It's just that I have a headache . . ." A headache named Griff. And another headache named whatever those men with the voices were named.

"Your grandmother always said the cure for a headache was a brisk walk down one side of Beacon Hill and up the other."

Which had never made sense to me, because if you went down one side and up the other, then you'd have to walk all the way around the bottom in order to do it. Why couldn't you just go down and up the same side?

"It will do you good to get some fresh air. Come on. We won't take no for an answer."

Oysters and clambakes! If Griff weren't so set on going out all the time, then maybe I'd actually be able to save him. It would serve him right if he got murdered while we were having dinner!

At least we didn't have to eat oysters. Father obeyed that "never in a month without an *R*" rule to the letter, so we had clams. And sarsaparilla to wash them all down. I'd persuaded Father to sit at a booth way back in the corner and insisted Griff sit beside the wall in the deepest part of the shadows. But then the waiter recognized Griff and told the manager, and then the manager must have told the cook, because pretty soon everyone in the restaurant had come over to talk to him about football. I might as well have just put a target on his chest.

I tried sitting right next to him and leaning forward so

anyone trying to get to him would have to go through me first, but he just put his arm up along the back of the booth and pulled me in close to his chest, talking over my head to all of his fans.

Honestly—I don't know why I was trying so hard to save him!

I stuffed more clams into my mouth than I should have, trying to hurry things along and get dinner over with, and then I had to figure how to chew and swallow all of them without gagging.

But he took his time.

Once he'd finished, I was all for going straight back to the house, but they wanted to walk to Faneuil Hall.

"Why?"

"Because it's a nice night. And there's no reason to hurry." My father was decidedly lacking in urgency.

Griff bumped my arm with his elbow. "Can I buy you an ice cream?"

"No!"

He blinked.

"After all that food? I couldn't eat another bite. And neither should you." There. Could we go now?

"I think I could manage."

"But—but—it isn't safe. Just—look at all these rough characters!" I gestured about, but the passersby didn't look very dangerous. Just then, however, a tall man walked into view. "See!" But . . . it was a policeman. One who looked a lot like Jack. I tried to hide behind Griff, but the cop kept coming closer.

"Janie?"

It was him! There was no use hiding now. Caught between trying to get Griff home in a hurry and trying to keep him from Jack, I decided Jack posed the greater danger. I stepped toward him, away from Griff. "Janie. Yes. She's . . . well . . . she's doing well. Very well." I linked my arm through his and drew him away from my father and Griff. "As well as can be expected, her mother dying and all."

"What are you talking about?"

"Stop talking."

"But why—"

"Stop it!"

He frowned. Griff was watching us, so I smiled and patted Jack's hand. "I'm sure she'll be happy to know you inquired about her. I'll tell her when she gets back." I stood on tiptoe, intending it to look like I wanted to kiss his cheek.

He obliged by stooping.

"Just don't ask me any questions right now. About anything!" I whispered the words into his ear and then kissed his cheek. "Bye."

He caught me by the elbow. "What kind of game are you playing?" He was looking beyond me at Griff. "Isn't that—"

"*Not* who you think it is."

Griff was peering at us. "Ellis?"

"Ellis? Again?" Jack was looking down at me. "Was he in that play too?"

Oysters and clambakes! I smiled again. "I wish I could tell you more, but I haven't heard from Janie myself. Don't worry though. Like I said"—I pulled my arm from his—"I'll tell her I saw you." I turned around, grabbed hold of Griff's arm, and tugged him away.

"Who was that?" He was looking back over my shoulder at Jack.

"One of Janie's friends." So to speak. He was a friend I'd made while I was pretending to be Janie.

"Janie . . . ?"

"Winslow. Cook's daughter. You remember—she's the one who always—"

"Warned us not to do whatever it was you always wanted us to do. I remember. And you know what?"

"What?" I dared a glimpse back over my shoulder. Jack was still standing there watching us.

"She was always right."

Yes, of course Janie was always right! Except for this one time. She'd come up with a plan that was much more like me than it was like her, and look where it had landed us all. In big trouble!

16

Griff escorted us to our front door that evening, then came right inside and ambled into the parlor. I had to follow him; Father had already disappeared into his office, and I couldn't just leave a guest to wander around by himself.

By the time I joined him, he was pacing in front of the fireplace. "I was wondering, Ellis, how come you never come to the football rallies?"

Football rallies? The last one had been way back in November. Why was he worried about football rallies? "Maybe I do and you've just never seen me."

"You never come."

Why should I? And see all the girls throw themselves at his feet? "Honestly, I figured so many co-eds attend already, you'd never miss me."

"I always miss you."

The truth was, I never quite knew what to say to Prince Phillips, star of the Harvard football team. He was so tall and so handsome and just so . . . so . . . *perfect*. He always made me nervous. I much preferred the Griff I knew from

Beacon Hill, the one I'd grown up with. "How can you miss me? Thousands of people in the city come to cheer for you."

His mouth twisted in annoyance. "They're cheering for someone they call Prince. They're not cheering for me. They don't even know me."

"I didn't know it mattered to you, whether I was there or not."

He sat down on the sofa, leaning forward to rest his elbows on his knees. Then he glanced up at me. "Do you know what they're saying in the Finance Commission?"

I shrugged. Something to do with numbers probably. I sat on the sofa beside him.

"They're saying I ought to run for state legislature in a few years, once I graduate."

"Do you want to?"

"I don't know. I've known that's what people want, but it makes me feel trapped. You know? Like . . ." He sighed and slouched into the corner of the sofa.

I knew exactly what it felt like! "It makes you feel like it's all been decided, and you have nothing to say about it. Like maybe you never wanted to do those things in the first place and maybe you wouldn't even be good at them, but nobody cares what you think or what you want because all they can think about is themselves and what they're good at and what they want." I wished people wouldn't be so selfish all the time!

"The thing is, maybe I would be good at it. And maybe I do want to, but what if I wasn't good at it? What if I lost my elections or made bad decisions? What if the only thing that happened is people ended up being disappointed in me?"

I never started out doing the wrong thing on purpose either.

It always just kind of happened along the way. "Maybe you should just do something else. Or run away even." But not to Hollywood. Because I was going there.

He sent me a sharp glance. "Run away? Why?"

"So you wouldn't give anyone a chance to be disappointed."

"But wouldn't that be worse than not trying?"

It didn't seem like it to me.

"What if it's something I actually want to do, and somehow it turns out I'm just . . . not good at it? Do you think it would be worth the risk in that case? What if I could do some real good in a position like that?"

"*Could?* You can!" Griff could do anything. And even if he couldn't, even when he lost football games, for instance, everyone always seemed to like him anyway. "I know you can. And I think you'd even be good at it." Unlike me, who was never good at anything. That was the difference between us. And that's why I was leaving and why he ought to stay.

"But I'm not like you, Ellis."

Thank goodness for that!

"I'm not very good at being myself."

What did he mean by that? "What—what are you saying?"

"You're more yourself than anyone I know."

No I wasn't. At least, I didn't want to be. I woke up every day telling myself I was going to try hard *not* to be myself. That's why I needed to leave. "I don't think I—"

He sat forward and took up my hand. "That's why I need you. To remind me who I am. I need to know there's one person who truly knows me and, in spite of it, in spite of everything, likes me still."

"But . . ." I looked down at our hands. His was so big and

nice and *firm*. He'd never been one to give a floppy old fish of a handshake, and I'd always liked that about him. He wasn't like some fellows. He wasn't even like *any* fellows. He was just always . . . himself. I looked up from our hands into his eyes. "I don't know if I can be that person."

He drew back.

"I mean, not the one who knows you and still likes you, because I am *that* person, but I'm not the person that's good at being herself. I don't think you know me very well. Or maybe you've mistaken me for someone else." Someone like Julia. Or Louise or Martha. Someone a thousand times better than me.

He smiled as if I'd said something funny. "I know you better than anyone."

"But if you really knew me, then you'd know you can't count on me." Especially now. Especially since I was heading to Hollywood. "And then you'd understand that you really, truly shouldn't need me." The thought he might, that he even suspected he did, sent panic spiraling through my stomach. I couldn't be trusted. Didn't he know that by now? "Maybe you should need someone else. Someone more reliable." Someone who wasn't going to California.

"Don't you know about griffins?"

The way he was looking at me was doing queer things to my chest. I'd never had trouble breathing before the way I did right then. "No." The word came out in a croak.

"They're meant to stand watch over priceless treasure."

"They are?"

"You're my treasure, Ellis."

A priceless treasure? Me?!

"And they only mate once, for life. You're the one for me. You always have been."

"But—"

"Griffin?" We both jumped at my father's voice and turned to see him standing in the front hall. "You're still here?"

Griff stood. "I'm sorry. I was just—" He cast a glance down at me. Sighed. "I was just leaving."

And thank goodness!

The way he'd looked at me on the sofa, that thing he'd said about griffins, made me want to say all kinds of things I knew I shouldn't. If I stayed in the city much longer, then I might never leave at all. In fact, if he hadn't needed saving, I'd beg Doris to let me stay with her for the next week and a half and leave right this minute.

My father saw Griffin out and then came back into the parlor. "I hope you're packed and ready!"

"Ready for . . . what?"

"For the shore! We'll leave tomorrow morning!"

Had he said the shore? My ears didn't seem to be working; my cheeks were still too warm from all those things Griff had said. "I can't." I couldn't. I couldn't go to the shore when I had to stay in the city to look out for Griff. He was safe as long as he was at work or at home, but who knew where he'd go if he stayed the weekend in the city?

"Of course you can. Tomorrow's Saturday. And we'll be back on Sunday night."

"I really don't think that's such a good idea."

"Whyever not?"

"What if—what if the train broke down and I couldn't get back in time on Monday?"

He looked at me with a frown. "Your mother and I decided to support your efforts, but I have to confess I was looking forward to some time away from the city. I wish I could ask your mother . . ." He looked faintly put out about it. "Why have I never had a telephone put in down there?"

Because it would cost about a thousand dollars, and if a messenger could be found, a telegram would do. But that still left the matter of Griff and some king trying to kill him. I couldn't leave town! But maybe . . . "Could Griff come with us?" If he tried to talk to me again about treasures and griffins, I'd just have to try hard not to listen and remind myself what I was doing was for his own good.

"Griffin? *Phillips?*"

"It would . . . it would give Lawrence someone to play tennis with."

"I suppose I could make the request." He scratched at his ear. "But the Phillipses always used to go away in July, didn't they? And aren't these things supposed to be sacrosanct?"

"We always go away in July, but now we're away in June too. And besides, it wouldn't be *going away*. It would just be . . . taking a break from the city."

"I don't know . . ."

I couldn't leave Griff behind! I decided to play the one card I knew would trump all of his objections. "Poor Griff. It must be so lonely there in that big house without his mother. And with his father being gone all the time in Washington . . ."

"Yes. Of course you're right. I'll ask. It's awfully late, though . . ."

"I'm sure he won't mind!" I smiled and stood on tiptoe to kiss him as I started up the stairs.

He stayed me with a hand on my arm as he looked at me with a quirked brow. "There's something . . . different about you lately."

The dark circles under my eyes? My fountain pen–darkened eyebrows?

"You look more responsible somehow. And serious. That work seems to be doing you some good." He patted me on the cheek. "We'll leave on the eight o'clock train."

Sleeping until seven gave me very little time to pack and no time at all for breakfast. I was just lucky I'd lost half my wardrobe over the course of the year. It wasn't very difficult to decide which shoes to take when you only had three choices and one of them a pair of satin dancing pumps and the other a pair of galoshes. I wrestled a satchel from my closet and tossed in skirts and blouses and a sweater to ward off the ocean breeze, a night slip, and Lawrence's old robe.

I dragged the satchel down the hall to the bathroom and threw my toothbrush into it after I'd finished brushing my teeth. My father was waiting by the car as I dashed down the front steps.

At my approach, the driver opened the car door to reveal Griff already sitting in the middle of the backseat. I paused. "Maybe I should sit in front."

Father got in on the far side. "Nonsense. Plenty of room."

There might have been if Griff's legs hadn't been so long and if Father had been willing to move over just a little. As it was, I traveled to the train station holding on to the door handle so I couldn't be accused of pressing myself against Griff.

But he leaned close as he stretched his arm across the length of the bench, his breath fanning the hair that hung over my ears. "Thanks for inviting me."

Hadn't Father said *he* would send the note? "I just thought maybe Lawrence would like some company. And that it would do you good to get away."

The shore always seemed like a good idea until we got there. That's when I remembered how primitive it was. As the car skidded on the sand-strewn road, the house came into view.

Fairview. Pride of the Etons.

Rather . . . pride of the wife of one of the early Etons. Though it might have actually had a view at one time, it didn't anymore. Dunes blocked the shore in the front, and in the back a curtain of trees had grown up in what once must have been a meadow. It seemed rather shabby and forlorn now, its shingled sides gone gray from a century's worth of battering by wind, sun, and sand. Its front portico listed a bit toward port and the back screened porch listed toward starboard. In between, the structure seemed beset by indecision in exactly the same way I was whenever we were there. Yes, there were tennis and swimming and boating without end. There were Saturday night dances and trips into town for ice cream.

But there was also an unrelenting breeze, swarms of mosquitoes, and sand that was everywhere and got into everything. As well as an old-fashioned water closet that refused to work half the time. And a whole house filled with people who insisted on getting up at the most ungodly of hours.

The driver halted the car opposite the front stoop. Mother

must have been watching, because Lawrence came out to help the driver carry my things up, something he never would have done without duress. But then he took one look at Griff and dropped my bag to pick up his. How was that for family loyalty?

"Let me." Griff picked my satchel up off the ground and carried it into the house.

Lawrence hightailed it up the front stairs at his heels. I went into the parlor and dropped into a chair . . . quite a bit farther than I was used to dropping.

Mother sighed. "Mice."

I shot off the cushion. "Mice?"

She shrugged. "They've been eating the stuffing out of the cushions."

As I looked closer, I could see where a hole had been chewed right through the fabric. At least the place had been aired out. The breeze coming off the bay stirred the air and that stale, salty, closed-up beach house smell was gone for the moment.

At suppertime, the driver took us in shifts to the Yacht Club.

There was a band playing, but the dancing was halfhearted, it being so early in the season. I took my shoes off and walked down through the grass toward the docks, taking a stroll in the moonlight. Going to Hollywood, this might be the last time I'd see Buzzards Bay for a while. I couldn't decide whether I'd miss it or not.

I heard the brush of footsteps through the grass, and soon Griff caught up with me.

Though I didn't really want to talk to him, I didn't send him away either, and he seemed content just to walk beside me. We could still hear the band, the sounds of laughter, and the clink of silverware on plates, but it seemed so far away. And Boston farther still.

I'd never really belonged here. Not with all these people who seemed so set on being so proper. On keeping track of who was related to whom and how the families all linked together. I just didn't fit with them . . . and I probably never would.

"Thanks again. For inviting me. I'd forgotten how much I missed this place."

Poor Griff. "You have the house here. You could come yourself. Later in the summer, maybe . . ." When I wouldn't be around any longer. By then, I hoped, he would be safe.

He picked up a twig and tossed it toward the water. "Can't. I have my job."

"Would they really mind?"

He seemed to consider the question. "They might not. But I would. It's important, the work I'm doing."

Of course it was. That was the reason a king was after him. Along with two Irish.

Henry and Marshall soon found us. Griff played with them on the lawn while I went down to the dock and sat, dangling my feet over the edge. As I looked out across the bay, I decided I probably would miss it after all.

Griff and I were driven back in the second shift along with my father.

I was dead-tired from my week at the switchboard and didn't waste any time heading for the stairs, right behind my father, but Griff grabbed my hand as I passed him. "I'm going to get up and go out later tonight. There's something I want to see."

Later? It was dark already. "There won't be any light to see by."

"Would you come with me?"

I supposed I had to, didn't I? In order to keep him safe? Although he was probably safer here at Buzzards Bay than at home. In spite of his eyes asking all kinds of questions I didn't want to have to answer, having him come with us last minute had been a brilliant idea on my part. If anyone had been watching him back in Boston to discern his habits like they did in the movies, they must have been outwitted.

"Please?"

I sighed, supposing it was better to be safe than sorry. "Tap on my door at . . . ?"

"One o'clock."

One o'clock. Of course he'd want to get up at one.

"Go away." Someone was tapping at my door much too early. In fact, it wasn't even morning yet. I rolled over and pulled the pillow over my head.

The tapping turned to knocking. I was going to string my nephews up by their toes. I pulled the blanket up over my head as well and now I was going to suffocate and wouldn't everyone be sorry when they found me in the morning: poor Ellis, dead before her time.

"Psst—Ellis!"

That voice wasn't Henry's or Marshall's, it was . . . "Griff?"

Now I remembered! I'd promised to go out with him wherever it was he was going.

I heard the door squeak open, then footsteps creaked across the rickety floor boards. "Hurry. We're going to be late."

Why was everyone always in such a rush? I pressed the pillow to my face. "Go without me."

"No."

"I'm not going."

I felt the bed rock as he sat on it. "Yes you are."

It was really enraging he could be so sure about what it was he thought I was going to do. "No. I'm not."

"I've carried grown men much larger than you halfway down a football field before."

I peeked over the top of my pillow. His features were grave in the moonlight. "Are you threatening me?"

"Do I need to?"

I propped myself up on an elbow and relegated the pillow to my side. "Why do you want me to go so badly?"

He glanced down at me, then looked resolutely over toward the opposite wall. "Because I need some cover. Are you coming or not?"

He needed some cover? Maybe he *did* know some Irish! "You don't need to get so touchy about it."

"If you don't get out of that bed right now, I might just . . . do something we'll both regret."

With all his talk about griffins and his trying to put his pin on me, it wasn't very difficult to figure out what he was saying. I pulled the covers up to my chin as my cheeks warmed.

"I'll just wait"—he gestured to the door—"out there."

Jeepers! The moment he shut the door, I leaped from bed,

grabbed a blouse and skirt, and shimmied into them. Then I pulled my sweater over the top for good measure. Asking Griff to come had definitely been a *bad* idea. I gave the belt of my sweater an extra firm tug and pulled my hat down tight over my hair. Oysters and clambakes! A girl ought to be able to sleep in peace. Especially at the shore.

17

Where are we going?" And why were we doing it in the middle of the night?

"You'll see."

I had tired of mysterious men. "I can't see much of anything in the dark. And you *will* tell me, or I just won't go at all."

"To the beach. Or nearly. And if we don't hurry, we might miss it."

Well. There was nothing very objectionable in that. I lifted my chin and started on again along the well-trod path through the grasses.

"Only . . ." Griff was talking from behind me.

I turned.

He was scratching at his head. "About that cover I was speaking of . . ."

I put a hand to my hip.

"There might be some people out there. And it might be good if . . . well . . ." He opened his mouth and then closed it as his brow furrowed.

"For a person worried about missing something, you don't seem to be in that much of a hurry."

"It might be good if we pretend to be sweethearts."

I couldn't help my brow from rising.

"If that's all right with you."

There was something very dear and completely charming about Griffin Phillips standing in the moonlight asking my permission to pretend to be my beau. I almost kissed his cheek. But I wasn't about to make it easy on him. He had, after all, woken me at one in the morning. "And how do you suggest we do that?"

"Well . . . we could . . . I mean, if you don't mind . . . maybe we could . . . hold hands?"

"Hold hands . . ."

"Or—or—maybe just . . ."

I walked back, took his hand in my own, and tugged him along toward the water. "Like this?"

"Well . . . no. Could you . . . maybe hold it like you mean it?" His eyes were making all kinds of appeals.

Now how was I supposed to leave with no regrets if he offered up his heart on a silver platter? Again?

As I'd been standing there, he'd threaded his fingers through mine. Now he pulled me up the path toward the top of the dunes and put a hand about my waist as we descended the other side. The scent of beach roses hung in the air. "Griff, would you wait just—"

He stopped so suddenly, I rammed right into him. But I might have been a Yale football player for all that he moved. "Hush." He crouched down into the waving grasses, pulling me with him. "There's someone out there."

"Where?" I crept forward to look over his shoulder.

In front of us, someone was standing on the beach, sweeping a light across the waves that were slapping onto the sand.

"Who is it?"

"Rumrunners." He said the words as if he were assuring himself of something.

"What are they doing?"

"Waiting for a boat. And when it comes in, they'll off-load the liquor and then take it into the city to sell."

"Can they do that?"

"They're not supposed to."

"Griff . . . you're not going to do anything dangerous, are you?" There was something in his voice, some note of determination, that made me suspect he just might.

He glanced away from the beach and looked back at me. "What?"

"You're not going to get yourself into trouble, are you?" Any more than he already had?

"Not with you here."

We watched in silence as the light stopped its sweep and the chug and gurgle of a motorboat came closer.

"But you might."

"Hmm? Might what?"

"If I weren't here, you might get yourself into trouble. What would you do?"

He was staring out into the darkness. A man in the boat rose and gestured farther out into the bay.

"I don't know. Tell somebody, maybe."

"But . . . somebody else might not like that. And so many

people drink these days. Do you really think it's worth it to get involved? Does anyone truly care?"

"I care. If there's a law, then people ought to respect it."

"I know, I just—this kind of thing can be dangerous. And I don't want you to get hurt."

"I know what I'm doing."

No. He didn't! That was the problem.

"Look, Griff, I—"

He turned around, grabbed me by the shoulders, pulled me to his chest and . . . and . . . kissed me. And then he kept on doing it. And it was . . . it was . . . it was very nice.

"What are you doing here?" A voice interrupted us.

I let go of Griff as a flashlight bathed us in sudden, and not very welcome, light.

Griff put a hand up in front of his eyes. "We were just—" The light bounced away, providing the blessed relief of darkness as Griff's hand dropped to grasp mine.

"Don't pay us any mind." The man turned away. "We won't be long. Sorry to disturb you." He left us with a laugh and the stench of his cigar.

"I thought I might see him here." Griff seemed very satisfied with himself.

Him? Him who? "Who was that?"

"*That* was King Solomon."

It took me a moment to understand what he was saying because I was thinking about his lips. Who knew that chiseled mouth of his was so soft? Or that the taste of licorice could be so intoxicating? Or that Griffin Phillips could kiss so well! What was it he'd said? Something about—"*King* Solomon"? *The* king? If that was the king, then I'd led Griff *into* danger, not away from it! "But—but—" Why had we stopped kissing? And . . . why couldn't I concentrate! "How do you know him?"

"Someone pointed him out to me once. He sent someone to see me at school. Wanted to pay me not to play ball next year."

"Pay you—?" But Griff loved playing football. It was practically all he did.

"He organizes the rumrunning from here up to Maine. And he does some gambling on the side. College sports are big business. Guess he wanted to hedge his bets."

Griff *knew* King Solomon?

A voice came floating up toward us from the beach. "Need me to go up and take care of them, King?"

As Griff pulled me into his side, I took refuge against him, throwing an arm around his waist and burying my head in his shoulder.

"Naw." We saw the glow of King's cigar arc up into the sky and then go sailing into the surf. "Just a couple of sweethearts, rolling around in the grass. Here. Give me one of those."

A shadowy figure handed something to him.

King turned back toward us and raised his arm.

Griff pushed me to the ground and threw himself on top of me.

"Hey, kid—here!"

I squeezed my eyes shut. I'd done it again. I'd failed. We were going to die right here on Buzzards Bay!

But the only thud came from a bottle landing in the grass beside us.

Griff grasped it by the neck, stood up, and waved it in the air. "Hey—thanks!"

As he knelt back down in the grass, he pushed it into the pocket of his pants. "I'll use it as evidence."

"Do you have to?"

"You want to drink it?!"

"No! I just wish—can't you leave this all alone?"

"If I don't do this, then who will?"

I didn't care if anyone ever did, just so long as he didn't.

We walked away from the shore, arm in arm, just in case anyone decided to follow us, and we didn't go directly home either. Griff led us up and over a dune and across the road past the house. Once we reached the tree line and the moon ducked in and out of view between the branches, I had no idea where we were.

"Griff—stop. I've got something in my shoe."

He offered his hand as I took my shoe off and shook it out. "Did you know those people would be there?"

"I thought they might be. I'd heard they were using the cove."

"But why does it matter so much? As long as they leave us alone?" And *he* left *them* alone. "As long as no one gets hurt?"

"Because people decided they wanted Prohibition."

"But what if it's a law no one wants?"

"Somebody wanted it. That's why we have it."

"I'm starting to get the idea no one really wants it anymore."

"Then they should work to change it, not try to figure out how to get around it."

I was so very tired. I sat down on a stump. "Why can't people just . . . let people do what they want?" Why shouldn't Irene be able to make a fool of herself if she wanted to? And why couldn't Janie take off work when she had to? And why was economics so all-fired important anyway? "Is anyone truly getting hurt?" If I could find a nice mound of grass, I might just curl up on it and fall asleep.

"We're all getting hurt! Everything's upside down and backwards."

"Like how?"

"Like . . . policemen. When we were growing up, they were the good guys. The nice guys. Everyone looked up to them. You knew you were safe if there was a cop around. But now they're the bad guys. They're being paid by people like King Solomon. And if they're not, it's even worse. They've been made into jokes."

"So you agree with Prohibition?" Is that what he was trying to say?

"I might or I might not, but until it gets changed, I have to uphold it. Any decent person does. That's why the commission is trying so hard to get rid of the mayor. He thinks the law is what he decides it should be."

"And you think you can get him fired?"

"We have evidence. And now," he patted his pocket, "maybe I have enough evidence to get King too."

"You're not thinking of testifying against him?"

"You bet I'm going to!"

"But that could be dangerous!"

"Dangerous for them."

"For you. You can't just go poking your nose into other people's business! And—how are you going to be governor someday if you go and get yourself killed?"

"The mayor is supposed to work for me. For all of us.

That makes what he does everybody's business. And King is nothing but an old-time outlaw."

"I just don't want you to get hurt."

"I won't. Besides, why should anyone care what I do?"

"Everyone cares what you do!" Even me. Even when I shouldn't.

He rested a hand on my arm and put a finger to his lips. Sitting there on the stump in the dark, I listened to the sweep of the wind scraping the sea grasses out on the dunes, to the hoot of an owl, to the slow, steady breathing of Griff as he crouched beside me.

"I think we're safe now." He put a hand into his pocket.

Oh, crumb. I'd forgotten all about that pin!

With a rustle of paper, he brought something out. "Want some licorice?"

I tried to sleep in, but the ancient house came awake with creaks and groans much sooner than I would have liked, along with the laughter of the boys and Julia's accompanying screeches. With my waking came the memory of Griff's lips on mine . . . and the sharp smell of . . . licorice?

I sniffed at my fingers.

Yes, licorice. I licked them clean as I contemplated the day.

I'd fallen into bed with my clothes still on, and when I got up, I found my sheets were filled with sand. I tried to brush it off onto the floor with not very satisfactory results. And when I put up a hand to rake my hair back, I discovered sand on my scalp as well. A bath was in order. Or at least a swim. But if King Solomon was here, then I had to keep Griff inside and out of sight. At least until we went to the train station in the evening.

So, no swimming, then. A bath would have to do.

Surely Julia had run the rust out of the pipes by now.

I pulled on my sweater and tiptoed down the hall, trying to avoid the boys, but they had reached the bathroom before I had. There might not be any rust-colored water in the bathtub, but there were all manner of turtles. And lizards.

I shuddered as one of them stuck out a forked tongue at me.

Downstairs, in the dining room, Mother was still eating breakfast. She put down her tea as I entered. "Ellis." She took a long look at me. "There is a wardrobe in your bedroom. If you would bother to hang your clothes up, it wouldn't look as if you'd slept in them."

"I'm sorry. Are the boys . . . ?"

"They're out."

Thank goodness! I went through to the kitchen and begged a piece of toast from the cook, along with a hard-boiled egg. She followed me back into the dining room with a teapot and poured me a blessedly full cup once I'd sat down at the table.

As I rolled my egg across the tablecloth, Mother frowned at me. I supposed she wanted me to give it a polite whack with the tip of my knife, but I'd seen Irene do her eggs this way and I liked the feel of it under my palm as the shell finally gave way.

"About Griffin . . ."

I paused in my rolling. Had she heard us last night?

"It was very thoughtful of you to extend an invitation to him. I don't believe the Phillipses have summered away from Boston since Maude died. I just want to take this opportunity to say I've been heartened by the changes I've seen in you lately."

I felt a twinge of guilt knowing she thought I was helping out at the orphan asylum. "About my job, Mother. I should really tell you—"

"I should tell *you*, Ellis, how proud I am of you." An actual, honest-to-goodness smile curved her lips. "I don't get the chance to say that very often. I truly feel you've started to turn a corner. Keep it up. That's all I wanted to say."

I was letting her believe something that wasn't true, but I'd tried so long to make her proud of me, I just couldn't bear to dash her hopes again. It would be something she could remember after I was gone: that one day I was good back when I'd traded places with Janie when I was little and that one time I'd made her proud when I'd worked at the orphan asylum. I smiled back at her and then started peeling the shell away from my egg.

"Oh—and the boys wanted to go swimming today. Maybe you and Griffin could take them."

"No!"

Her brows flew up into her forehead.

If King Solomon were still in the area, then the only safe place for Griff was here, inside the house. "*I* can take them, but I don't think Griff would want to go. He's . . . been working so hard. I'm sure all he wants to do this weekend is sleep."

"Goodness." Mother drew her sweater tight at her throat. "I hope he takes good care of himself. Sometimes fatigue can turn into ague. Maybe that's why he's not up yet."

He was still sleeping? I was of a mind to stomp upstairs and rattle his door to wake him up, but I was hungry. Apparently early morning walks required a lot of energy. I devoured the egg, ate the toast, and downed my tea. If I was lucky, I'd have an hour or two of peace before the boys returned.

I wasn't lucky. I was never lucky.

Just as I'd settled down on my bed with a magazine, the boys barreled into the house and up the stairs. Someday they were going to punch a hole right through the old floor.

The footsteps paused at my door. "Auntie Ellis?"

I put a finger in the crease of my magazine and closed it. "She's not here."

"She is too."

"Not."

"Too."

"Ellis!" Julia pushed open the door with a bang. And a frown. "Where have you been all morning?"

"Sleeping. And eating breakfast." And enjoying myself.

"The boys want to go swimming."

"Isn't it almost lunchtime?" Or near enough that there wasn't time left to go swimming.

She sighed. "After, then."

I'd come up with some excuse to keep Griffin here at the house. And at least then I'd have time to get the sand out of my hair . . . before it got replaced by more sand. The boys were hopping from foot to foot as if they'd got some mischief hidden in their pockets. They probably had. "I heard the cook was baking pie for lunch."

"Pie!" They raced off down the stairs.

"Really, Ellis. I'd think you'd be more helpful."

Helpful! I'd been helpful all week long, trying to work

Janie's job and keep Griff from getting killed. If I were any more helpful, I might well help myself to an early grave. "Some people come to the shore for a break."

"Yes. And I'm one of them!"

If she hadn't married one of those down-on-their-fortune Otises, then maybe she'd have been able to hire a nurse for the children and get all the breaks she wanted.

"Clarence was going to come this weekend, but then he changed his mind."

He always seemed to be changing his mind about coming to things.

"Really, I'm just about at my wits' end. And you of all people ought to be the person to help me."

Me of all people? She said it like I was to blame for her entire life. I was about to get mad, but then I realized how drawn and tired she looked. "I already said I'd take them after lunch, and I meant it."

"Thank you." Her sigh seemed to drain all the energy from her body. She turned and went along back down the hall. But then Griff came to take her place. He was in his shirtsleeves, with his suspenders hanging from his waist. Sleep had mussed his hair, freeing it from the confines of pomade to hang about his face. He scooped it back with a hand. "There are some . . . uh . . . turtles in the bathtub. . . . I just thought someone ought to know."

The boys were waiting at the entrance to the dining room at lunchtime like a pair of wriggly puppies, but Mother wasn't about to let them pass. "I've decided on a picnic for our luncheon." There was much exultation from the boys and a frown from Julia. An offer to help carry something from Griff and a polite, but firm, refusal from my mother. "Ellis said you've been fatigued lately."

Now I understood why we were picnicking! Mother's cure for everything was a big dose of fresh air. Preferably accompanied by a stiff wind to drive it deep into the lungs. I took up a blanket to carry.

Griff's brow was wrinkled in puzzlement. "She did?"

Standing behind Mother, I was bobbing my head like some organ-grinder's monkey.

His brow cleared, though he gave me a skeptical glance. "I have been working awfully hard. . . ."

"Probably better, then, that you stayed in your room this morning and had a good rest." That was quite a concession from a woman who believed the righteous had no business sleeping past six in the morning. Mother was gesturing for Father to take the hamper from Griff. "Julia? Why don't *you* take the boys swimming after lunch? I have to go into town and that way Ellis can stay here in case Griffin has need of something."

"Why do I have to—"

Mother's steely-eyed glance put an end to Julia's complaint.

Griff pulled the blanket from my arms and started after the picnic hamper, which was making its way to the shore in my father's hand. We were accompanied along the way by shrieks from the boys, who'd run off down the path.

Griff couldn't be outside. This wasn't what I'd planned at all! "Wait!"

He turned while the others kept on going. "Forget something?"

"*King Solomon.*"

"What?"

"You know. *Last night*. What if they recognize us?"

"They're probably back in the city by now."

"But what if they aren't? What if he's still here?"

"Don't worry. I'll keep an eye out. And anyway, that's why I . . . well . . . one of the reasons why . . ." Was he blushing? "King never really saw my face. We were too busy . . ."

Too busy. That was one way to refer to it!

"And really, I ought to apologize."

"Apologize?"

"It wasn't very proper of me."

"Proper?"

"Taking advantage of the situation like that."

As I followed him down the path, I couldn't quite help being a little sorry he was sorry. Deep down, in a part of me I was supposed to be ignoring, I'd been kind of hoping he'd kiss me at least once more before we left.

I spent the picnic on the lookout for King and suspicious men of any sort. I didn't see any. And by the time I'd finally decided there were none, Father and Mother were taking a stroll along the beach, Griff had found a football from some- where that he was tossing around with Lawrence, and the boys were eating the last piece of pie.

That's what you got for trying to keep someone from being killed.

At least in Hollywood I wouldn't have to do things like try to stop someone from being murdered. Maybe only for pretend, once in a while. But I'd have real-life experience now, which would be a good thing to go along with my talent of crying at nothing at all and my ability to laugh on cue, with great hilarity. I tried one out. It was extremely gratifying when the boys looked up as if they'd missed out on a joke.

Julia frowned. She was always frowning. "Is there something funny? About being stuck out here on Buzzards Bay with two small boys? For the entire summer?"

Looking at Julia's face, I rather thought not. "No." Now I'd gone and done it. She was crying. "I'm sorry, Julia, I didn't think—"

"You never do. That's the problem with you, Ellis. You never think about anyone other than yourself!"

Well, that wasn't true at all. I thought about other people, didn't I? I thought about Jack and how to get him to tell me the things I needed to know. But I suppose I couldn't really count that, since I was doing that as Janie. I thought about Griff and how to keep him from giving me his pin, even though if I were staying I might just change my mind . . . so I shouldn't probably think about him at all really. Except to keep him from getting killed. Who else was there to think of? And why should I spend time thinking about people who didn't think very much of me? "Do you mean to say . . . am I terribly selfish?"

"Ellis!" The word came out as something between a laugh and a cry. "Are you really asking me to tell you what I think about you? After I just told you that you never think of anyone but yourself?"

Was I?

"Just . . . go away."

Well, I was planning to. And soon!

O n the way back to the house as we crossed the dunes, we saw a car filled with men drive down the lane. One of them tossed something out the window. When we came up to the road, we saw the stub of a cigar, its tip still aglow, lying in the road. Father ground it into the sand but not before it brought back all the things I'd worried about over lunch.

When Julia told the boys to go put on their swimming trunks, I knew I had to think fast. "Why don't we all spend the afternoon at home?" I walked into the parlor and sat down on that mouse-eaten chair just to make sure they understood what I was saying.

Julia and Mother looked down at me in horror. "With the boys?"

"Lawrence can play with them."

When they looked in his direction, Lawrence mumbled something about taking the boat around the bay and ducked outside.

"At *home*?" The boys made it sound as if I'd proposed to torture them.

"Just for the afternoon." Until it was time to catch the train.

Julia looked as if she was going to kill me. Maybe the murder I ought to have been worried about was my own.

"We could . . . play sardines!"

My mother was adjusting her hat. "You can do what you want to. In any case, your father and I are expected at the club."

"And I'm going along with them." Julia was already practically pushing them both out the door.

"Sardines?" Marshall was looking at the door with longing. "But Auntie Ellis, it's a great day for swimming."

"But I have to start packing so I'm ready to go back to the city tonight. Now, who's going to hide?"

The boys debated between themselves until they nearly came to blows.

"I'll hide." Griff sent me a wink.

"We'll count to a hundred, then."

"By tens?" Marshall looked hopeful.

"By ones. But . . . Griff hasn't been here in a long time. Maybe we should count to five hundred instead."

"Five hundred?! I can't count that high. We'll be here *forever*!"

I looked up at Griff. "Find someplace easy."

"No!" Marshall was indignant. "He's supposed to make it really hard!"

As I closed my eyes, I held a hand up to them, making sure there was a crack between my fingers so I could peek now and then. "One, two . . ."

I wished I'd thought to sit down before I'd decided to count to five hundred. We'd had to start over twice so far. I wasn't quite sure, but I thought Griff might have gone upstairs. I'd heard a creak or two out in the front hall.

"Four hundred and ninety-four, four hundred and ninety-seven—"

"It's not four hundred and ninety-seven, it's four hundred and ninety-four." Marshall took after his mother. He was always quite certain he was right.

"We already said four hundred . . . and . . . four." And so did Henry.

"We said that back a long time ago. Now it's four hundred and ninety-five."

If I didn't step in, we'd be counting to five hundred all day. "Four hundred and ninety-six."

They counted the rest of the way along with me, then shouted five hundred in triumph. And only . . . I looked at the clock on the mantel . . . forty-five minutes after we'd begun.

I clapped. "Go find him!"

Henry started for the stairs, but Marshall stopped him. "He's not upstairs."

"How would *you* know?" Henry asked with all the disdain of a four-year-old.

"Because if he'd gone up the stairs, we'd have heard him. Come on, let's go check in the kitchen." They raced around the corner, leaving me in blessed peace . . . and with the question of where exactly Griff had disappeared to. I crept up the stairs, leaning heavily on the banister, stepping only on the side of the treads nearest the wall. And I skipped the fifth step completely.

The hall was another matter.

I slunk down the first five feet, then hopped from one side of the hall to the other to avoid creaks. I pushed open the door to the first bedroom with a finger.

No Griff.

I picked my way farther down the hall to Lawrence's room. I crept inside, stooping to look under the bed. Then I opened the door to his wardrobe, pushing aside his shirts, running my hand along the back.

Nothing.

I went on to Julia's room and bent to look under the bed. There was nowhere else to hide, so I turned to leave, but then I spied an old Eton sea captain's locker. It had been a favorite hiding place back when Lawrence and I had been younger and the house had been filled with our friends. I remembered showing it to Griff one rainy summer day when we'd played cards all morning and had nothing else to do that afternoon but play sardines. Back then, we'd both been much smaller. But maybe . . . I tiptoed over and threw up the lid.

He smiled up at me. "What took you so long?"

"They're never going to find you here."

"I don't care if *they* find me. I was hoping *you'd* find me." He shifted, stretching his legs out over the side of the chest, making room for me. Then he held up a hand. "Come on in."

I sat beside him, tucking my skirt around my knees and then leaning back against the chest and hooking my legs over the side too.

He sent me a glance. "Do you remember when you first showed me this trunk?"

"They never did find us, did they?"

"And when we finally gave up and went looking for them, they were gone."

I smiled as I remembered. "They were out in the rain, mucking for clams."

"And then they all came down with a summer cold."

I had forgotten that part of it. We'd spent the better part of a week, just the two of us, sailing in the bay, swimming, and playing tennis. We talked over memories for a while as we waited for the boys to find us.

Griff leaned back against the side of the chest. "We were quite a pair. That's what my mother always said. You always talked me into doing more than I should have."

"And you somehow always talked me into doing less than I wanted to."

"I'm glad you invited me here." He shifted again and stretched an arm across the back of the trunk. "I was beginning to think you were avoiding me." When he looked at me like that, I had to remind myself I was leaving. And now, after the previous night, I would have to write him an even longer letter in order to explain my going.

"About last night . . ." He knocked my knee with his. "I'd meant to tell you what a fine girl I think you are and how I've never met anyone like you and . . ." He'd been looking at our knees, but now he turned and looked into my eyes. *Deep* into my eyes. And then he put a hand up and pushed a lock of hair behind my ear. "I meant to tell you how glad I am to know you and *then* ask if I could kiss you. The way it happened wasn't what I'd wanted for our first kiss."

First kiss? Did that mean he planned a second one? If he did, then I really shouldn't be sitting next to him in an old sea chest, should I? But then why couldn't I seem to get my legs to move?

"What I'd hoped would happen is . . ." His hand cupped my neck and he leaned close.

My visions of Hollywood disintegrated as I closed my eyes and lifted my lips to his.

"Ellis!" My sister called out from downstairs.

I jumped.

The front door slammed. "Ellis?"

"What?" I stood and scrambled out of the trunk. What was she doing here? She wasn't supposed to be back until later. *Much* later!

"Ellis Eton!"

Maybe . . . maybe I'd just pretend I wasn't here. No one had found us. We could still play sardines.

But now there were footsteps on the stairs. Too late! And Griff had already come to stand beside me and . . . suddenly I realized we were in a bedroom.

Together.

Alone.

I moved toward the door, but Julia opened it first.

She looked at me. She looked at Griff. And then her mouth fell open.

"We were playing sardines. With the boys."

"I leave the boys with you, and you have a—a—petting party!"

"No!" Both Griff and I shouted the word in unison.

"How could you even *think* of making the same mistake that—" She clapped a hand to her mouth.

Mistake? What mistake?

"That's the last time I'll ever trust you with anything again!"

"Julia?" My mother's voice came floating down the hallway.

"Did you find them?" My father's voice joined hers.

"I can't believe—! I don't even know—! How could you?" Julia stormed out of the room and down the stairs.

I followed.

Griff came along too, trailing behind me. "I didn't mean . . ."

There was raucous laughter down in the front hall. Who on earth was that?

Julia was standing at the bottom of the stairs, wringing her hands. "Look at them. Just look at them!"

I did. The boys were laughing like loons, clutching each other as if they might otherwise fall over. Marshall was holding a bottle much like the one King Solomon had thrown in our direction the previous night. "What's wrong with them?"

"They're drunk!" Julia flung the words at me like an accusation.

"It's not *my* fault!"

"You were supposed to be watching them, Ellis!" My mother was nearly shouting.

"We were playing sardines." The whole point was *not* to watch anybody.

"Do you know where I found them?" Julia gestured at Griff and me. "Up in my *bedroom*!"

Mother's eyebrows nearly shot right off her head. "Julia, go ask the cook for some ipecac and a bucket. Several of them. And Griffin . . ." He seemed to shrink before her gaze.

Father broke in. "Griffin—why don't you and I go see if we can figure out where they found that bottle."

Which left me alone in the hall with my mother.

"Oh, Ellis." She let out a long sigh. "I thought—I was beginning to think I could trust you. But now I see—" Now she was wringing her hands too.

"We were not—"

She looked at me, her brows cocked.

"—doing whatever it is Julia thinks we were. We were waiting for the boys."

"For *three hours*?"

"Three hours . . . ?"

"We left at one o'clock. It is now almost four o'clock, and we have to leave for the train station in less than two hours."

"I guess . . . we lost track of time. . . ."

"I've heard about all those terrible dances and . . . and . . . petting parties, but I told myself even though you might sometimes be flighty, you have a good head on your shoulders. I've always believed you have more common sense than Julia, so I've refused to think you would ever betray my trust . . . but tell me the truth, Ellis. Do I have anything to worry about?"

"Mother!"

"I have nothing against Griffin; indeed, I have always hoped you two would come to an understanding one day. But that doesn't mean—"

"Mother, I am not lying. We were just playing sardines. We didn't do anything." Why wouldn't she believe me?

"I've never liked the idea of that game. Hiding in the dark, going to find someone, and then sitting down on top of them. Or—" she shuddered—"lying down beside them."

"It was not dark and we were not—doing any of that!"

There came a horrible retching sound from the kitchen.

It was immediately followed by the sound of wailing, which soon broke off into hiccups.

"I don't think this mixing of boys and girls nowadays does anyone any good. When I was your age—"

"When you were my age you always did exactly the right thing at exactly the right time! You just don't understand: I'm not like you, and I *never will be*!" I left the house at a run, slamming the door behind me, just like Colleen Moore in *Flaming Youth*. But it didn't make me feel any better. Neither did seeing Father and Griff on the path, coming toward me.

I just wanted to be alone. This was why I'd planned to go to Hollywood in the first place: so I wouldn't hear "Oh, Ellis!" anymore. Or witness disappointed looks or . . . bad grades. Spending so much time with Griff this weekend had almost made me throw my plans to the winds.

Wandering down to the beach, I kicked at the seaweed the tide had left stranded until I spied a big piece of driftwood. I sat down on it and stared out at the bay.

Why did he have to be so nice, and why did he have to insist on liking me so much? Couldn't he see how I always messed everything up? Why couldn't he just be like everyone else and hate me?

I heard a cough and turned to see Griff. Of course it would be him. It was getting to be a habit. He sat at the other end of the log, facing away from the bay, looking at me.

I threw a glance at him. "Did you ever think maybe things would be better if I weren't here? At least then people wouldn't be mad at me all the time."

"I'm not mad at you. I'm more mad at me. I should have realized the boys would wander across some liquor with all the smuggling that goes on around here. And I shouldn't have put you in that situation up there in the . . . in the bedroom." A flush stained his cheeks.

"But that's just what I mean. I always get people into trouble. Even people who don't mean to be or want to be. Everyone would be better off without me, don't you think?"

"I've never thought that. Not once. And *I* definitely wouldn't be better off without you."

It was nice of him to say that, but I'm sure he didn't mean it. And I wouldn't let it dissuade me from my plan. Just because Griff had said all those nice things about me and just because he was good at kissing didn't mean I should stay. And besides, he had started down the path that would lead, as it had done for everyone else, to a full-fledged "Oh, Ellis!" I wasn't good for him. Anyone could see that.

When I got home that night, I pulled my Hollywood scrapbook out from underneath the mattress and went through my plan again. Once I got there, I'd go straight to Famous Players-Lasky Corporation and refuse to work with any director but Alan Crosland, because he was the best there was. And there would be palm trees and Spanish villas and swimming pools and tennis courts and . . . why didn't it sound as perfect as it used to?

I closed the scrapbook with a sigh. It would all be worth it—I knew it would be—and Griff would thank me for it. Someday when he'd married himself a Lowell or a Warren, he'd thank God he hadn't married Ellis Eton. Although maybe, from time to time, when he'd see me in a movie, he'd think . . . "What if?" He would be the hometown boy, and I'd be the girl who got away, and everything would be just fine. There was nothing to worry about. I was a good actress, and I'd be a complete success. I knew I would be. Didn't I have everyone down at the switchboard convinced that I was Janie?

"Why—you aren't Janie!" Some of the girls at my normal table were taking a correspondence class and had filled the table with books, so I'd sat down at a different table, and now one of the girls was peering over at me in the dining room as if I'd just revealed myself to be some awful ogre. All I'd done was ask did she know if there were any fish knives.

"Shh!" Miss Hastings was nearing, and I didn't want to be noticed by her any more than I already had been.

"But—where's Janie?"

I smiled in an especially Janie sort of way, with my lips closed and my mouth turned up only ever-so-slightly at the edges. "She's not here. But I am. She asked me to pretend to be her."

The girl looked at me askance. "Well . . . if it's all right with her . . ."

"Jane Winslow?" The supervisor looked out over the dining room.

How would Janie have answered? I stood, hands folded in front of me. "Right here, ma'am."

"You clocked in five minutes late both Friday and today."

Those who hadn't been watching us now turned around in order to do so.

"If this job isn't important to you, I'm certain I can find a girl to which it is."

"Oh! It is. I promise you it is. I won't be late again. Ever. I promise!"

She sent a doubtful look my way and then left.

I made my way to Doris's table with shaking hands.

She greeted me with a frown. "I told you to stay out of her way."

"I'm trying!"

"Being late is not the way to do it."

"I'm not trying. To be late, that is. But I *am* trying. I'm really trying." I was!

"Well, you better try harder, or Janie's going to be out her job."

The other girls were glaring at me as if they agreed.

"And she really needs this, now that her mother's passed." One of the girls crossed herself.

"I know she does." That's why I'd agreed to help. I just had to get through to the end of the week without messing up again . . . and then I'd buy my train ticket and I'd go to Hollywood just like I'd always planned.

After work, back by the orphan asylum, I climbed inside the car and let it take me home. Father hadn't returned, so I ran upstairs, pulled the receipt with the telephone numbers from my desk drawer, and took it down to his office to start making telephone calls. You'd think it would have been easy, just calling up sixty different telephone numbers, but an hour later, I wasn't even halfway through.

"Tremont-4621."

"One moment, please."

The telephone went silent before someone on the other line picked up. "Hello?" A woman.

"Is the man of the house in, please?"

"Naw. He's still at work."

I hung up and then drew a circle around the telephone number. I'd decided if I couldn't get a man on the phone the first time I called a number, I'd call again later. I put a hand to my back and stretched as I looked at my list. I'd made twenty telephone calls, and I still hadn't recognized a single voice.

I picked up the handset again and put it to my ear.

The operator picked up the call. "Hello?"

"Tremont-4577."

"One moment, please."

Another silence and then a new voice. "Hello?" A man!

"Hello. This is Miss Smith. Is John there?"

"John? I think you got the wrong number, miss."

Something sounded familiar about his voice. If I could just get him to say *royal*. Or *picture*. "Are you sure this is the wrong number?"

"It is if you're asking for John."

"What if—" Think! "What if I weren't? What if I were asking for someone else?"

"Who you asking for?"

"What if I asked for you?"

"Is that what you're doing?"

Was I . . . ? "Sure. That's what I'm doing."

"So whadda you want?"

"I want to . . ." How could I get him to say the right word? "I want to . . ."

"Listen, I haven't got all day."

"I know. I'm sorry, I just was wanting to know something about . . . about hanging pictures." Hanging pictures? Oysters and clambakes! He was going to think I was some kind of nut.

"Pitchers?"

It *was* him! "Yes. And I was thinking . . . what I thought was . . . maybe we could . . . meet."

"Pitchers? You want to meet to talk about hanging pitchers? Is this some kind of a prank?"

"No! No pranks. Someone gave me your name and said you were good at hanging pictures. King did. King was the one. He gave me your name."

"King! King said that about me? I guess, I mean I've put up pitchers before . . . but . . . who are you again?"

"He said I could count on you." What on *earth* was I saying?

"For pitchers? That's a new one."

A female voice called out somewhere in the background.

When he spoke again, his voice was low and hushed. "Listen. I'm kind of busy right now. But I could slip out later. Where you want to meet?"

Rats! I hadn't thought this far ahead. "We could . . ." It couldn't be any place too obvious. I wanted to see him, but I didn't want him to see me. "We could meet . . ." Where?! Not at the Common or the Public Garden. And I didn't want him anywhere I'd normally be. "Why not at that—" I lowered my voice—"speakeasy. By that grocery in the North End."

"The grocery in the North End? There's about fifty groceries in the North End. Who did you say you are again?"

"It's just . . . I can't remember the name. It starts with a Z."

"The one by Zanfini's? Sure. I know it. Give me an hour, and I'll meet you there."

An hour? I didn't even know if I could find that grocery again. And now I had to be there in an hour?

Someone rapped on the door.

I pushed the telephone away, palmed my list, and folded my hands in my lap. "Come in."

A maid curtsied. "Your father is waiting in the dining room, miss."

Thank goodness he hadn't come into the office! "Tell him . . . tell him I won't be eating tonight."

"Miss?"

"I won't be eating supper." At least not here with him.

"Are you—are you sure?"

"Quite. And besides, I have to run out. For work. You can tell him that if he asks."

I went up to my room and replaced my dress with a middy blouse and skirt and exchanged my satin pumps for my galoshes just in case I had to do some running. I only hoped I wouldn't have to dodge any bullets! Grabbing one of my mother's old hats and my pocketbook, I tiptoed down the servants' stair and found the driver playing cards out in the garage with the gardener.

They both stood as they saw me.

"I need to go to the North End."

"Where did you say again, miss?" The driver was squinting out the front window.

"To a grocery."

He drove down a street that seemed impossibly narrow and then jerked to a stop. "Is it this one?"

Was it? I bent to peer out the window. "No."

"But . . . you're sure it's here? Somewhere?"

"I'm sure. It starts with a Z. Zanetti's . . . Zeffanini's . . . something like that."

He turned a corner and came face-to-face with a brick wall. "I'm afraid—"

"It's got to be around here somewhere." We were in the North End. I could smell it: coffee, garlic, and . . . something rotten.

"Yes, miss." He reversed, turned the car around, and headed down the street in the opposite direction.

"Perhaps . . . that way." I pointed to the right.

"We've already been that way." He turned left.

Really? All these streets seemed the same.

He drove down one block. Then another. "Is it this one, miss?"

I looked through the window. Zanfini's. "That's it!"

"Should I wait?" A rough-looking character out on the street gave the car a long look as he passed by. "Are you going to be long, miss?"

"I rather think not." Although . . . I didn't know. Not exactly. The man had said to meet him in an hour, but how dependable would he be? "Maybe . . . could you park around the corner?"

He raised a brow, but he did as I had asked.

Now I had to figure out where to stand. There were lots of people walking past, but they were all Italians. I pulled my hat down a bit lower in order to hide my face. A mistake. I had to be able to see.

But not *be* seen.

I didn't really fit in, even in my skirt and blouse. And no one else was just standing around, and definitely not beside the speakeasy. Those who came slipped down the stairs and disappeared inside quick as you could say . . . well . . . quick!

I looked up the street and then down. There wasn't any place to hide. I glanced at my watch, but it wasn't there. I'd forgotten to put it on. And that man might be here any minute!

Maybe I could go inside the grocery. It was on the corner. If I stood in just the right place, I might be able to see the street and the entrance to the speakeasy. I stepped across the alley and went into the store.

A man was standing near the door. He smiled.

I smiled back. It smelled heavenly. Like a giant bowl full of . . . something really good. An old woman was stirring a pot that sat on a stove against the back wall. My, but there were an awful lot of vegetables. And fruit. Fruits. Was it fruit or fruits? Fruit and vegetables or fruits and vegetables? I'm sure I ought to have learned that somewhere. Fruit or fruits? I suppose . . . they served a fruit salad at the club, not a *fruits* salad. So there was an awful lot of *fruit* in the grocery. Some very nice-looking strawberries. I reached a hand toward a small basket filled with them.

The man stepped from the corner and lifted it for me. "You would like?"

"No. No, thank you. I'm just looking."

Over across the way were some gorgeously shiny grapes. I picked a bunch up.

He stepped over and held out his hand like a teacher waiting for an examination booklet.

I put them into it.

"Not this one." He put it back and picked up another bunch. "You like this one."

They both looked the same to me. I nodded though. It didn't seem like he understood I didn't want to buy anything. I pointed toward the window at the corner.

"You want one of those?" He went to stand beside a crate filled with green clumpy things that looked like they had warts on them.

No. I didn't. At least . . . I didn't think I did. I didn't know what they were. I wished he would just leave me alone. I smiled and then walked past him toward the window. Standing there, right in the corner, I could see the entrance to the speakeasy. Perfect! Now I just had to wait for someone who seemed like he was waiting for someone. And then I'd know who one of those people on the telephone was and who to keep a lookout for when I was around Griff. Although . . . I still wouldn't know his name. But I knew his telephone number, and when I went to work tomorrow I could look it up.

As I stood there, a tall, large man with a cleft chin walked by. If the man I was looking for was anything like him, then I didn't think I needed to know his name. At all. I'd surely never forget what he looked like. Why, if his hair were darker and he were more clean-shaven and dressed in a suit instead of a sweater . . . if he didn't have that cleft in his chin and his eyebrows were thicker, then he'd look just like the actor Tony Moreno! I thought he might be the telephone man, but he went right on past the speakeasy and never once turned around.

My, but whatever was cooking smelled good!

I glanced over my shoulder toward the stove. The old woman was still stirring that pot. Someone had come in and looked as if they were buying a bowl of it. Opening up my pocketbook, I collected the change from the remainder of the previous week's allowance, which had fallen to the bottom as I kept an eye on the window. Eighty-three cents.

I wondered . . . was it enough to buy a bowl?

A couple of men sauntered past. I let the change fall back into the pocketbook. Maybe later I'd buy a bowl. Right now I had to keep an eye on the speakeasy. And I would have, except at that moment a young woman walked over.

"You are fine?"

I glanced over at her and nodded.

"I help you?"

I shook my head, wishing she'd just go away.

"You want fruit? Vegetable?"

Maybe . . . I reached back into my pocketbook for the change and then handed it to her. "Is it enough for some of that . . . a bowl of . . . ?" I gestured toward the stove with my chin.

"Ah! You want minestrone?"

"Yes." If it would keep her from distracting me.

Her smile lit up her face making her look almost beautiful. "Mama make the best. I bring you."

She took the coins from me, and I turned back toward the window. There was someone loitering by the stairs now, but he wasn't very suspicious-looking. He seemed more like a gardener than a murderer in his coveralls and his dirty cap. In the movies all the bad guys wore fedoras and suits, inside which they always seemed to hide their guns. This man didn't look as if he could hide anything at all, he was that skinny.

He started down the stairs several times, but he always turned around and came up again.

"Take." The woman was holding a bowl out to me with both hands.

"Thank you." I dipped the spoon in and took a taste. It was even better than it smelled.

"You like." It wasn't a question but it deserved an answer. "Yes."

"*Bene.*" She nodded and then turned and stood next to me. "You watch someone?"

I nodded.

"Come from there?" She pointed toward the speakeasy. "Yes."

"Not good people. Lots of smiles. Lots of laughs. From here." She pointed to her mouth. "Not from here." She pointed to her heart.

She seemed rather smart for a foreigner. The man was still out there, and by the time I had finished the soup he hadn't left. Was he the telephone man? I wished I'd remembered my watch. It seemed like I'd been inside the grocery for a while, but there was no way to be sure. Shadows had begun to devour the stairway to the speakeasy—it must be getting late.

The woman whisked the empty bowl from my hands and then took it back to the stove. She conferred with the man who'd tried to make me buy things and then came back. "I'm sorry. You leave now."

"Not yet." I wanted to wait a few more minutes to see if anyone else came.

"You leave now. We close."

Oh. "Oh! I'm sorry. You're closing."

"*Sì.*"

"Uh . . . well . . . thank you."

She was standing, hands folded atop her apron. Waiting.

"I guess I'll just . . . I'll go now."

"*Grazie.*"

She followed me to the door, then locked it right behind me.

As I stepped out from under the awning, the man in front of the speakeasy looked at me and then his gaze drifted onward. Was it him or not?

I guessed there was only one way to find out. I walked in his direction, and when I got to the speakeasy, I stopped. And then I tried my very best to be Janie. "Excuse me. Do you have the time?"

He'd stepped down onto the stairway, which led to the basement entrance. Squinting up at me, he pulled a watch from his pocket. "Sure."

Sure? Sure didn't tell me anything. I had to get him to say pictures. Or royal!

"It's seven."

That late? "It's a very nice evening."

"Yeah." He eyed me and then stepped up and out of the way. "You going in?"

"Me? No. I don't think so." I didn't want to, but how could I get him to say those words? "Why? Are you?"

"Don't know. I'm waiting for someone."

Maybe he was waiting for me!

He squinted up at me. "Some doll. Say, you don't need any help with pitchers, do you?"

"Pitchers?" It *was* him. I tried not to smile. "I don't think so."

"Forget it. Forget I mentioned it. I guess she's not coming."

I backed away toward the alley, where I hoped the car was still waiting. "Thank you. For the time."

He gave me a wave as if to say it was nothing. But he'd given me something after all. An up-close look at his face.

O h, I wish I could shimmy like my sister Kate." I did a quick dance around the Phillipses' parlor as I hummed the song later that evening. I'd come over to make sure Griff didn't go out anywhere. "She shimmies like a jelly on a plate . . ." I'd decided to do a dance for my auditions in Hollywood, as well as a reading. I hadn't decided on a scene yet, though. In fact, I was thinking I might write a scene for myself. I wanted something that would let me use my talent for crying real tears.

I backed up to the divan in order to try the dance again.

But then I paused. The divan. A divan might be just the thing. . . . I slipped out of my shoes, stepped over the arm, and arranged myself on top of the cushions in a languid pose. Or maybe . . . I put my wrist up to my forehead. That was better. I would look ever so much more pitiful that way. Maybe I could pretend to be an invalid. I almost started crying at the thought of it: my whole life ahead of me and nowhere to go. How terrible! I nearly started crying real tears for real. But maybe I shouldn't be quite so pitiful after all. Maybe . . .

maybe I could just *pretend* to be pretending to be an invalid. I could vamp it up a bit in that case. I turned onto my side and put my palm beneath my chin. Tried fluttering my eyelashes. That was better. I could be helpless *and* seductive that way.

"Would you please stop, Ellis?"

I looked up to find Griff watching me. But instead of the frown I expected, he was looking at me rather . . . strangely.

"Sorry."

"It's just . . . I would much rather take you out somewhere than be stuck in here going through these numbers."

"Can I do something?" Besides trying to keep him from being murdered?

"No. Yes . . . maybe."

Which was it? I got to my feet and did another shimmy while I waited for him to decide.

He slammed the book shut and threw down his pencil. It hit the tabletop, then vaulted through the air, landing tip first on the carpet.

I did the Charleston over to the pencil and picked it up. Then I did a foxtrot over to the table and set it down in front of him.

He sighed as he picked it up. "I just wonder if this is really worth it."

I dropped into a chair beside him.

"One of the fellows on the commission presented his evidence yesterday to try to get an arrest warrant for one of the mayor's assistants. We had everything we needed—more than we needed—and the judge wouldn't even read it. Refused to look at it. So does it really matter if I can prove what the mayor's done? The police and the judges and the councilmen are all on his side."

I thought about all those people I'd seen at the speakeasy drinking liquor, breaking the law, and loving every minute of it. "Maybe people are tired of being told what to do and what to think all the time. Maybe the laws don't make any sense."

"But how can it make sense to appoint liars to the government and cheats to the state bench? It's as if . . . right has become wrong and wrong has become right."

"It can't be that bad."

"It *is* that bad. It's worse. Why bother to have laws at all?"

"If that's the way you feel, then of course your work is worth it." I pulled the book from his hand, opened it back up, and shoved it under his long face. "If people keep electing the crooks, then you have to tell them why they ought to stop. If you think it makes a difference, then show people why."

"*You* agree with me, don't you?"

"I think I do." I did, didn't I? "It's just that . . . you can't really force people to do what you want them to, can you? Even if it is for their own good." The talk of laws and morality was just plain dull, and it looked as if it was depressing as well. At least to Griff. "So . . . what are your plans for the summer? Other than working with all these numbers?"

"I don't really have any."

"None?" But those men had been clear about doing whatever it was they had planned out in the open in order to send a message. What had they said? . . . "*In plain sight of everybody so there's no mistake about it.*" So they weren't just going to drive up here to Beacon Hill and kidnap him. They were going to do something in front of a bunch of people. That meant they had to know something about Griff's plans, which I didn't. "What about . . . the Fourth of July?"

He shrugged.

"You're not doing *anything* this summer?"

He tapped his pencil against the table. "I get to cut the ribbon at the hospital opening next week."

That didn't sound very exciting. "Why?"

He shrugged. "It's a memorial for Mother."

That wasn't any grand thing that would have lots of people attending. "What else are you doing?"

"Working. And sleeping. And pretty soon I'll start football practice."

Football practice and cutting hospital ribbons? "There has to be something else."

"Why?"

"Because . . ." Because? "Because . . . you're Prince Phillips for goodness' sake! And the captain of the football team ought to be out more." Or *not*! I wasn't supposed to be encouraging his going out. That would only make it easier for him to be murdered. Normally I'd be pleased he was so boring, except that he had to be doing *something* out where everyone could see him, because apparently that was the plan. Otherwise, I'd been mistaken about everything.

As I left Central the next evening, Jack was waiting on the sidewalk, which was perfect because I was hoping maybe I could slip the name James McDonnell of Tremont-4577 into our conversation. That was the man who belonged to the telephone number, and he lived just a couple blocks up on Milford Street.

"I thought we could go back to the North End this evening." He started off down the sidewalk in the direction of the elevated railway station.

The North End? I caught up with him. "I thought you didn't want to be seen with me."

He glanced over at me. "I changed my mind."

"What if I have other plans?" Plans that didn't include falling-down drunks and billowing clouds of cigarette smoke?

"Do you?"

"No, but—"

"Then let's go."

"How come we always do what you want to do?"

"Because I'm paying, and I'm supposed to keep an eye on you. And besides, a fellow deserves to have a drink now and then. And . . . I'm a little bit worried about things."

I stopped walking.

It took him a few steps to realize I wasn't beside him. Once he did, he turned around. "You're not coming?"

"I can't stay past eight."

"But the party doesn't even start till ten, baby!"

"The last time, I had to sneak back into the house. And . . . I don't want my mother to worry." Because she *would* worry if she ever found out.

He raised his hands. "Fine."

Forty minutes later, I was regretting my decision. It had taken some quick thinking to send the car back home without Jack realizing what I was doing, and now that we were at the speakeasy, there hadn't been even one minute when I didn't have to yell to be heard. It was no good trying to carry on a conversation with him. "Tell me again why we're here."

"To have a good time." He yelled the words at me.

A waiter brought Jack a coffee cup, and he downed whatever was in it. Then he leaned back against his chair and loosened his necktie. What was it about liquor that made everyone want to part with their clothing? It didn't seem decent.

"Ellis!"

I moved my chair closer to Jack's and tried to hide behind those big, broad shoulders of his.

"Yoo-hoo! Ellis Eton!"

Jack poked my arm with his elbow. "Looks like your friend's here again."

Sounded like it too.

"Ellis!" Irene lunged forward and tried to kiss my cheek. She missed. But she did manage to splash whatever she was drinking all over the front of my dress. And of course it had to be a deep golden amber color.

"Sorry." She pulled a napkin from the table and tried to blot it up, but only succeeded in stumbling against the table, sending Jack's cup skidding to the floor. "Sorry." Bending to reach for it, she over-stretched and then collapsed, giggling, onto the floor.

I got up and reached down to lend her a hand.

She grasped it and then pulled me right down on top of her.

"Irene!"

"Sorry. Sorry, sorry, sorry." She snickered as she tried to push me away.

I rolled off her and pushed to my feet, giving her my hand.

She reached right past it, then tried again. "Stop moving, Ellis."

"I'm not!"

Ignoring my offer of help, she got on all fours and then grasped at the back of my chair and pulled herself up. She started to leave, but couldn't seem to make her feet go in the right direction.

"Honestly, you shouldn't drink so much! Do you want some help?"

She tried to brush my hand from her arm, but she missed again and ended up pawing at the air beside it. "Don't need any help, thank you."

"Are you all right?"

"Fine. Fine as a—fit as a—" Some hairs had gotten caught in her lipstick, and she tried to blow them away. It didn't work. She finally took an angry swipe at them. "I'm fine."

She didn't seem to be, but she'd brushed off all my offers of help and I didn't want to risk her convincing Jack I really was Ellis Eton. I watched her lurch from table to table until she disappeared into the crowd.

21

Later, as I was headed toward the entrance, I ran into Irene again. She was standing by the door, her face an alarming shade of gray.

"Irene? Are you okay?"

"Ellis?" Her eyes nearly rolled back into her head as she looked at me.

I put an arm around her shoulders as she swayed.

"I don't—don't feel—Ellis? My head's not right." Her knees buckled as I tried to keep her on her feet.

"Jack!"

I wasn't strong enough to hold her up on my own. I tried to shake some sense into her, but she began to slip from my grasp. "Help me—somebody!"

There was no pause in the drinking or the laughter or the music.

"Jack!"

Nobody came. Nobody even noticed.

I pulled her to my chest, wrapped my arms around her, and just tried to hang on.

"Ellis?"

"It's all right, Irene. Everything's going to be fine."

"Always wished—always wished I were you."

At the moment I would have collapsed from her weight, Jack appeared and lifted her from my arms. I followed him out through the door and up the stairs.

"We have to do something!"

He set her down on the curb. "She probably drank some bad gin. Best thing to do is let her sleep it off."

"Irene?" I squatted next to her. As Jack let go of her, she slumped forward toward the street.

I tried to push her back and prop her up, but she kept falling over. I looked up at Jack. "Do something!"

"What do you want me to do?" Jack was backing away toward the speakeasy steps.

"Call the police. Get an ambulance—" Something!

"First of all, I am the police. Second, we can't ask the ambulance to come here."

Irene's eyes weren't opening, she wasn't talking. In fact, she hadn't moved at all. "Jack, she's not waking up!"

"Oh, come on—" He took her by the shoulders, lifted her up, and shook her. The toe of one of her shoes got caught in a crack on the sidewalk and came off. "Hey—!" He gave her another shake. "What's her name again?"

"Irene."

"Hey—Irene! You got to wake up now."

Her head lolled to her chest.

Jack bent and set her on the ground, letting her fall onto her side. Then he grabbed me by the arm and tried to haul me off down the street, but I wasn't going anywhere. "We can't just leave her here!"

He kept walking, although he did slow down long enough to turn and talk to me. "If she's really dead, she won't care."

"Dead! What are you saying?"

"She's not breathing, baby."

"She's just—she's—she's sleeping! She's going to wake up; she just needs more time. And we can't leave her, because when she wakes up, she's bound to wonder how she got to the sidewalk, and if we aren't here to explain, then—"

"Trust me, eventually someone will call an ambulance, and you don't want to be here when it comes. They'll ask a whole bunch of questions you really won't want to answer. And then the newspapers will catch wind of it, and then the reporters will come. . . ."

"So you just—you're just going to leave her here?"

"Best thing to do. *Only* thing to do."

"Well, I'm not going. I'm staying right here!"

"You can't."

I sat down beside her. "Just watch me."

He swore and walked back to us. "Fine. But I'm warning you: If she's found in front of the club, they'll shut it down for sure."

"I don't care what they do. I'm not leaving."

"I can't stay."

"Then go."

As he walked off down the street, I sat next to Irene and cradled her head in my lap. She couldn't be dead. She wasn't. Any minute she was going to wake up and ask me where the party was. And then I'd tell her what I thought about places like that speakeasy, and she'd sigh with a frown and probably ask me to find her a cigarette. And sooner than you knew, next autumn we'd be back at the dormitory together, laughing about all of this, because she wasn't going to be mean next year. We were going to be friends again. I smoothed the skirt of her dress down over her knees.

That's where the ambulance found us: sitting on a curb.

Two men got out and took her from me, placing her on a stretcher.

"Is she . . . ?" I couldn't finish the sentence.

"She's dead."

They pulled a blanket up over her face. Once they drove off, Jack came back and sat down beside me. He took my hand into his.

Twisting away from him, I pulled it from his grasp.

"I called the ambulance from a shop down the street." He put a hand to my cheek. "Listen, baby, something I learned in the war: When someone throws a grenade into your trench, the best thing is not to be there when it explodes."

"I don't think she was breathing."

"It happens sometimes. You drink too much. You get a bad batch. Something goes wrong."

"You don't think she . . . she's not *really* dead, is she? I don't think she is . . . I'm pretty certain . . . I mean . . ."

He sighed, took my hand, and pulled me to standing. "Let's get you home."

I pushed at him. "I don't want to go home with you." When he wouldn't leave, I beat at him with my fists. "Go away!"

He didn't budge. "Someone's got to take you home."

When I turned and started walking away down the street, I could hear him following me.

Irene was dead. She really, truly was. She'd been alive just two hours ago and then she'd—she'd died. She'd practically died in my arms. No . . . not practically. That's what she'd actually done. She'd died as I was holding on to her. I was the last person she'd ever talked to, the last person she'd ever seen. I was the person she'd wanted to be. She'd wanted to be *me*. But—but—why? *I* didn't even want to be me. Especially not now. Not anymore.

Jack slipped his suit jacket over my shoulders.

In spite of the fact I didn't want him anywhere near me, I nestled into the warmth of his jacket, drawing the sleeves up around me.

"You're shivering."

I was? But it was summer. I opened my mouth to try to deny it, but my teeth wouldn't stop clattering together.

"Here." He came forward, wrapped one of his big, strong arms around my shoulders, and pulled me to his side. "Poor little bunny."

"She-she-she . . ." Why couldn't I talk? Why was I crying? What was the matter with me?

"She's dead. She died, all right?"

It wasn't all right. It would never be all right. People didn't just—just—*die*!

"Sometimes things happen, and you can't help it. You can't do anything about it, and you can't stop it. Sometimes people just die."

Not from drinking! "You're a policeman. And you were

253

there too, right along with them, breaking the law the whole time." There ought to be something wrong with that.

"It's a law I don't believe in."

"It shouldn't matter! Because that's your job: to make people obey the law."

"And how am I going to do that, baby? There's one of me and there's . . ." He craned his neck as he looked up and down the street. "There must have been a hundred people in the club. At least."

"You just . . ." I moved away from his embrace and looked down at his waist. "You take that gun and . . ."

He put a hand on it as if fearing I might do that very thing. "No one but a gangster pulls a gun on anyone. Even in the war there were things you just didn't do."

"There. See? Rules. And you obeyed them, right?"

"Well . . . no. Not all of them. Because there were a lot of stupid generals in Washington and a brand-new Joe College in charge who didn't know hooch from a haircut trying to tell us what to do. So we saluted, stepped lively, and did what we had to." He reached into his shirt pocket, pulled out a cigarette, and lit it with a trembling hand. "But you didn't live very long if you didn't look out for yourself." He took a long draw on the cigarette and exhaled. "Who's got the right to tell me what to do anyway? And what's the harm in a drink or two? Why should I stop anyone from having a good time?"

"A good time?"

He took another draw as he looked around. "What would you have wanted me to say to all those people in there anyway? 'Shame on you. You shouldn't be drinking that stuff'?"

I wasn't quite sure what I would have wanted him to say.

Or what I would have wanted him to have done. I'd never really thought about laws before. Not until Griff had started talking about his numbers. I'd always just . . . obeyed them.

"Baby, they'd laugh right in my face. Half of them are older than I am. Besides, who am I to tell anyone else what to do?"

"You're the policeman!" And if *he* didn't, then who would? "What about—what about all those people who get shot by gangsters? Like in—like in Chicago?"

"What about them? Gotta hope they died happy, doing exactly what they wanted to do."

"Irene wasn't." She might have been doing what she'd wanted to do, but she hadn't been happy.

"You didn't kill her."

"But I was there."

"And thank goodness. Did you ever think of that? Maybe that's the best thing that could have happened. If you weren't there, who would've been?"

I thought about that for a minute, but then realized he was just trying to be nice. "She wanted to be me. Did you know that? That's what she said."

"People say lots of things when they're dying and—"

"Don't you dare say they don't mean them! If you only had a few words left to say, why wouldn't you want them to be the truth?" Why wouldn't you? "But . . . why would she want to be me?"

"Living up there on Beacon Hill with all those rich people? Who wouldn't want to be you?"

Me, that's who!

"People always want what they don't have."

255

Irene had wanted to be me, and I wanted to be a Holly-wood movie star.

"Listen, baby, it's tough luck—but if people make choices, then they have to live with the consequences." He flicked the cigarette away and then held out his hand toward me.

"But what about me?" I couldn't stop my chin from trembling. "How do *I* live with the consequences?" I didn't drink and I obeyed the law, but it hadn't stopped Irene from dying in my arms.

He took me by the hand, but I pulled it from his grasp. "Don't touch me."

He held up his hands. "Fine. I won't touch you. But you can't blame me for any of this. She knew what she was doing."

Had she, though? Had she really known it would end like this? "You didn't even know her."

He shrugged, then stuffed his hands into his pockets. "If a bullet's got your name on it, no use trying to dodge it."

"This is not the war! She didn't have to die." There were no bullets and no trenches and no stupid g˜ ˜rals. There was just . . . jazz music and cigarette smoke and crowds of laughing people. And none of those were supposed to get you killed.

"Listen. You're in a war, you survive, you come back, and you figure you got to take whatever you can get, whatever way you can get it. Life's a gamble. One day you're here and the next? . . . you're gone."

"That's it? That's all you're going to say?"

"Come on. Let's go home."

"This is not about you or your wars or your—your dumb luck! It's about Irene and how she still ought to be alive."

"I'm not saying—"

"Or maybe it *is* about you and how you're supposed to be this great cop, this hero, and you know what? You're not! You're just a—just a man who doesn't have the courage to do what's right. So I don't want you, Jack Feeney. I don't want to speak to you, I don't want to see you, I don't want you to take me anywhere ever again."

"All right. Fine. Just keep your nose out of my business, and it's been good talking to you."

I tossed his jacket back at him.

He caught it. "Just—take care of yourself."

Take care of myself. I guess I'd have to if the police department was filled with cops like him. It was every man—and woman and child—for himself. Or herself. I was on my own.

When I got home, I put "That Old Gang of Mine" on the phonograph. For a long time I sat there in the dark, trying not to remember the way Irene's hair had felt beneath my palm, or the way she'd looked at me just before she'd collapsed in my arms.

But closing my eyes just made it all worse, and leaving them open meant it was all real.

I pulled out my Hollywood scrapbook, but this time the pictures of Mary Pickford's mansion and palm trees and swimming pools didn't transport me anywhere. And visions of sharing a marquee with Douglas Fairbanks or Rudolph Valentino didn't make me want to climb out my window and hop a train to California. Life wasn't *Through the Dark* or *Mabel's New Hero* or even *The Ninety and Nine*. I lived in a place where the good guys had become bad guys and the bad guys had turned into good guys. There weren't any Keystone Cops, and I wasn't Mabel. There were just people like Jack and people like me. People who had sat around and watched while a girl like Irene had drunk herself to death. I needed to talk to someone, and there was only one person I could think of who would understand.

Though it was after nine o'clock, the butler let me in when I knocked at the Phillipses' door. A few moments later Griff greeted me from the parlor. He gestured toward the table. "I'm still working on the books. There's lots of different accounts to go through, so it's slow going." He glanced over at me, but I still didn't quite know what to say, so I sat down on the divan and did nothing at all.

He worked for a while, making notes on a sheet of paper, and then he put down his pencil. "What is it, Ellis?"

"What is what?"

"Whatever it is that's on your mind. You've been sitting there for a full quarter of an hour."

"I'm tired."

"You're never tired. You're always doing something. And right now, you're not even fidgeting."

"Can I . . . ask you a question?"

He closed the book and rubbed at his eyes. "Sure. Ask me anything."

"When your mother died . . . how did you go on? How did you stop remembering?"

"I didn't. I haven't."

"Then it—it never goes away?" It felt like the bottom of my soul had dropped out and left me with nothing at all.

"It changes. You start remembering other things too. Things besides the death. You start remembering the life."

"The good parts?" Irene and I'd had fun when we'd roomed together. I wouldn't mind remembering those parts.

"And the bad parts. All of it. Together."

"Were you there when she died?"

"No. She was quarantined, along with all the others."

"What if you had been? What would you have said? What would you have done?"

"Nothing . . . at least, I don't think I would have . . . maybe . . ." His gaze slipped from mine. "I might have told her I loved her."

Had I said anything to Irene? I couldn't remember.

"I don't know . . . I just . . . as much as you might want to, you can't stop people from dying."

But that was just it. Maybe I could have. If I'd dragged Irene out of the speakeasy when I'd first seen her, insisted that she come, maybe she wouldn't have died. I should have made her take my help. I should have told her I didn't like that Floyd of hers or the way he treated her. I should have done *something*.

"You can only . . . I guess, when they're leaving, actually dying, you can . . ." He swallowed. "You can let them know how much they meant to you. You know?"

"I was at one of those . . . one of those speakeasies—"

"What!"

"And—just listen. Don't say anything. While I was there, Irene died."

"Irene *Bennett*?"

"She . . . I don't know . . . maybe she drank some bad liquor or something."

"Irene is dead?" He spoke the words as if he couldn't quite believe them, and then he slammed the book shut, making me jump. "That's why all this has to end. One way or another! And the sooner it happens, the better. For all of us."

"Just . . . will you listen? Please?"

"I'm sorry." He looked contrite. "I won't say anything else."

"Nobody even noticed. She was there, she was laughing and dancing and then, all of a sudden, she wasn't." She was alive and then she was dead. Had she even known what was happening?

"Are you thinking it's your fault?"

"I don't know, Griff. I mean, it wasn't me who gave her the drink. I'd told her she oughtn't be drinking. But I was there."

"It's not your fault."

"But whose fault is it?" Didn't it have to be someone's fault she'd died?

He rested a forearm on the ledger. "It's the fault of people who made a law that can't be enforced and the fault of the people who could enforce it but don't and people like the mayor who ought to care but look the other way instead. But most of all, it's the fault of all the people who think it just doesn't matter. All the people who don't care what happens to others just as long as it doesn't affect them."

"What would you have done? If you had been there."

"At that speakeasy?"

I nodded.

"I would have tried to get her some help."

"But what if it was too late? What if there was no time?"

"Then I would have taken her to the hospital."

"But what if there was no way to call an ambulance?"

"Then I would have carried her there myself. I would have done what any decent person would do."

Maybe that was the problem. Maybe there just weren't

any decent people left anymore. "You wouldn't have left her? Even if you could have gotten in trouble if you'd been there?"

"Is that what people did?"

"I . . . don't know."

"As if her death might spoil their good time?"

"I don't know that it was really like *that*."

"Then what was it like? Did they just refuse to notice because it would have been inconvenient? Is that how it was?"

"You wouldn't have left her there." He wouldn't have. I knew Griff wouldn't have.

"No. I wouldn't have." He peered over at me. "You're shivering."

Was I? I just couldn't seem to get warm anymore.

He shifted in his chair, swinging his legs to the side. "Come here."

I flew to him, to that sure and certain goodness that was Griff. He wrapped his arms around me, and suddenly I was crying into his starched white shirt. "I just . . . I didn't . . . I couldn't . . . oh, Griff . . ."

I stayed there for a long time. Well past the point when I stopped crying. Long enough for my hiccups to go away. For my breathing to match the strong, steady beat of his heart. To pull my knees up and curl into his chest. Long enough for him to encircle me with his arms and tell me everything was going to be all right.

But it wasn't. I knew it wasn't. Irene was dead and that changed everything.

Nothing would ever be the same.

I almost told him, right there, sitting in his arms, that I loved him, because I did. Really and truly. But I had to go to Hollywood now because I couldn't stay, not with what had happened to Irene. So I didn't say anything at all. And after a while, Mr. Phillips came home from wherever he'd been, and I slipped off Griff's lap, said good night, and went home.

I still couldn't sleep. I couldn't get Irene out of my thoughts. I could still feel the awful weight of her body as I tried to hold her up. I could still see the glossy waves in her hair and smell the perfume she wore.

Was it like Jack said? Were people entitled to do what they wanted? Or was it more like Griff insisted? Was the law meant to be obeyed and upheld?

And whose fault was it when people like Irene died?

Jack had been to war and come home. And then he'd become a policeman, for heaven's sake. He was a real, honest-to-goodness hero. But Jack had done nothing at that speakeasy, and Griff would have done everything he could have.

It was all so confusing.

I rolled over and wondered what the actor William Hart would do. The right thing, probably. But I was starting to think that only worked in the movies. This was real life with real people. And sometimes it was difficult to figure out what the right thing actually was.

Why didn't people just do what they were supposed to? Why didn't they just obey the laws? Then no one would ever drink and no one would ever die.

From drinking, in any case.

Because everyone died eventually. Griff's mother had died

of the influenza. Janie's mother had died of a heart attack. Irene had died from a drink.

You couldn't force people to choose the things you wanted them to. You could hope. I guess . . . you could make laws that punished them if they did the wrong thing. But you couldn't make their choices for them.

Even God Himself had always let people choose, hadn't He?

But that didn't seem quite right, just leaving everyone to their own devices. That's what all those people in the speakeasy were doing. But weren't we supposed to be our brothers' keeper?

That's what Griff was trying to do. He was trying to look out for people.

And what *was* the wrong thing, anyway? Jack said a fellow deserved a drink once in a while. It didn't seem that terrible of a thing, to want to have a drink. People drank in their own homes all the time. Why shouldn't that be okay?

Because of the law.

It was the law that had turned them all into criminals, whether they drank at a club or whether they drank in their own dining room.

So maybe . . . maybe the problem was the law. Maybe if there wasn't a law, then everything would be all right.

I thought about that for a while, but that didn't make any sense either.

I beat at my pillow to punch it into shape and then lay back down again. Nothing made any sense anymore. I wished I weren't so stupid. It seemed like there was something about it all I couldn't quite understand. If the law was working, then people would be better, wouldn't they? They certainly wouldn't be worse. But then why were there so many speakeasies? And people like King Solomon? And why were there smugglers out in Buzzards Bay?

The law *wasn't* working.

But I couldn't figure out why.

It just didn't seem fair a person like Irene had died from just one drink. Or one of many drinks. She'd probably had more than one. But was it right that just one drink could kill someone?

Maybe the problem was speakeasies. If there weren't any speakeasies, then people just wouldn't drink. But even as I thought it, I knew that wasn't right. Of course they'd drink. They'd just do it somewhere else.

People *wanted* to drink.

That was the problem.

There was a law, but people were stubborn. They just kept breaking it. So maybe there shouldn't be a law. But then what would happen? People would just drink any old thing whenever they wanted to and wouldn't that be even worse than now?

But didn't you have to draw a line somewhere? Didn't you have to look out for other people when they weren't willing—or weren't able—to look after themselves?

Why did people have to be so . . . people-y? Why couldn't they see drinking didn't do them any good? The problem was definitely people. They just didn't know what was good for them, and they wouldn't make the right choices.

As I drifted off to sleep, I knew I'd figured it out: The problem wasn't drinking. The problem was people. And what they needed wasn't a new law; what they all needed was a new heart.

23

As I left Central after work the next evening, Jack fell into step beside me. "Don't look at me."

Too late. I already had. As he nudged me toward a diner, I gestured to the driver to wait for me.

Jack grabbed my forearm, opened up the diner door, and shoved me inside. He could have done it a little more gently. "What do you think you're—"

He marched me over to a booth in the very back. And then he plunked me into a seat and sat down across from me. "Something kept bothering me after I saw you down at Faneuil Hall that night. It was the guy you were with, that Joe Brooks. He looked familiar. And I kept thinking about it and thinking about it and then I remembered where I'd seen him before: *at a football game*. So you know him." It wasn't a question; it was a statement.

"We're neighbors."

"So that bit about wondering what was going to happen to the kid I was talking about . . . you knew I was talking about him."

I nodded.

He ran a hand through his hair. And then he swore. Looked up at me. "Sorry."

It was nothing I hadn't heard in the dormitory.

He pulled a torn bit of newspaper from his pocket and pushed it toward me.

I picked it up. It was Irene's obituary.

"I thought she was just some bearcat, but she was a co-ed! Why'd she have to get mixed with all of this? And what am I supposed to do now?"

I shrugged. "What were you supposed to do before?"

"Nothing. Unless I thought you knew something."

"And what if I did? What were you supposed to do then?"

"I was supposed to let them know."

"Who? King Solomon?"

He grimaced as he grabbed a menu. "Doesn't matter."

I pulled the menu from him and stuffed it back between the salt and pepper shakers. "It matters to me. And I'll just bet it would matter to you if you were me too. But you're not the one in danger of being murdered!" I waited for him to deny it, to tell me those people, whoever they were, had no such plans, but he didn't. Which made me even more angry. "What are you doing going around with people like that anyway? You ought to be ashamed of yourself!"

"What am I supposed to do?"

"What are you supposed to do? What am *I* supposed to do? And what's *Griffin* supposed to do?"

"Who's Griffin?"

"Prince!" Good grief. They may be bad guys, but they sure weren't smart guys!

"Just . . . calm down. Give me a minute to think about all this."

The waitress came by with a coffeepot and held it up.

"Sure." Jack took the cup in front of him from its saucer and turned it right side up.

She moved to turn mine over too, but I stopped her. "No, thank you." After she left, Jack picked up his cup. He must have drunk a good half of it in one long swallow.

"Isn't that hot? Doesn't it hurt?"

"Never mind. We have to figure this out."

"Just tell whoever the person is that doesn't matter that I don't know anything."

"But you know him. You know that Prince Phillips kid." Jack put his head in his hands and sat there staring at his coffee cup. "It wasn't supposed to be like this. I wasn't supposed to know you. You weren't supposed to know anything . . . no one I knew was supposed to get hurt, see? It wasn't supposed to matter because . . . it didn't matter. I'm just doing a favor for a friend."

"So you're telling me it's all right to do the wrong thing as long as it doesn't hurt the wrong people?"

"I don't know what I'm saying. Just . . . let me think."

I'd already let him think, and it didn't seem to be doing much good.

He looked up at me. "Could you just get the kid to do what he's supposed to?"

"What he's *supposed* to do or what you want him to do?" Somehow I didn't think they were the same thing.

"Just tell him it's for his own good."

"No."

"You understand what's at stake here, don't you? He's going to end up getting himself in trouble."

I already knew that! I knew all of it. That's why I was trying to keep him *out* of trouble. "You're telling me you want him to stop doing the right thing so the bad guys won't do the wrong thing?"

Jack stared at me for a long moment. "Yeah. That's what I'm telling you."

"But he's been working so hard at all of this—"

"Working . . . ?"

"And he's found some really—"

"Found some . . . ? Why should I care what he's found?"

"Because it's important."

"Listen to me: *It doesn't matter.*"

"Something has to matter. Don't you care that the mayor—" Wait a minute. Something wasn't making any sense. "If it doesn't matter, then why should anyone care? If no one was worried, then . . . they wouldn't be worried. But they are. So it does too matter!"

"If you would just listen to me, then no one would get hurt."

"Stop shaking your finger at me! Why can't you just tell those—those—bad people to stop?"

"Stop?" He snorted. "What, you want me to tell them to just . . . be nice?"

"I wish . . . I wish people would just do what they're supposed to. Why can't they just . . . obey the law?"

"Because they're people. And laws that can't be enforced just . . . can't be enforced. Do you know how many Feds there are in the city to enforce the Volstead Act? Less than forty."

That few? "How do you know?"

"They offered me a job, but I turned it down. Couldn't live on what they wanted to pay me. But listen: There are over a thousand speakeasies. Close down one and three more start up to take its place. How do you expect me . . . how do you expect anyone to do anything about that? This law has turned everyone into a crook."

"But . . . I'm not a crook. I'm honest."

He raised a brow. "Sure, *Janie*. I don't even think that's your real name, is it?"

"I'm only trying to do a favor . . ." A favor for a friend, the same way he was doing a favor for a friend. Could I really say my favor was any different than his?

"So it's all right for you to lie and do favors for people, but it's not all right for me? Where's the difference?"

"I don't know."

"Good. So now you're back to being the I-don't-know girl. I liked you better that way anyway."

"Better than what?"

"Better than the too-good-for-the-likes-of-you girl." He downed the rest of his coffee.

"I never said I was—"

"Oh yes, you did. In more ways than one." He nodded, jammed his hat on his head, and walked out of the diner.

Another sleepless night. Even bigger circles under my eyes the next morning. Pretty soon I wouldn't have to use a kohl pencil to look like Theda Bara. As I was eating breakfast, the butler came in and laid an envelope down beside my plate.

"For—for me?"

"Yes, miss."

I opened it to find a telegram.

TO: ELLIS ETON
BEST OF LUCK STOP COMING TO SEE YOU
MOTHER

"Are you sure this is for me?"

He took the envelope from me and turned it over. "Miss Ellis Eton. Louisburg Square. Boston."

I'd never received a telegram before. Whatever did it mean?

Father came into the dining room, newspaper in hand. I might have asked him, but he didn't give me time to say anything. "Good luck, Ellis!"

" . . . thank you?"

"We're very proud of you."

"Thank you." I supposed I needed all the luck I could get, only . . . what on earth was he proud of? I finished my tea and left the table puzzling over what had come over everyone all of a sudden and why Mother was coming back, but I soon put it out of my thoughts. I still had my eyebrows to draw on and my teeth to brush. And by the time I was finished, the driver was waiting for me.

It was nice to be wished the best, though, and I walked into Central with a veritable spring in my step.

I remembered to turn my beads around.

I remembered to put my headset on.

I remembered to flip my switches and remove my cords. And to write down all my numbers before I transferred to them. It was almost easy. I'd finally become a real hello girl!

Only my inability to figure out what those men intended to do to Griff marred what was an otherwise perfect day.

The supervisor tapped my shoulder around noon and I followed Doris up the stairs.

"Well, look at that!" Doris was staring at the lunch counter.

"What is it?"

"They're serving giblets. Things are looking up!"

I asked for extra and then I sat down with the girls. I ate while they talked about the latest Valentino movie. I hadn't even known it was out.

Someone started playing "Hinky Dinky Parlay Voo" on the piano, and we gathered around and sang until someone whispered that the supervisor was coming. The tune changed to the much more sedate "Linger Awhile." I was really going to miss these girls when I left for Hollywood.

As Doris and I headed toward the switchboard after lunch, we saw a commotion outside on the street. "I wonder . . ." I craned my neck, trying to see beyond her. She turned to look, then gave a dismissive wave. "It's just the orphan asylum."

"Orphan asylum?"

"Sure. They're having some kind of pageant today, and all the bigwigs are coming to see it. Clogs up the traffic. Happens every June."

I picked up my headset and put it back on. Spying a blinking light, I picked up a cord, wrote down the number, and patched the call through. The board stayed busy until about three o'clock; then all the lights seemed to go dead. A rare moment of peace. No one was talking on the telephone.

I hoped the street traffic would be back to normal by the

time the driver came to pick me up. It was amazing a pageant at the orphanage would cause such a stir. Poor little orphans.

Orphans!

Good luck? Best wishes? *Coming to see you?*

Oh no!

No, no, no, no, *no!*

I was supposed to *be* at that pageant. At least, that's what my parents thought. That's why they'd wished me good luck. I ripped my headset off, bounded from the stool, and dashed—right into the supervisor.

"Where do you think you're going?"

"I have to—"

"Your shift doesn't end for another two hours."

"I have to go."

"If you want to keep your job you'll—"

"I'm sorry." I pushed past her and rushed toward the door.

Please, please, please!

I suppose it was a kind of prayer.

Please may they not have noticed I wasn't there.

There were still an awful lot of fancy cars parked on the street.

I walked up the steps of the orphan asylum and pushed open the door, crept in, and then tiptoed down the hall. It sounded like . . . I walked toward a buzz of conversation and peeked around the corner. A reception was still taking place. If I could just sneak over to the punch table and pick up a few cups, then I could make it look as if I'd been helping out.

My mother and brother were talking to the Oliver Bradlees.

SIRI MITCHELL

I sidled over toward the refreshments table and then veered away when sour old Miss Mary Adams appeared. I knew her. She knew me. And if she were in charge of the table, then I had no hope at all of making it look as if I'd been helping.

What could I do?

I found what I assumed to be an orphan and started up a conversation. She turned out to be a Quincy. We were related. At least . . . I think we were. Somehow. Back a few hundred years ago. I supposed . . . I could try to do something in the kitchen. That would look good, wouldn't it?

I started out in that direction.

"Ellis Eton!" My mother's voice cut through the murmur of polite conversation. There was no point in trying to hide now. I squared my shoulders and turned to face her.

Everyone else in the room did too.

"Ellis Eton . . ." At least she'd lowered her voice as she'd approached. She indicated the door with a twitch of her head. "To the car. Now!" She was eying my ear as if she'd like to take a good tug on it.

I covered it with a hand. "Wouldn't you care for some punch?" As long as we stayed at the asylum, she wouldn't dare to berate me.

Lawrence was making faces at me behind Mother's back.

"No, I would not. We're going home."

275

It was a very silent, very torturous ride back to Beacon Hill, and it was made worse by Lawrence poking me in the ribs.

"We'll discuss this when your father gets home" was the only thing my mother would say.

"But I—"

She held up a hand. "I only wish to hear your explanation once."

I'd assumed Julia and the boys had stayed at the beach, but when we got back to the house, I discovered I'd been mistaken.

"How was it?" Julia didn't even wait until the front door was closed until she asked.

Mother told her exactly how it had been.

"She what?" Julia's eyes were nearly popping out of her head.

"She wasn't there. She lied to us." Mother looked significantly around the room. "To all of us."

"But—you mean—!" Now Julia's eyes were being swallowed by her eyebrows. "I can't believe—" She stamped her foot and then turned and marched up the stairs. A long moment later, we heard a door slam somewhere up on the second floor.

Mother was looking at me in that straight-lipped way she had. "It was a bit of a trial dislodging the boys from the shore in order to come back here for what we thought would be your pageant."

"I'm sorry. I never actually said I was working at the orphan asylum. You just kind of assumed . . . and then you kept saying how proud you were of me, and I just couldn't . . ." There was no point in saying anything else.

"You'd better go apologize."

"To Julia?" I'd much rather apologize to the boys. To practically anyone else but her.

Mother inclined her head in the direction of the staircase.

I went. Shrieks from the attic told me where the boys had gone. I wished I could have walked past my sister's room and gone to play up there with them instead, but I threw back my shoulders, gritted my teeth, and tapped on Julia's door.

"What!" She threw the word at the door like a dart.

"I just . . . it's me. I wanted to apologize."

"Fine. You have. So now you can go." Those words were less vehement and muffled somehow.

I turned the doorknob and pushed the door open. She was lying on the bed, her arm flung over her face. Her hair was splayed about her head, and she looked very un-Julia-like.

"I just . . . I didn't realize that . . . I didn't . . . realize." I hadn't realized anything. I'd thought drinking didn't really matter as long as I wasn't doing it, and I'd thought working Janie's job would be easy and that letting Mother believe a lie would never harm anybody at all.

"What you don't realize, Ellis, is what it's like to be me, at the beck and call of two small boys, married to a husband who always begs off doing anything with your family. What you don't realize is how most of the time I just want to throw back my head and scream. What you've *never* realized is that you have absolutely no idea what it's like to be yanked out of school in order to be married and then wake up with children. And *responsibilities*! What it's like to always feel you'll have to apologize forever for a momentary indiscretion. I would like to say I have a sister I can count on to help out with things now and then, but she's too preoccupied and selfish to even notice me, let alone help me. I hate my life. And it's all your fault!"

"*My* fault? You're blaming me for having to marry Clarence? And having children?" I was used to being blamed for things, but normally I'd actually done them first. "I don't know why you always have to bring the boys along everywhere or why you always have to be here. You're married, for goodness' sake, with a house of your own."

"What else am I supposed to do with the boys? I'm not going to leave them somewhere when I know they'd be laughed at or scorned. The circumstances of my marriage aren't their problem. And why am I always here? Why should I spend any time with Clarence's family? All they ever do is look down their long blue noses at me and make jibes about Clarence's hopes and dreams coming to nothing, as if it were my fault he . . . well . . ."

"The Otises have always been like that! They look down their noses at everyone. Still, I don't think it's fair that—"

"*I* don't think it's fair all my plans and dreams were cut

short by one thoughtless, stupid indiscretion. Everyone was doing it, but then I got pregnant and—" She let that sentence hang in the air for a moment before she clapped a hand over her mouth.

She . . . ? I heard myself gasp. "But . . . I'd always thought you *wanted* to get married to Clarence."

"Wanting to get married and having to get married are two different things."

"But . . . where?"

"Where what?"

"Where did you do it?"

"Ellis!" A blush had swept Julia's face.

"I mean . . . well, I just . . . can't quite picture . . ." In the movies people were always falling all over themselves onto a bed or some conveniently placed sofa. It seems like you'd need a room to do that sort of thing, wouldn't you? And it's not as if they would have just excused themselves and gone to Julia's room after Sunday dinner. Besides, I'd been a regular brat; I'd always followed them around everywhere they went. Except when they went on their drives on Saturday afternoons in order to get away from me and—oh! "It was in his car, wasn't it?"

Julia's face flamed even brighter, but she refused to answer.

It was. They'd done it in his car. And—oh! I'd heard girls at the dormitory talk about the backseats of their beaux' jalopies, but I'd never actually . . . now my face was the one to flush. Had they *all* done it? Even—even—oh my goodness! Is *that* what was going on back there?

"I thought going to Europe would let people forget about it. But people *know*, Ellis. I know they know, even if they don't say anything. And the worst of it is Father and Mother know. And how is Clarence supposed to feel about coming over when he knows they know and . . . and how would you feel? Knowing people were whispering about your wedding? Knowing your parents paid for your tour because they were ashamed of you?"

They had? They were? Then why were they always bringing up Julia and throwing her in my face whenever I did something wrong? And—hey! No wonder they always sent the driver to take me to and from school.

"Would *you* want to go around out in society with everyone knowing all those things about you?"

"Why don't you move away?"

"To where?"

"I don't know. Calif—" No! *I* was going to California. If she was going to California, it would defeat the whole purpose of going away. "What about Texas?"

"Texas! We're from Boston. And Boston people stay in Boston!"

She didn't have to sound so huffy about it. I was only trying to help.

"Besides . . . wouldn't that be like lying?"

"It's not like anyone there would ask you when you got married and how many months later Marshall was born."

"Ellis . . ."

"And it's not like you're ever going to introduce yourself by saying you're Julia Otis and you got pregnant before you were married and Marshall was the result and what do you think about that?"

"Ellis!"

"I don't see why it's anyone's business but yours."

"It wouldn't be . . . if we hadn't . . . done what we'd done."

"But you love Clarence . . ."

"Of course I love him. He's a good man. He did the right thing. It's just . . . complicated. Now we're not quite respectable. And once you're not . . ."

Once you're not, Boston never let you forget it. Which is exactly why I was headed to Hollywood. "I've always thought Clarence was a good sort."

"He is! But we might have waited a few more years to marry. And I would have graduated from Radcliffe like all my friends, and he might have been able to find a better position. But now . . ."

Now he was still one of the down-on-their-luck Otises. "Well, good grief! You're married to the guy, so stop apologizing for him. What's done is done. It'll all work out. I'm sure it will."

She half-laughed, half-sobbed. "When? When will it work out? Because I'm tired of being this—this—scarlet woman. I'm tired of always apologizing for myself. And I'm just . . . *plain tired*."

"Then don't be."

"You don't understand, Ellis."

"Sure I do. You're only some shamed woman because you think you are. And if you think you are, then why wouldn't everyone else believe you? The trick is, you have to decide to believe something else."

"Like what?"

"Like . . . in the new Corinne Griffith movie. You might be a woman with a sordid past—"

"Ellis!"

"—*but* you can put it all behind you. It's not like anyone can blackmail you about it like they did in the movie because everyone already knows, so you can just skip over the entire second act, but the point is—"

"Ellis, I don't have time for—"

"—the point is, sometimes you have to *make* people give you a second chance. They're only treating you that way because it's the role you're playing. If you start playing a different role, they'll treat you differently."

"But I've never been good at acting like you are."

"You won't be acting. You'll just be yourself. You aren't meek and mild, Julia. No wonder you're so tired! You're good and smart, and you've never minded telling people so. You have to start being yourself again. Don't you see? People only snub you because you let them. If you didn't let them, they wouldn't be able to do it."

"And how am I supposed to not let them?"

"Ignore them. Whenever they try, think, 'That couldn't possibly be a snub because I'm Julia Otis, and I'm here to help, and who wouldn't want me as a member of their committee?'"

"Just . . . like that?"

"Just like that! And you'll see: They'll start to believe it."

"Julia Otis. I always thought I would be different once I actually married Clarence. But I'm not. I just wish—"

"You can wish or you can do." That's what the dean always said. "You might have done the wrong thing in the first place, but you don't have to do the wrong thing in the second place." That's what *I* always said.

"If only we hadn't—"

"But you did. So it can never be the same as it might have been, but it *can* be different."

There was a loud crash somewhere up in the attic, followed by the patter of feet on the back stairs.

Julia sighed as she pushed to her feet. And then she did something she'd never done: She embraced me and kissed me on the cheek. "Thanks, Ellis." She left me standing there, mouth hanging open as she intercepted the boys in the hall and took them by the hands and led them off toward their room.

"You're . . . welcome?"

Father came into the parlor after work with a merry salute. "So how was it?" At least he didn't seem perturbed by anything . . . although I was sure he soon would be.

"It wasn't." Mother didn't mince words when she was mad.

"What . . . wasn't?" He'd paused in his step and looked as if he wasn't quite sure where to put his foot down next.

"The pageant. Ellis wasn't there."

His brows sank toward his nose. "But . . ." He turned his gaze to me. "You left the house this morning. I saw you go."

"She hasn't been there ever. Have you, Ellis?" There seemed to be a hopeful, wistful glimmer in her eyes.

"No."

The glimmer disappeared.

Father had run a finger across his mustache, then crossed his arms over his chest, nodding as he'd listened to us. But now he was shaking his head. "I'm afraid I don't understand."

"She lied to us."

He fully understood that.

"She's been lying to us this whole time."

He was frowning now. "Ellis? Is this true?"

"I . . . hadn't meant to." That was the truth, at least.

"Hadn't meant to what?" Mother's words exploded with frustration. "Be precise, Ellis. Because if you tell me you hadn't meant to work, well then, I'd say you had succeeded." Clearly it wasn't a success she particularly admired.

"I hadn't meant to lie. And I *have* been working these past few weeks. It just wasn't . . . there."

"Then where was it?"

"I would rather not say."

"But you said quite a bit two weeks ago. And those words convinced me you had turned a corner. I was, dare I say, quite proud of you. And now both my girls . . ." She let her words trail off.

"I *am* working a job, and I *am* helping someone less fortunate than me."

Mother scoffed.

"It's just not a real orphan. I mean, I thought she was at the time. But I never did say I was working at the asylum. You just assumed it. And I have to finish up the week at work. I have to go in tomorrow. I have to!"

"And how are we to know you're telling the truth this time?"

"Because I am."

Mother just kept looking at me with those sad, woeful eyes. And then she shook her head. "I'm going back to the shore tomorrow with Julia and the boys. Do what you want. You will anyway."

"I'm . . . sorry."

Mother raised her head as if she were imploring heaven

to help her. "At some point, I would like to hear something else come out of your mouth. You have so much potential, and you've had so many advantages. If you would only—"

"I'm sorry I've been such a disappointment to you."

Her face softened. "You're not the disappointment. It's just your complete failure to—"

"To do anything at all? I know. Nothing I do ever comes out right. May I leave now?"

"Ellis—" My father held out a hand as if to restrain me.

I left the parlor and ran up the stairs to my room. Pulling my Hollywood scrapbook out, I went over my plans once more. I couldn't wait any longer. After this, knowing I'd lied, the next time I went to the shore my mother would keep me there for the rest of the summer. The moment Janie returned, I would have to leave. That meant I only had a few days left to discover exactly what that telephone call had meant.

The next morning, I tried to decide what to say to Miss Hastings. She seemed like one of those people who was used to getting her way. A lot. In fact, she was really bossy. So I should probably apologize first thing to get it over with, then promise to do better in the future. And really, I would, because in just a few more days, I wouldn't be me anymore. Janie would be back and everything would be perfect again.

I wondered if the supervisor would yell at me. Hopefully not. At least she didn't know my real name; I wasn't in danger of receiving another, "Oh, Ellis."

Humming a tune, I picked up my timecard. At least I meant to, only it wasn't there. That was funny. Maybe I'd put it in the wrong slot the day before. When—oh! I hadn't punched out the day before. It was probably in the wrong slot then. It had to be. I sorted through all the cards, but Janie's wasn't one of them. I'd definitely have to talk to Miss Hastings. Only I couldn't right now—my shift was about to start. I'd do it at lunch.

I flung my beads around to the back of my neck and tangoed down the hall and into the switchboard room, but I stopped when I saw my stool. Someone was already sitting in it . . . and it wasn't Janie. I walked over and tapped her on the arm.

She looked over her shoulder at me with a frown.

"You're sitting on my stool."

She took her headset off. "But . . . the chief just put me here."

"She must have been mistaken." I pulled the headset from her hand and put it on my head.

Beside me, Doris had slipped off her stool. "Actually . . . Miss Hastings hired her to replace you."

"Replace me? Why?"

"Because of yesterday."

"I know I was gone for a while, but—"

That girl tugged the headset from my ears and put it around her own neck. Of all the nerve! I tried to take it back, but she ducked away and wouldn't let me.

I put a foot to the stool step and tried to push her off with a shove of my hip. "I'm afraid there's been a misunderstanding. Why don't you go talk to the supervisor and straighten it out while I get to work?"

She wouldn't budge. "Why don't *you* go straighten it out?"

SIRI MITCHELL

"Because I have a job to do, that's why!"

"Well, so do I." She gave me a shove of her own.

I shoved back.

Doris pulled on my arm. "Janie, you were fired!"

I tried to ignore the stares of the girls around us. "I was not fired. Something came up. I had to leave, but now I'm back." I addressed myself to the girl. "I'm sorry for the inconvenience and I hope you didn't have to come far, but I'm here now and I'm ready to work if you'll just . . ." With a heave of a hip and plop of my bottom, I pushed her off the stool.

She landed on the floor with a cry, and I might have felt bad except she'd been so stubborn about the whole thing. Really, there was only one job to be had and I already had it. Why couldn't she understand that?

As I adjusted my headset, a light started blinking. Pulling a jack out, I moved to plug it in. But the girl shoved at me with both hands, nearly knocking me from the stool. I had to drop the jack to hold on to the board. "Of all the—!"

"This is *my* job."

Why did she keep saying that? "No, I don't believe it is. And if you're uncertain, then I think the person to ask is—"

"*What* is the meaning of this!" Miss Hastings was standing, arms akimbo, glaring at us both, which really wasn't fair. It wasn't my fault that girl seemed to think she'd been given my job! "You!" She was pointing her finger at me. "You were fired yesterday. And you—" she now swung that finger toward the girl—"were hired yesterday."

"What!" She'd hired someone? For *my* job?

"I don't know how you have the nerve to return after running out the way you did yesterday afternoon."

"The nerve—? But—it's *my job*!"

"It's my job. And I can give it to whomever I like." Miss Hastings yanked the headset from my neck and put it on the head of that other girl.

While they were fiddling with the adjustments, I launched myself at the stool, landed belly-first, wrapped my arms around the seat, and clung to it for dear life. "You can't fire me!"

"I already did." She put a foot to the stool step and started peeling my fingers away from the seat.

"You can't fire me because it's not my job."

"Exactly. It's not your job."

"It's Janie's. Please!"

"It *was* yours, Janie. Now it's hers."

I pushed my toes against the floor, using them to turn the seat around so she couldn't get at me.

"Stop moving!"

"I will if you give me my job back."

"This is not some child's playground, Miss Winslow. And if you think you'll ever work for this company again, you're sorely mistaken!"

"Never?" She couldn't do that to Janie, could she?

"Ever!" She marched off.

I followed her into her office, drawing the door shut behind us. "Please. You can't fire me!"

"I most certainly can."

"But I promise I'll do better."

"You promised that last week and look where it got me yesterday."

"But you don't understand! Janie's mother just died and she, well, there's a Mr. Winslow, you see, and Janie just wanted to make sure he knew because he's her father, you know, and all she wanted was—"

Her face seemed to soften for a moment. She rose from her desk, walked over, and patted my arm. "I can see you're overcome with emotion. Perhaps you need to see one of those analysts who can provide some kind of . . . clarity . . . for your grief."

"But I promised Janie I could do this job!"

"And clearly, *Janie*, you can't." She leaned forward. "You do realize you *are* Janie . . . ?"

"Please!"

"I must ask you to leave now. There's work to be done and telephone calls to be patched through. By girls more competent than you."

When I got home, the maid handed me a message as I walked in the door. "For you, miss. It was a telephone call from Miss Winslow."

"Janie?" I unfolded the sheet of paper. *I cannot meet you on Sunday. Will come by on Monday afternoon.*

Well, that was a relief! It would give me more time to figure out what to do about her job. Only I still hadn't figured it out by the time my father tapped on my bedroom door later that afternoon. "I'm going to need your help tonight, Ellis."

My help? "With what?"

"Oh . . . there's a benefit tonight, postponed from early May, and I volunteered your mother to help because usually she would be here since we don't go to the shore until July. Only I forgot to tell her before she left this morning, and now it's too late. She did say to tell you she'll come for you sometime next week and to make sure your things are packed. In any case, the benefit's tonight, and she can't come back to the city and . . . well . . . she's not here."

"How can I help?" I couldn't make as big a mess of things as I had down at Central . . . could I?

"You don't have to do everything. Hopefully you won't have to do anything. Edward Coffin's wife is the hostess. All you have to do is assist her."

I would have assisted Mrs. Coffin if she'd been there, but she wasn't. Her dyspepsia was acting up again, so the responsibility for the evening had fallen to my mother, which in turn had fallen to me. And now the head waiter was standing in front of me, waiting for directions.

"I suppose . . . hadn't people ought to be seated?"

"Yes, miss. Only we don't have the seating chart."

"Well, where is it?" My goodness, did they have to be told everything? If they didn't have it, then why didn't they go and get it?

"Mrs. Coffin was working on it."

"But she had to have finished it, didn't she?"

"I couldn't say, miss. She never gave it to us."

I felt my brows rise as I surveyed the gathering crowd. How many times had I seen my mother pore over her seating charts as if they were battle plans? It wasn't nearly as easy to seat a dinner party as it sounded. If I didn't know better, I would think Mrs. Lodge should be seated by Mr. Codman Jr.—who was eighty years old if he was a day—because she never stopped talking and he might as well be deaf. Only Lodges and Codmans never got on, so that could never do.

Oh dear.

I could work on a seating chart for days and never be able to get it right.

Maybe if I . . . no. That would never work. Or—! No, that wouldn't work either. What if I told everyone to sit at tables according to who their great-greats were? No. Mr. and Mrs. Lawson liked to pretend no one knew they were first cousins.

"What are you serving for dinner?" Maybe it would be canapés, which everyone could eat standing up. That way no one would have to sit down.

"Standing rib roast with jus and Yorkshire pudding. With peas."

Oysters and clambakes! Why did everything always have to be served with peas? Now everyone would have to sit down. I'd just have to wade in and do what had to be done. Make no apologies. Broach no recriminations. As long as people thought there was some order to the thing, then maybe there would be. "Can you get me a piece of paper?"

While he was gone, I surveyed the crowd, trying to figure out who to seat together. A poorly executed arrangement would be a disaster that would be remembered for years. I could just imagine it. *Do you remember that time when old Ellis Eton . . . ?"* Thank goodness I was already planning to leave for Hollywood!

If this dinner was going to be the last one I enjoyed, then why shouldn't I eat it with people I liked? When the waiter returned, I wrote out my table first and filled it with our family friends, and then I distributed the rest of the guests around the remaining tables.

Walking out to the hall, I posted the seating chart, and then I borrowed my father's glass and tapped it with the handle of a knife. The crowd quieted. All except for Mr. Codman Jr., who couldn't hear anything.

"I apologize for the delay in seating. Tonight, to go along with the theme of the dinner, you are being seated according to a criteria of which only I am aware. At the end of the evening, I hope you will be able to guess what you had in common with each of your tablemates. Thank you."

There. That ought to give everyone something to talk about!

Father and I stayed until the very end of the evening, since I had acted as hostess. I tried not to look at my watch too often, but really, you'd think nobody had ever worked a day in their life, the way they were still carrying on well past eleven o'clock!

I tried to speed things along by thanking people for coming, but I got caught up in ever so many conversations. Each table seemed to want to tell me what they'd discovered they had in common. The first table had all attended the first Chautauqua Assembly back in the summer of 1874.

"Oh! Except for me. I couldn't because that was the summer I came down with scarlet fever. But I'm sure you couldn't be expected to know that."

How could I have? I'd been born thirty years too late to remember.

Mrs. Rice was beaming as I approached her table. When she crooked her finger, I bent close. "Clever girl! How our conversation has taken us back. How did you ever know?"

I simply smiled.

Another woman at the table beside theirs tapped me on the arm with a slender, beringed finger. "I had no idea you were so well-versed in our family's history."

Neither had I.

"It's encouraging to find a young person taking such an interest in these things."

"Well, it's . . . interesting."

"It is. Thinking that but for a suitor's change of heart we might all have been each other's aunts and uncles, instead of just cousins. Very well done."

Each other's aunts? And uncles? I looked over that group, trying to figure out how that could possibly ever happen, but time was too short and the hour too late and I had never bothered much to listen when everyone went on and on about their family tree.

As I left that table, Mrs. George Emerson reached out from the one behind it. "Do you know what he did?" Her crooked, trembling finger was pointing at Mr. John Perkins, who happened to be my great-uncle.

"I can't say that—"

"Of course, she must." Mrs. Andrew Peabody had pinned me with a piercing gaze. "Why else would she have put us all together at the same table?"

Whatever he'd done, Uncle John didn't look nearly as upset about it as the women did.

"And *that man*!" She turned her finger on the other gentleman at the table, who seemed to be pretending not to hear.

Now Mrs. Emerson's entire body was trembling. "Let's just say it's high time they were found out for it. And we have you to thank!"

Oh dear. I'd always liked my Uncle John, and now it looked like I'd gotten him into trouble. "I would say . . . maybe by-gones ought to be bygones . . . ?"

Mrs. Peabody sniffed.

Or maybe not.

We got back around midnight, but even so, the telephone's shrill bell rang out as we set foot inside the house.

Father strode toward his office. I followed him down the hall and stood in front of the desk as he took up the telephone. He listened for a moment. "Elizabeth?"

It must be my mother.

"You're—" He paused, and I heard the squawk of Mother's voice coming over the line. "But why are you at the Win-throps'?" Another pause. "But do you know how much it costs?" He grimaced as he held the phone away from his ear. "Yes, of course. For emergencies. I'll ask to have a telephone put in tomorrow."

He sat in his chair.

I reached over and plucked the hat from his head, setting it down on the desk in front of him.

"The dinner benefit? Is that why you're calling?" He picked up a pen and tapped it against his blotter. "No. I had no ex-pectation you would stay for it. I simply forgot to tell you—"

He put the pen down and began setting the papers on his desk straight, at right angles to the edges. "No. Her dyspep-sia was acting up again." He frowned. "Her *dyspepsia*. So I asked Ellis to take over the duties."

"What!"

Even I had no problem hearing her voice.

"It turned out just fine. She did everything wonderfully. You would have been very proud of her." He paused again while Mother spoke and then glanced up at me and offered me the telephone.

I shook my head.

He offered it once more.

Though I took it from him, I had a bad feeling about it.

"Ellis? Are you there?"

"I'm here."

"I'm sorry you were left in charge. I've told your father not to volunteer me for these things!"

"It went well."

"I'm sure it couldn't have been too bad or I would have heard about it by now. Just so long as it wasn't a disaster."

"It wasn't. It was a resounding success. Everyone enjoyed it." Well . . . most people had enjoyed it.

"I'll come back next week and make sure everyone understands you were just filling in on an emergency basis. I can try to correct all the mistakes you made."

"But I didn't—"

"Don't worry. It will all be fine."

I gave the telephone back to Father and went upstairs to get ready for bed.

I'd pulled it off. I'd done something right for once! It was something Mother really could have been proud of. But she wouldn't believe it. It was as if she couldn't even comprehend the possibility. She'd been prouder when she'd thought I was working at the orphan asylum than she was when I actually *did* do something right.

Every day, in every way, I'm getting better and better.

I thought about that as I lay in bed and I decided I wasn't. I wasn't getting any better, and I might not ever get any better. But maybe that was all right. I'd done something well tonight, and I didn't do it the way other people might have—but if other people had done it the way it was supposed to have been done at the last minute like that, then it mightn't have worked out at all.

E llis!"
   I looked up from my dinner plate the next evening to find my father staring at me. "Pardon me?"

"I've been wanting to do something for Janie Winslow, since her mother died. I can't see that just handing her a check would do much good, but I'm told she's an excellent employee, so I've asked if she can be employee of the month. That way—"

I knew what he was going to say. He'd said it so often before. *"That way, it would be a reward for hard work."*

"—it would be a reward for all of her dedication and hard work."

"I'm sure she'll be thrilled to pieces."

"I hope so. In any case, would you like to come?"

"Come? Where?"

"Down to the telephone company. When I give her the award."

"When?"

"On Friday."

Friday! "*This coming* Friday?"

"Why wait when there's good to be done right now? And I wanted to do it before you went to the shore for the summer."

"You *can't!*" Because Janie didn't have a job anymore.

"But . . . I thought you and Janie were friends."

"We are. But . . . the telephone switchboard is an awfully busy place. At least, that's what I've heard. So I'm not so sure you ought to interrupt her job just to give her a check."

"It's a very generous check. I hardly think anyone would begrudge her a short ceremony."

"You know how shy she is. Why don't you just have them put it in her normal paycheck?"

"Because the rest of the telephone employees need to know hard work will be rewarded."

"I really don't think she'd want to stand up in front of everybody."

"Then she can sit. So . . . do you want to come?"

"I . . . guess. Yes?" What else could I say?

The whole thing had been a lark. At least for me. I had thought it would be easy, just another role to play. How hard, after all, could transferring a telephone call be?

Very!

Much harder than I had expected. I hadn't applied myself, I'd left my post, and now I'd lost Janie's job. She didn't deserve to be punished on account of me. And she was going to return in just two days.

But what could I do?

Maybe . . . maybe I could find her a job somewhere else.

I could interview employers for her and then, when she got back, she'd have a choice. She could decide what she wanted to do next. How could she not like that? Only . . . I had a feeling she wouldn't.

But, until I could think of something else, that's just what I'd have to do.

The next morning after church, I asked the maid for the newspaper and flipped through the pages until I came to the employment section. My, but there were an awful lot of jobs! I didn't know how I'd decide which ones to choose.

I read through the columns, circling the positions that were for women. Nurses, typists, secretaries. Telephone operators. Although . . . if I'd gotten her fired from one position at the telephone company, it wasn't very likely they'd let her take another.

I marked a big dark X over that one. And then I marked it over again just so I would remember.

I doodled a flower-covered vine in the column's margin, then turned the page. There were positions available for nurse-maids, schoolteachers, housemaids, shop clerks. Even for librarians.

What would I like to do if I were Janie?

I drew a picture of a sailboat as I thought about it. Janie was rather quiet, wasn't she? So she probably wouldn't want to work in a place that was too noisy.

I circled the advertisement for a librarian.

Although . . . Central was very noisy, and she'd liked it well enough there.

I circled all of the advertisements for typists.

Did she like children?

I circled all of those for schoolteachers as well. If the position paid well enough, she probably wouldn't mind them.

That left the . . . secretaries, shop clerks . . . I turned the page back over. Nurses, nursemaids, and housemaids. I couldn't see her as a nurse. I wouldn't want her to have to take care of sick people every day. And I couldn't see anyone wanting to be a nursemaid, changing soggy diapers all the time.

Shop clerk?

That seemed too ordinary.

A secretary?

I thought about it for a while as I went through my desk drawer, lining up all my pencils and arranging my blotting papers in a neat stack. After everything was put away, I finally decided Janie probably wouldn't want to be a secretary, taking notes for somebody all day.

The next morning I got up early, skipped breakfast, grabbed my gloves, and folded the newspaper pages I'd marked up and put them into my pocketbook. Then I went to find the driver. There was no time to waste. I had to find Janie a job before I saw her later that evening.

"May I help you, miss?" The woman who greeted me sat behind a large desk, and she had to nearly shout her words to be heard above the clattery, clackety sound of typewriters, which came from somewhere down the long hall behind her.

"Yes. I'm here about the job." I raised my voice as well.

"Which . . . ?"

"The . . . um . . ." Which one was it? I'd decided to try for all the typists first and then all the schoolteachers. And after that, the librarian. But then, on the way down into the city, I'd realized it would be smarter to tackle the jobs by area instead. So that meant . . .

"Was it the secretarial position?" She asked the question with a smile.

"I don't believe so, no." I'd decided Janie didn't want to be a secretary, hadn't I? "Maybe . . . could you tell me what positions you have available and then I could decide?"

The woman blinked as her smile disappeared. "I . . . suppose so. We have positions in the mailroom, and—"

"I'm quite sure it wasn't the mailroom."

" . . . and in the typing pool and—"

"Yes! That was the one."

" . . . and on a private telephone exchange as a switchboard operator."

"Oh. Yes! That one too, only . . ." If this company asked the telephone company for a reference, they wouldn't be able to give a good one. "Maybe . . . no. No. Just the position as a typist."

By this point she seemed to be regarding me with a suspicious tilt to her head. "Would you like to fill in an application?" She asked the question as if she were hoping I would say no.

"Yes, please."

She handed me one with a frown.

I sat down on a rickety old chair in the corner to fill it out. As I was smoothing it out over my pocketbook, another girl came in. She asked for an application for the typing position as well.

The woman who had frowned at me smiled at her and offered her an application.

I raised my pencil. "Excuse me. I was here first."

The woman hardly deigned to look at me. "We're taking applications all week long."

I smiled the smile my mother always used when she was determined to get her way. "I'm sure Janie's going to get it, though." I looked at the girl who'd just come in. "So there's no need for you to apply."

"Please." The woman was waving the application toward the girl. "Take it."

The girl snatched it out of her hand, took one last look at me, and left.

It wouldn't do for the position to be filled before Janie returned. Now then. I addressed myself to the application. Name.

Well, that was easy.

E-l-l-i-s-E-t-o-n.

Oh dear. I ought to have put down Janie's name. I snuck a peek at the frowning woman. She'd gone back to whatever it was she'd been doing. I hated to have to ask her for an eraser, but I didn't have one on my pencil.

"Excuse me. Do you have an eraser I can borrow?"

Her frown appeared once more and then immediately deepened, but she placed one at the corner of her desk.

"I've put the wrong name down on this one."

"The wrong *name* . . . ?"

"Yes. You see, I'm filling it out for a friend."

"I don't think that's allowed."

"But Janie is completely different than I am. She's a very nice girl. And quiet. Very neat and tidy and she always says please and thank you." That was the mark of a well-raised child in my mother's opinion. "She would be perfect for your job."

"I suppose . . . if she's not you. Does she have experience as a typist?"

"Well . . . I don't know, really. I don't think she has. But she might. You'll have to ask her on the first day."

"I'm afraid without the requisite experience, she won't have a first day. Didn't you read the advertisement?"

Yes, in fact, I had. But I'd decided experience didn't really matter. If they could just meet Janie, they'd like her. Everyone did. I took the eraser and made the correction.

This time, I filled it out properly . . . although I didn't know what address to give, so I put in my own. And I didn't know when Janie had been born and I had no idea what prior jobs she'd held—and I really didn't think I ought to put down the switchboard job—so I just left all of that blank. Then I put my gloves back on, slipped my pocketbook over my wrist, and turned in the application.

"But—" The woman turned the page over and then flipped it back. "It's not filled out!"

"Janie can fill in the rest once she returns."

"But I don't know anything about her!"

I pointed to the application form. "Janie Winslow. That's her. Right there."

I was secretly hoping it would turn out I'd done Janie a favor. Maybe she hadn't liked her job, and if she hadn't, now she'd have the time to look for a new one. So . . . maybe she wouldn't hate me after all. Maybe she'd end up thanking me. But filling out applications was much more difficult than I had imagined. The first woman seemed to be right; you weren't allowed to apply for a job on a friend's behalf. After that became apparent, I simply went round collecting applications for Janie to fill out herself later in the evening. Experience seemed quite important to everyone, and I didn't really know if Janie had any in very much of anything. At one of the schools that had advertised for teachers, I asked if it was absolutely necessary to have a teaching certificate.

"I'm afraid we can't hire anyone who doesn't have one."

"But I just know my friend would make a wonderful teacher."

"That's what the certif⌐⌐⌐ is meant to do. It ensures that anyone who gets one is, in fact, a wonderful teacher. I'm sure you understand we can't hire just anyone."

"Janie Winslow isn't just *anyone*. She's about as kind and loyal and . . . and *good* as anyone you'd ever want to meet!"

"I'm sure she is. But that still doesn't mean we can hire her."

I had no idea it could be so discouraging to look for a job. And I wasn't even looking for one for myself!

Yet.

A wave of absolute horror washed over me. I wasn't looking for a job for myself now, but very soon I would be. Would it . . . would it be like this? Was everyone going to keep harping on experience and certificates and all those sorts of things?

Would I be able to find *anyone* who'd be willing to take me at my word when I said I was a terrific actress?

Everyone had to start somewhere.

But if even Janie—who was smart, nice, and good—had trouble finding a job, who was going to hire me?

28

Janie came by the house later that afternoon just like she'd said she would. I embraced her and then hurried her up the back stairs to my bedroom and closed the door so we could talk.

"Did you find your father?"

She shook her head. "He'd left for the fishing grounds already and won't be back until later in the summer."

"Then . . . you had to bury your mother by yourself?"

She nodded.

"All alone?" That was tragic! I moved to embrace her again, but she was straight-armed and stiff-bodied.

"It was fine. It's done. Thank you for filling in for me."

"You're welcome. But . . . there's something you should know, and I feel as if I should tell you, right now, before you say anything else."

She was standing there, blinking. "What is it?"

"I . . . lost your job."

"You what?"

"I lost your job."

"My—but—*how*?"

"It wasn't on purpose, but it's all my fault. All of it."

Janie dropped onto my bed as if her bones had suddenly disintegrated. "I spent the last of my money on the train ticket."

"Well—here!" I went to my pocketbook and took her pay out of it. Which left me . . . nothing. But I'd lost her job, and she needed it far more than I did. "Here." I placed it in her lap. "We got paid."

She offered it right back. "And I told you I would let you keep it."

"But I lost your job. You need the money more than I do." Hollywood would just have to wait. I didn't know how I'd tell my parents about failing the economics class, and I'd have to somehow find the courage to tell Griff I couldn't accept his pin, but I couldn't take Janie's money. "It's yours. Take it. And let's get to work finding you another job. I went around the city this morning and got bunches of applications for you." I took them from my desk and set them beside her. "For typist positions. And librarians. I tried to pick up some for teaching positions, but you have to have a teaching certificate first, so I didn't think that would work. . . ."

"But there's nothing else I can do but answer telephones! It's the only thing I've ever done."

"Well, to tell you the truth, that's what I thought. And I was going to apply for a position for a private switchboard, but then I thought they might contact the telephone company, and if the telephone company had to say they'd fired you, then I thought maybe you oughtn't apply for another switchboard job."

"So . . . you lost me my job and now I can't apply for another one?!"

I sat down beside her. "There must be something. Some job you can do. I mean, you're so, so. . . . *good* and everything. All the time!" It had never ceased to amaze me.

"That's not a skill, Ellis. It's a personality trait."

"Then we'll just have to figure out what job needs someone who's good." I thought for a few moments, and then I had a brilliant inspiration. "Sunday school teacher! You'd be an excellent Sunday school teacher."

"You don't get paid for that."

"I really wish you could be a regular teacher. I think you'd be really good at it."

"I would love to go to college for a certificate. I've always wanted to go to college, but I don't have the money." She got up from the bed and walked toward the door. "You're no help at all. You lost my job, and now I have nothing. Literally."

"I feel really bad, Janie." I did. Extremely bad. "I didn't mean to lose your job. I really wish there was something . . ."

"You just don't understand, do you? Life isn't all . . . songs and dances. Or—even a movie! Some of us have to work for a living. And not by responding to invitations to dances and lectures or by packing up to go to the shore every summer. The only thing that matters to you is *you*! And the rest of us exist only at your pleasure and only when you want us to. So thank you for your time and thank you for your momentary interest in my dull and sorry life, but I have to go join the rest of the girls out on the street looking for work now."

"But—"

"You have no idea how having money, even just a little,

changes everything. I was working in order to save enough to go to school. But it turned out I couldn't really save anything at all because I had to do things like eat. And buy clothes to wear. And now, since Mother . . ." Janie lifted her chin even as it began to quiver. "Now I have to pay for an apartment too, because I can't stay with Doris forever. And even if I did save up enough money, I'd still have to eat and have clothes to wear and pay for an apartment, and I'd have to pay for college as well . . . and figure out how to do it all without a job. Because I wouldn't be able to go to class and work at the same time."

"I hadn't realized before I met the girls—"

"You've never realized anything. You've never had to!" She gripped her pocketbook tightly with both hands and held it to her chest. "I might as well just get married, because I'll never be able to do anything else now."

"I wish I could—"

"You've done enough for me already, Ellis. Please, *please* don't think you owe me anything else."

"I only want to help you."

"No, you don't. You only ever do favors in order to help yourself."

I thought long and hard after Janie left. About everything. She'd been right. I was a mean and selfish soul. If I'd had anything to sell, I would have done it and given the money to her, but that still wouldn't have made things right. If I wanted to make amends to Janie, I needed to replace what I'd taken from her. I needed to find a way to give her back her life.

If I'd ever needed to buckle down and apply myself to a problem, now was the time. I was hoping somewhere inside my stupid head was a solution, but I was terribly afraid there was not. Nobody had ever counted on me for anything before. Not really. And not for anything important. Janie herself wasn't even counting on me now.

But I was. And I knew this time, I would have to come through.

What could a smart, good girl like Janie do?

That was the question.

She could . . . marry a minister. That would be perfect! Only . . . she'd have to know one in order to do that. And why should she have to get married just because I'd lost her job? Wouldn't that be heaping punishment upon punishment? Marriage was out of the question.

Maybe she could . . . still be a typist! In a secretarial pool! But . . . she'd said she didn't know how to do anything other than answer telephone calls. Surely if she had taken secretarial courses, then . . . oh. She'd said she'd wanted to go to school, but she'd never had the money to do it.

In order to do something else, *any*thing else, it seemed like she needed money.

That check my father had been going to give her really would have helped. But that still wouldn't have been enough to pay for a place to live and for food. Or clothes. And goodness knew how expensive those could get!

There ought to be a scholarship or something she could qualify for. Irene had gotten one. If Janie could get a scholarship *and* my father's check . . . maybe that would be enough. Would she be able to go to school then? Going to school was just another step on the path that had been laid down long ago for me, but for a girl like Janie, I supposed it could change just about everything.

Mother had come back to the city on the afternoon train in order to find out what problems I had caused at the benefit on Friday. I asked her and Father if I could speak to them after supper. They sat on the sofa in the parlor, exchanging a worried look as I stood in front of them, trying to figure out what to say.

"I know I haven't exactly made you proud of me this summer."

Their worried looks changed to frowns.

Perhaps I hadn't chosen the best of beginnings.

"What is it you're trying to say, Ellis?" My mother looked as if she was on the verge of leaving the room.

I'd have to tell them the whole truth if I wanted them to help at all. "The job I had these past few weeks was Janie's, and—"

"Janie's? Janie *Winslow's*?" Mother was sitting up a bit straighter now.

"Janie Winslow's. After her mother died, she needed to go back up to Maine and have her buried, only the telephone company wouldn't let her."

"Did she ask? I can't imagine the company would—" Father was sitting up straighter too.

"Of course she did! And they said no. So she came to me and asked would I pretend to be her and work her job so she could go. So that's what I did. Until Thursday, when I got fired and lost her job."

"Oh, Ellis!"

"It's just that I had to leave my shift early to go to the pageant and—well, you know the rest."

"So . . . that check I was going to give her . . . ?"

"She might have gotten it—Janie came back this morning—except she doesn't work for the telephone company anymore. But the point is that I still want to help Janie, only I want to do it in a way that lasts. I want to send her to college."

"College?" Now my father was completely mystified.

"Janie and all the others like her down at Central. There are a lot of smart girls there, and they'd love to go to college, and they're trying to save money, but they don't have enough because they can't save enough. And then even if they do get enough, they have to keep working so they can—can still eat and have somewhere to live. So if people like us don't help them, they'll never get a chance to . . . well . . . do anything at all!"

"People like *us*?" Mother was looking at me suspiciously.

"Well . . . me. People like me."

"And how do you propose to do this?" At least Father looked a little, tiny bit interested in what I was saying.

"I was thinking that you still have the check you were going to give to Janie before I lost her job. And if you give it to her, that would help. Quite a bit."

"It might."

"But what I was hoping is that you would establish a scholarship. Or a foundation. Or maybe . . . a scholarship foundation."

"You're asking me to give quite a bit in order to bring this scholarship into being, but what about you?"

"What—what about me?"

"What are you going to give?"

"I don't have much of anything to offer."

Father shook his head as if in disappointment. Clearly I'd chosen the wrong answer.

"I don't have any money." I'd given it back to Janie. "At least . . . not until I'm given my allowance." But that usually disappeared, since I spent it on movies and magazines. "Perhaps instead of giving it to me . . ."

Mother was looking at me, one brow raised.

"Perhaps . . . I could give it to the scholarship fund. Maybe I could get the other girls to chip in too. Instead of going to the movies or buying ice cream sodas, we could skip them and give the money to the fund instead. And—and maybe we could even canvass for the fund. At the football games! Or we could—"

"And what are you going to call this fund?" Mother was trying hard not to smile. I could tell by the way she was biting her cheek.

There was only one rule among Boston's first families about the naming of things resulting from a donation. That they not, in any way, be connected with the donor. "How about . . . the . . . Irene Winslow Scholarship? For girls looking to change their role in life."

29

The next morning I slept in longer than I had for ages and finally stumbled down to breakfast at ten o'clock. Afterward, as I sat in the parlor working a crossword puzzle, I heard the doorbell ring. I ignored it. Someone would get it. And besides, I needed to think of a seven-letter word for "faces."

Aspects?

I filled it in, but it didn't match up with the word that ran across it. Oysters and clambakes! I erased it.

Facets?

No. That was only six letters. But . . . maybe the puzzle was misprinted. If I marked over that last box, then it would fit just fine. I started coloring in the extra box with my pencil.

"Miss Eton?" The maid called from the front hall.

"Hmm?" There. Almost done. *F-A-C-E-T-S.* Perfect! Now I just needed to find a five-letter word for enraged that ended in an *S*. But . . . I couldn't really think of any words that ended in an *S*. At least not for enraged. *Were* there any? Maybe I shouldn't have marked out that extra box.

"A Mr. Feeney is here for . . ." She took a step closer. "Janie Winslow."

" . . . a Mr. Feeney?" I ought to go root around in Mother's sitting room for a dictionary. There had to be a word that ended in an *S* in there that had five letters and meant the same thing as enraged. I wondered if anyone ever checked these puzzles for spelling errors. Maybe the word wasn't really five letters. Maybe they had misspelled it. Wouldn't that be rotten luck? I didn't know how anyone ever finished one of these! I tossed it onto the desk, then turned around to face the maid squarely. "I'm sorry. What were you saying?"

"I told him Janie doesn't live here, but he keeps saying she does."

"Janie?"

The maid colored. "Miss Winslow."

"Who is looking for her again?"

"A policeman. Mr. Feeney."

Jack? Here?! "I . . ." Jack couldn't be here! He still thought I was Janie, and I needed him to keep thinking that until I could figure out how to save Griff. I leaned out to look around her but didn't see anyone. Good! That meant he couldn't see me. "Tell him you can pass a message to Janie for him. I'll see that she gets it."

"Miss?"

"If he gives you a message, then we'll forward it." And when she went back to the hall to speak with him, I'd hide behind the desk.

"If you say so, but with Mrs. Winslow dead . . ."

"I said we'll get it to her and we will. Now . . . go on!"

320

I moved to duck behind the desk, but then the maid reappeared . . . with Jack right behind her. Too late to hide!

The maid gestured to him. "I was just going to get him something to write a message with."

"There you are!" Jack stepped in front of her and came over toward me. "I kept being told you weren't here."

I motioned for the maid to leave.

She screwed her face up in a puzzled frown, then turned around and left.

"I came to—"

"Ellis? Ellis!" My mother's footsteps sounded on the stairs.

Oysters and clambakes! I grabbed Jack by the hand and pulled him down behind the desk with me.

"Why are we hiding?"

"Because . . . because . . . because I'm not supposed to be here."

"Why?"

"Because I'm Janie. And Janie doesn't belong upstairs. So if she finds me . . ." I held my breath as I heard my mother's footsteps fall silent.

"Who finds you?"

"My moth—I mean—that woman."

"Why would she want you?"

"Why wouldn't she?" I wished Jack would stop asking questions!

The footsteps went away down the hall, and I heard the door to the office shut.

I stood and pulled Jack up beside me, then pushed him toward the door. "Time to go."

"But I didn't even—"

"Let's talk outside, shall we?"

"But—"

I opened up the front door and shoved him out. Or tried to. My, but he was tall! "I told you—I'm not supposed to be here."

"Fine. I'm going."

I went with him. Or I was going to until I saw Griff jog down the front steps of the Phillipses' house. What was he doing home at this time of day? He turned. Raised a hand. "Hey, El—"

I grabbed Jack by the hand and tugged him back into the house.

"But you just—"

"Hush!" I paused inside the door. Was my mother still in the office?

"Hey!" Griff's voice sounded closer. Was he coming over? I didn't dare to look.

I closed the door behind us. Now. Where to hide?

"Ellis? Is that you?" Halfway down the hall, the office door swung open. It was too late to make a break for the stairs. I sprang toward the parlor and the refuge of that desk, pulling Jack with me. "Get down!"

He crouched beside me. "Weren't we just here?"

"Hush." I put my hand over his mouth as I listened for my mother and peered out the window. Griff was there, standing on the sidewalk. He stepped forward. Stepped back. Raked his hand through his hair. And then he shrugged and went back toward his own house.

Thank goodness!

"Where did she go?" My mother. "Ellis?"

I heard the maid come back in. "Ma'am?"

"Have you seen Ellis?"

"She was here just a minute ago, but I haven't seen her since."

"When you see her, can you tell her I'd like to speak with her?"

"Of course, ma'am."

There werc two sets of footsteps now, going in opposite directions. I chanced a look. The front hall was clear. I couldn't risk the front door again because the maid was sure to hear me, and we couldn't go out the back because then we'd have to walk past the office and risk Mother noticing us. The only way out was up.

"How are you at climbing trees, Jack?"

"Trees?"

"Come on." I took his hand and led him out of the parlor, toward the front stairs. "Only step where I do."

"What are you—"

"Is that you, Miss Eton?" The maid poked her head around the corner.

Oysters and clambakes! I stepped off the first stair and planted myself in front of Jack. "No, it's not."

She blinked.

"And I have this police officer with me. He needs to inspect the windows. Upstairs."

"I do?"

"He does?"

I jabbed my elbow back and gave Jack a poke in the ribs. "Yes. So we'll just be going up now." I held my chin high and started walking up the stairs.

Jack lumbered up behind me, stepping on all the squeaky places as he went.

"Didn't I tell you to step where I step?"

"Would you let up!"

"Just—" I waved my hand toward the top of the stairs. "Come on."

Down below us, I heard a door swing open. "Ellis? Is that you?"

I took Jack's hand and hurried us up to Lawrence's room at the back of the house. And then I pushed aside the curtains and unlocked the window, inspecting it as I did so. It looked fine to me.

"Ellis is what that girl at the club called you. Why is everyone calling you Ellis?"

"Well, she . . . they . . . think I'm Ellis. She always has. Because I look like Janie."

"What?"

"She doesn't understand. No one understands."

"*I* don't understand."

"See what I mean? But that's not important." I hit the sash with the heel of my hand and then pushed up. There—finally! "What's important is that you leave. Now." I pointed toward the tree outside the window.

"You want me to climb out the window?"

"There's a tree. You'll have to lean forward a bit and then jump for it, but I think you'll make it."

"You want me to climb out your window? Like some thief?"

"Yes." To put a point to it.

"Tell me how I got mixed up with you again?"

I helped him put a leg out over the casement. "I was working down at Central and patching telephone calls through, except too many of them came in at once, and I meant to transfer one through except another one came in at the same time and I forgot to flip the switch for the first one and then—"

"Never mind."

"So if you just—see? Lean forward a little bit."

"I get it, thank you."

"And please don't come visit me here anymore."

He swung his legs, pushed off the ledge, and grabbed the tree branch. "But I wanted to tell you that—"

I pulled the sash down and locked the window.

"Janie!" He was still trying to say something.

I pulled the curtains shut and collapsed onto Lawrence's bed. Thank goodness that was over! But . . . why had he come in the first place? He hadn't ever said, had he? I thought about it for a minute as I stared at the ceiling. No, he never had. And it looked like a spider was building a web up there at the corner of the wall. I'd have to tell the maid.

I wandered downstairs and as I was going, my mother came out into the hall. "There you are!"

"Here I am. Did you need something?"

"I need you to start packing for the shore so you're ready to go by Friday." She turned and went back down the hall toward the office.

The shore. A long, bleak summer stretched before me. I was supposed to be getting ready to leave for Hollywood right now, only I didn't have any money anymore.

The maid came around the corner as she left. "Mr. Phillips stopped by. He asked for you. I told him you were having the windows inspected."

I thanked her and then went back into the parlor and found that crossword puzzle. I supposed I ought to assume the newspaper had gotten all the clues right and spelled all the words correctly. That meant I still needed a seven-letter word for "faces."

I worked at the puzzle while I ate lunch and tried to figure out what to do about Hollywood and Griff and that telephone call. I only had three more days before I'd be trapped at the shore for the rest of the summer. I'd already decided the men must have been mistaken when they'd talked about doing whatever it was in plain sight because Griff didn't seem to be planning to go anywhere with great crowds of people . . . although I really ought to make sure about that.

I didn't want to go talk to him at his house . . . but I didn't want to leave him on his own either, just in case those men tried something. Maybe if they saw someone   me—outside Griff's house, they'd think twice about whatever it was they were trying to do. In the movies, no one ever wanted a witness to their dirty work.

I put the puzzle down and went out to pace back and forth on the sidewalk in front of Griff's house for a while, but then my feet started to hurt. Solving a murder plot was hard work.

I heard the door open and ducked behind our front stairs.

"Ellis?"

It was Griff. If I stayed where I was, maybe he wouldn't see me.

"I see you."

I stepped out into the open.

"As long as you're there, could you maybe come in and help me with something?"

Perfect! Well, maybe. Was it better to be inside with him or outside where the bad guys could see me? "Why are you home? I thought you were working."

"I *am* working. But the office is too small for all the records I need to sort through." He led me into the parlor and shifted through a stack of ledgers, finally pulling several from the pile and opening them.

"Are you still not done with these?"

"It's not just one budget we're investigating; it's all of them. And since we tried for that warrant, they've been even harder to get." He pulled out a chair. "Could you read the figures in this column to me?"

I sat and read the numbers, then went on to the next column when he asked. With every number, he consulted his own book and then made a notation in a column of a third book.

"How long has this commission been after the mayor?"

"Years."

"Do you ever think maybe it isn't worth it? That maybe they should just let people be?"

"What do you mean?"

"Don't you think the mayor might get mad at you? And try to do something, maybe?"

"I'd like to see him try! Then we'd get him good."

"But what if nothing ever happens? What if he never gets convicted?"

"You don't give up at the beginning just because you're afraid of what might happen at the end. If it's worth it, then it's worth it, just like you said before. Nothing can change that."

Several hours later, Griff finally took the book from me and closed it up, stacking it on top of his own. And then he took my hand in his. "I've been wanting to know what you'd think about something."

Working all afternoon beside him, thinking about how truly terrific he was, I just knew if he pulled that pin out of his pocket right then, I might very well accept it. "I think . . . it's awfully swell it's the middle of June already, don't you?" I pulled my hand from his and stood, moving to place some distance between us. "You'll be done with all of this and back at school before you know it."

He gave me a look of such disappointment that it pierced my soul. "Just what is it you're afraid of, Ellis?"

An honest question deserved an honest answer. That's what my mother always said. "I just—I don't—I don't want to disappoint you." That was the truth of it. I hadn't wanted to disappoint him by leaving, and I didn't want to disappoint him by staying—because eventually that's what he would be either way: disappointed in me.

"You could never disappoint me."

"I disappoint everyone else. All my life, all I've ever done is disappoint people. 'Oh, Ellis!' this and 'Oh, Ellis!' that. How could I possibly not disappoint you?"

"What is it you think I'm expecting you to be?"

"Like everyone else. And I'm just not good at that. I try but—"

"Why would I want you to be like everyone else? Why would *you* want that? You're so good at being you."

"I'm *not* good at being me. Haven't you been listening? Nobody wants me to be me."

"I do."

"And what happens if I am? Do you really want me around in twenty years so people can say, 'Oh, Ellis.' Or—or worse! They'll probably say, 'Oh, Griff!' And then they'll say, 'What did you ever see in her?'"

"No one would ever say that."

"Why not?"

"Because you're the only one who ever calls me Griff."

"Well, then . . . then maybe *I'd* say it! I would. I just know it! In twenty years, I'd be so disappointed in myself that I'd disappointed you, I'd wonder why on earth you wanted me in the first place. In fact, you'll probably be asking *yourself* that question in twenty years: 'What did I ever see in Ellis?'"

He stood and closed the distance between us. "That would never happen. And the other reason I know it won't is because I hope you're around for *fifty* more years."

He wasn't listening to me. "How can you say that? How can—how can you stand there and . . . want me? Who am I supposed to be, Griff?"

"You. Just be who God created you to be."

"But I don't know how. And besides, I'm so much better at being someone else." In fact, I was better at being practically everyone else than myself.

"I know exactly who you are. You're the one girl who's refused to turn me into a prince and the only one who never stopped calling me Griff. And you'll always—and I mean forever—be my Ellis."

I felt a tear roll down my cheek.

"Golly, I didn't mean to make you cry. Don't cry." He put a thumb up to rub away the tear, but another rolled down to take its place. "Please don't."

I tried to stop, but I just couldn't. I was so tired of being me. It was just about the worst fate I could ever think of, but his words had made me feel as if I didn't have to try so hard to be someone else. As if Ellis Eton might be all right after all.

He took one long, searching look into my eyes as his hand slid to my neck, and then he bent and pressed a kiss to my lips. One single kiss. It reached down and tingled the very tips of my toes. It might not have been movie perfect, but it was exactly right.

When I opened my eyes, he was staring at me and I found, as I looked into those clear blue eyes, that I liked seeing myself reflected in them. But when he had closed his eyes and would have kissed me again, there came the sound of a discreet cough. "Mr. Phillips?"

Griff dropped his hand, and I tried to hide behind him as he turned.

It was the butler. "There's a gentleman at the door asking for you."

A man? At the door?

Griff sighed. "I'll be right there."

I grabbed at his hand. "Don't go."

"Why not?"

"Just—don't."

"Ellis—"

I grabbed onto him with my other hand. "Please, Griff. Don't ask me why, but just please, *don't answer the door.*"

He sent a look over his shoulder at the butler and then came back toward me, putting a hand to my shoulder. "All right. Fine. I won't." He tucked me into his side, then turned and sent the butler away. "You're trembling."

"I'm fine."

"What's wrong?"

"I'm just . . . worried about you. About—all those numbers and those books. What if someone wants to take you out of the picture?"

"Take me out of the picture? What a thing to think!" He was smiling as if I'd said something funny.

"You said you're trying to get the mayor fired. What if— what if he found out about it?"

He stopped smiling. Taking up my hand, he pulled me across the room toward the front bay window. "Let's see if we can tell who it is."

We crept to the window, peeking out between the holes of the lace curtains. We heard the door open. Heard the butler say something. Heard the door shut.

And then someone jogged down the front steps.

"It looks like . . ."

A cough sounded behind us. We turned from the window to see the butler. "A Mr. Freddy Brooks, sir."

Freddy Brooks? Who was Freddy Brooks?

"He left you a message." The butler was holding out a note.

"I thought Freddy'd gone back home for the summer. . . ."

Griff took the note, opened it up, and read it. "He's back, passing through town on his way to New York City. Wanted to know if he could stay the night." For the first time since I'd known him, Griff looked as if he were annoyed with me. "But . . ." he turned the note over. Turned it back. "I don't know where he went." He looked over toward the butler. "Did he say where he was going?"

"No, sir."

"Well . . ." Griff looked at the note and then at me.

"I'm sorry. I just didn't want you to get hurt."

"Honestly, Ellis, this isn't one of those movies you're always going to see."

That was the truth. It was much worse!

"I used to think you weren't like other girls, prone to all kinds of hysterics. But now I'm beginning to wonder."

"I had a good reason for asking you not to answer the door."

He raised a brow as if expecting me to tell him.

"A *very* good reason."

"Which is?"

I shook my head. "I can't tell you."

"Ellis! This kind of thing was fine when we were kids, but we're not ten years old anymore."

"I know, I just—" I shrugged. I couldn't really say anything else. "Well . . . what are you doing tomorrow? Maybe I could—"

He held up the message. "Trying to figure out where Freddy is! In between the hospital opening and the—"

Hospital opening? "Which hospital?"

"Massachusetts General. The heart wing. Remember? The one we built in Mother's memory?"

"Do you have to go?"

"Do I have to—! Of course I have to. Everyone's going to be there. Even the mayor's going to put in an appearance."

"Mayor Curley?"

"Which other mayor would I be talking about?"

"So it's . . . in plain sight? Where everybody can see it?"

"It's a big event. Father's been working with the hospital on the plans for the past three months."

"And everyone's going to be there?"

He nodded.

"I need you to promise me something."

"Will it make you leave?" He looked truly peeved now.

I walked up and took his hand between my own, and then I looked into his eyes, those gorgeous blue eyes that just a few minutes before had been looking at me with such hope and love. "Could you promise me you won't go? I can't tell you why. You'll have to trust me: It wouldn't be safe."

He pulled his hand from me. "No!"

"No, you won't go?" Well, that was a relief!

"No, I can't promise you. I have to go. Everyone's going to be there."

That's what I was so afraid of!

31

And don't forget." Father was watching me from his position at the head of the table as he poured some cream into his tea the next morning.

" . . . forget what?" After spending a sleepless night trying to figure out how to keep Griff from attending the hospital opening, I'd already drunk two cups of tea, though it didn't seem to be helping me to wake up.

"Your mother wanted to go to the heart wing opening today, down at the hospital. She thought we could all go over together after the ceremony. That way the crowds won't be as pressing, and we can actually go inside to tour it."

"After?"

"It seems like a good idea."

"I can't go after." After would be too late. Griff might already be murdered by then! "I think—is it all right if I go with the Phillipses so I can be there for the ceremony?"

He blinked. Frowned. "I suppose. Did they ask you?"

They would. And if they didn't, I'd ask them to ask me.

But I couldn't wait for an invitation. If I didn't have one by the time they left this morning, I might as well just dig my black dress out of the back of my closet and plan on attending Griff's funeral. I watched the front walk through the parlor window that morning, and when Griff stepped out, I ran to meet him.

"My mother and father aren't coming to the hospital until after the ceremony, and I would rather see the whole thing."

"Great." He started walking toward the car that waited for him at the curb.

"I mean—I was kind of hoping—"

"I'm glad you'll be there."

"But the thing is, I'd like to be there for the whole thing. The ceremony and everything. But you know how my mother is, and she doesn't think it's proper, and I think, actually, she's kind of sad about your mother dying." That thought had just occurred to me as I said the words. She *was* sad, wasn't she? Griff's mother had been her closest friend, and they'd lived right here next to each other for lots of years, and now Mrs. Phillips was dead. Not that she'd died recently. It had been a while. Quite a few years. Six of them. But she was still . . . she was sad. My mother, that is. Because Mrs. Phillips was dead. And that made *me* sad. And Griff was sad too. It was all just so *sad*!

"Ellis? I have to go." He nodded toward the car. "My father's already there."

"So . . . can I go with you? To the ceremony? If it wouldn't be too much of a bother?"

He was frowning. "We're supposed to be there early. You wouldn't want to wait around for the ceremony."

Would I ever!

"I'll just see you afterward."

"No!" That wasn't going to work at all. "Please. Please let me go with you. I promise I won't get in the way."

"I guess . . ."

"It's decided, then? Yes?"

He sighed. "Fine. But we really have to go now."

I stretched up to give him a hug. And then I kissed him right on the cheek. "Perfect. You'll be glad you said yes. I promise."

"Didn't you promise I'd be glad I said yes to your coming early with us?" Griff bent to help me pick up a tray of tiny tea sandwiches I'd knocked off the refreshments table. And then he handed me a fistful of napkins that had tumbled to the ground.

"Yes. That's what I said. And you will be glad you said yes." I put a finger to my mouth and licked off some of the cream-cheese filling. Mmm! I was glad he'd said yes too.

"Do you mind telling me *when* I'll be glad I said yes?"

"Soon." Right after I stopped him from being murdered.

"Because I wasn't very glad when you stumbled into the chairman of the board. And now there's this."

"I'm sorry. I'll just—" I put the last of the sandwiches back on the tray after I brushed some dirt off it. "I'm going to sit down right here, and I'll save seats for you." I walked up a few rows to the front and sat in one of the chairs that had been set up for the occasion. "And I promise I won't move."

"Just—don't promise anything. You aren't very good at it." He scowled and went off in the direction of his father.

That wasn't fair. I thought I was rather good at promises; I made quite a few of them. Like paying back the girls in the dormitory. And working for Janie. And looking after my nephews. I made promises all the time. I suppose, to be truthful, I didn't always *keep* them, but on the whole, I considered I was getting better at it than I used to be. Keeping that in mind, I did sit there and didn't move. Except for my feet. I practiced a new step I'd seen at the Yacht Club. One-two-three-*four*. One-two-three-*four*.

The seats in front of the stage began filling up around me, and a crowd began to mill in the open area behind us. But the hum of conversation ruined my rhythm. I stood up and looked around to see if I could find that man from the speakeasy, but I couldn't really see very well, so I stood atop my chair.

That was better.

I still didn't see him, but as I was standing there, everyone began to look at me and that was even better. I could see everyone's face now. He wasn't there, but there were more people still waiting to come in and sit down.

I glanced at my wristwatch, or meant to, but it wasn't there so I climbed down and asked the woman who was sitting behind me for the time.

"It's nearly ten o'clock."

It would start soon, then.

But . . . what if that man wasn't here when the ceremony started? What if . . . what if he came afterward? I might never see him until it was too late! So maybe I ought to sit in the back instead—or even stand with the rest of the crowd.

I got up, but then I remembered my promise.

I'd promised I wouldn't move.

But that didn't really matter, did it?

I sat down. Maybe it did. I'd promised, and I'd really meant it. But I'd forgotten about looking for that man. And Griff might be annoyed with me now, but he'd be really mad if he ended up dead. So maybe I *should* move.

I got up.

But Griff and his father came, sitting down beside me.

I leaned toward him. "I was going to—"

The mayor stepped up onto the platform.

Too late!

As he talked about Mrs. Phillips and the new heart wing, I kept an eye on the audience, swiveling back and forth in my seat.

Griff poked me with his elbow. "Knock it off."

"Sorry, I just—"

There was a burst of applause.

The mayor smiled and held out a hand, palm up, toward Griffin and his father. They both rose and walked toward the platform.

Where was that speakeasy man? Was I too late? Was Griff going to be murdered before I could do anything to stop it?

As Griff stepped up to the podium, I saw that man from the speakeasy slink around the edge of the crowd as he neared the platform. So that was one of the men, but where was the other? And what should I do about them?

Up to the left of the platform, one of the bystanders took the gum from his mouth and stuck it behind his ear just the same way Doris did whenever she started work at the switchboard.

The speakeasy man was getting closer now.

And there! On the other side of the courtyard, Officer Jack Feeney was edging along the crowd toward the platform from the other direction.

I half rose from my seat.

Over alongside the side of the platform, the chewing-gum man was staring over at Jack.

Gum!

Doris only put her gum behind her ear when she was getting ready to work. No one here was working. Or they weren't *supposed* to be working. They were just listening to speeches.

The only people working were the people intent on murdering Griff.

The speakeasy man. The chewing-gum man. And . . . my gaze crept over toward Jack.

He glanced at me and then looked away.

My hand flew to my mouth. He wasn't just some impartial observer. In spite of what he'd said, he was still *in on this*!

The man from the speakeasy put a foot to the back of the platform, reached a hand inside his coveralls, and began to pull something from it.

I couldn't wait any longer, and there was no way to be discreet about stopping the man, so I got to my feet, leaped onto the platform, and stood spread-eagle between Griff and the man. "Don't shoot!" I screwed my eyes shut, just in case he did.

But . . . there was no gunshot. In fact . . . I opened one eye . . . nobody had even moved.

Griff put a hand to my arm and bent to whisper into my ear. "Ellis? What are you doing?"

I pointed to the speakeasy man. "He was going to try and shoot you."

"He what?"

"With a gun! He has a gun in his pocket!"

Somewhere out in the crowd, someone screamed, and then everyone tried to leave at once.

The man turned around and jumped from the stage, trying to join the mad rush from the courtyard.

Griff took a running leap and landed right on top of him, knocking him to the ground.

They wrestled for a moment, and then Griff prevailed,

ripping the object from the man's hand. He took the man by the collar, yanked him to standing, and then proudly held his prize aloft as if he'd just scored another touchdown.

Only it wasn't a gun.

It was a . . . What was it exactly?

Cameras clicked and flashes popped as reporters who had been covering the ribbon-cutting turned their attentions to the man instead.

"It's a crowbar." I jumped at Jack's voice in my ear.

"A . . . *crowbar?*"

"Officer?" Griff marched the man over toward us as Jack pulled a pair of handcuffs from his pocket. Another policeman had joined us by then. He took the cuffs from Jack and the man from Griff as Mr. Phillips approached, scowling. "What is the meaning of this!"

I knew what the meaning was. I knew exactly what it was. "That man was trying to murder Griff! And that man—" I pointed out the chewing-gum man—"was in on it!"

Everyone's gaze swung in the chewing-gum man's direction. He tried to make a break for it, but Griff's father stuck out a foot and tripped him.

Jack laid a hand on my arm, but I brushed it off. It was time for the truth to be told. "Tell them!"

He gave me a long look before he stepped forward to answer. "No one was trying to murder your son, Mr. Phillips." He turned to look at me. "This is a ribbon-cutting ceremony, not some movie." He dropped his gaze. "It seems there was a plan to try to . . ." He cleared his throat. "Disable him."

"*Disable* . . . ?" Mr. Phillips said the word as if he'd never heard it before.

Dis-*what*?

"These men work for a local bookie." Jack shrugged. "Gambling on college football is big business."

"And how does my son fit into all of that?"

Jack held up the crowbar. "It seems your son had been approached this spring about throwing a game or two in the fall."

"But I told them I wouldn't!"

Jack clapped Griff on the back. "And he told them he wouldn't. The thought was if his leg were broken and he couldn't play next season, then maybe Harvard wouldn't be such a hard team to beat. And maybe some of the other football players would think twice before turning down an offer."

"They wanted to break my son's leg?" Mr. Phillips was staring at the crowbar in horror.

Jack shrugged. "At least they were planning to do it at a hospital. I don't think they meant to hurt him much. Just . . . put him out of the picture for a while."

The mayor stepped up and started clapping Griff on the back, congratulating him for catching a crook.

I'd heard everything Jack had said, but I still didn't understand what was going on. When was he going to talk about the murder?

Jack broke into the conversation. "Would you excuse me for a moment? I'd like to speak with Miss *Eton*. Alone." He didn't wait for anyone to say yes or no. He simply took me by the elbow and marched me over toward the edge of the platform. There, he leveled a stern look at me. "At any point in time, were you ever planning to tell me you're actually Ellis Eton?"

I shook my head.

"*Is* there a Janie Winslow?"

I nodded.

"Does she live on Beacon Hill?"

"No. Although . . . she used to. For a while, with her mother who was our cook, but then she got a job down at the telephone company, only when her mother died—"

He held up a hand. "Never mind. It's not important."

"Was this . . . this whole plan . . . Was it about breaking Griff's leg?"

He glanced over in Griff's direction. "Sure. Why? What did you think it was about?"

"I thought . . . I mean . . . you weren't worried about his job, then? Or the mayor? This was all about *football*?"

He glanced beyond me toward the Phillipses and then his gaze came back. "Yes."

"*Football?!*"

"Shh. Don't say it so loud."

"So there was . . . there was no murder planned?"

"Who ever said there was a murder?"

"You did."

"I never said that. I'd never get involved in anything like that. What kind of man do you think I am?"

Well . . . that was the question, wasn't it? He seemed to be better than I'd thought he was, but just a little bit worse than he ought to be, considering he was a policeman. "You're sure there's no murder."

"Murder!" He gave a snort. "No."

"But . . . what about you? Why were *you* here, then?" Before he could answer, I figured it out. "You were trying to stop them!"

His gaze slipped from mine. "Maybe."

"But . . . I thought you were part of it."

He frowned. "I was in the beginning. But . . . I had a change of heart. That's all."

A change of heart.

"Maybe . . . some of the things you said . . . about laws and people . . . maybe some of them changed my mind about some things."

"Are you telling me you've decided to become one of the good guys?"

He straightened. "Maybe. Mostly, I'm thinking it's time to move on. Do something else for a while." He looked down and gave me a wink. "So maybe I'll see you in Hollywood after all."

Hollywood. I laid my hand on his arm. "To tell you the truth, I'm not going."

"Not going? After all those things you said? And all those dreams you had?"

I looked beyond him toward Griff. Toward the man with strong convictions and a faithful, steady heart. I felt my mouth lift in a smile, and when I spoke it was in mimic of Jack. "Let's just say I had a change of heart. That's all."

He followed my gaze. "You could do worse. That kid's all right."

As we spoke, the speakeasy man was walked off through the courtyard by the other policeman. "What's going to happen to him?"

He sighed. "It's like this: The whole thing was supposed to send a message, out in the open in front of everyone. King wanted all these bluebloods to know he won't take no for an answer. Not even from them. So doing something to that prince here, where you'd think he would be safe . . ."

"What are you saying? What's going to happen to those men?"

"That's where I was supposed to come in. I was supposed to frog-march them out of this place and into the patrol car and then . . ." He shrugged.

"Then?"

"Then . . . let them go."

"Let them go! Just like that?"

"Except I got a different officer to help me, and he'll make sure they actually get to the jail."

I didn't like the way Jack kept avoiding my eyes. "And after that?"

" . . . they'll probably be out in a couple days."

A couple days! After trying to break someone's leg? "But what about Griff? Won't they just try again?"

"Naw. That's why I told Mr. Phillips about the plan and made sure everybody heard me do it. They'll find someone else's leg to break now. So don't worry about it."

My jaw must have dropped open, because he laughed. And then he kissed me on the cheek. "Been good knowing you, baby."

"Ellis?"

I whirled from Jack to find Griff standing before us, a puzzled frown on his face. He was looking between Jack and me. "You know this man?"

I looked up at Jack. "He's a friend of mine."

Griff stuck out his hand. "Griffin Phillips. Nice to meet you."

Jack shook it. "Same here." He put a finger to his hat, then winked at me. "I have to be going now. So long."

As Jack walked away, Griff took my hand in his. "Ellis, I really need to talk to you. I've been trying for a while, but something always seems to get in the way. I figure now is as good a time as any." His free hand dove into his pocket.

I felt the tips of my ears flush, and my heart thrummed in my ears. "Yes?"

"Ellis, would you—"

"Oh, Ellis!" My mother severed our connection, taking me by the shoulders and shaking me, and then she gathered me into her arms with a sob. "We came early, we decided to be at the ceremony after all, but what were you thinking?!"

"I didn't really—"

"How do you get yourself mixed up in these things?"

"I don't really—"

"There's been quite enough drama this summer. Now. I want you to come back with us and sit down so the ceremony can continue."

Half the attendees had already fled the courtyard, and it didn't appear as if they were coming back. If I'd just stayed in my seat like I'd promised, Jack would have stopped the man with the crowbar, Mrs. Phillips would have had her wing dedicated by now, and Griff would have already cut the ribbon. I'd messed everything up—again.

"Ellis?" My mother reached toward me, but I'd already stepped beyond her grasp. "Where are you going?"

"I think I'll just go sit in the car."

B oth of my parents were waiting for me in the parlor when I came downstairs for supper, and Griff was there with them. Humiliation heaped upon humiliation. By the time I saw them all, they'd already seen me. I couldn't turn around.

My father invited me to sit down across from them.

I sat.

"About the ceremony, Ellis . . ."

I didn't want to think about the ceremony. I didn't want to think about the pageant at the orphan asylum or how I'd lost Janie her job down at Central. Or Irene. *Or* my failed economics test. My life was one long series of disasters. "I'm sorry." I looked up at Griff. "I ruined everything, didn't I?"

"You stopped Griffin from getting his leg broken." My mother looked as if she couldn't decide whether to frown or smile. "It wasn't all bad, and actually—"

Father interrupted her. "Actually what we wanted to know was how you discovered the plan in the first place. And why you didn't tell anyone."

I got up from my chair. Maybe I would run away to

Hollywood after all. I could find Jack and ask him to lend me some money, and we could go together. That wouldn't be so bad. Only . . . as I looked at Griff I knew I wouldn't. I couldn't. Griff was one thing I'd decided I wouldn't run away from. I didn't want to. Not anymore.

"Ellis?" Father prompted me with a steely-eyed look.

"It all started with Janie." But . . . had it really? "Actually, it all started with Hollywood."

My mother's eyebrows put a fine point to her skepticism. "Hollywood?"

"I was planning to run away."

"Run away? What—!"

"Just listen. Please? I've been planning it for a while. I'd been saving up money for the trip, but then I'd spend it. So I'd borrow money, and I'd spend that too. When Janie's mother died, Janie had to go back up to Maine for the funeral. Only they wouldn't let her go, like I told you, so she needed someone to take her place down at Central. I said I'd do it as long as I could have her two-weeks' pay."

Mother gasped. "*Run away?* But—why?"

"Because I've never been able to do anything right. In fact, I'm not good at anything at all. I never apply myself, I'm incapable of buckling down, and I'm—I'm not even smart."

"Yes, you are." Dear, sweet Griffin. Always my champion.

"I'm really not."

Mother extended her hand toward me. "I think you'll find if you just try harder—"

"I *do* try."

"Maybe if you studied more. If you applied your—"

350

"I can't. I've tried. I've studied, or tried to, but I just can't
do it. I will never be the kind of daughter you want me to
be. The only thing I'm good at is acting."

Father had been listening to me, head cocked, eyes narrowed. "So . . . you wanted to go to Hollywood to act?"

"Yes."

"In . . . movies?"

"Yes! I want to do something I'm good at."

Mother laid a hand on my father's arm. "We didn't realize
you felt so strongly—"

They didn't realize anything! "Just let me finish. I started
working Janie's job, and it was hard! That first day, while I was
trying to learn the switchboard, I listened in on a telephone
call accidentally. I didn't mean to. And that's when I found
out about the plan. Only I thought it was about someone
wanting to murder Griff, not trying to break his leg. And
then I met Jack, he was the policeman, and I would have told
someone, only they'd have wanted to know where I'd heard
it, and I didn't want anyone to know I was working Janie's
job because then I'd have to say why and I didn't want any
of you to know I was planning on leaving for Hollywood."

"We certainly would have found out sooner or later."
Mother was looking at me as if she didn't quite know who
I was anymore.

"I know. But I was going to explain it all in a letter. Then
I'd have time to think of what to say and wouldn't sound
like . . . well . . . like this."

"You stood up for what was right. . . ." It sounded like
Father wanted to add a *but* to his words.

"And you *did* stop Griff from being hurt. . . ." It sounded like Mother did too. "But . . ." There it was. "I wish you would have told us you were so unhappy. To run away . . . we would have missed you terribly."

"I'd hoped it would make life easier on all of you."

"Easier isn't always better. I admit you're prone to outbursts, and you're full of surprises, but you are an Eton, after all. . . ." Mother's eyes had gone suspiciously shiny. "Just don't run away. Please."

"I won't." I ventured another look at Griff. "I don't want to anymore."

"We can work all these things out." Father sounded as if the problems were fixed. "All we ask is that you do the best you're capable of."

"And apply yourself, Ellis. That's all we really want."

Hadn't my mother been listening? "I'll try." I'd do my best for Janie and the scholarship foundation. "But I won't promise anything." I'd promised myself, after the ceremony, that I wouldn't make any more promises. Not until I knew I could keep them.

Father got up and walked toward the front hall, patting me on the arm as he passed. "Griffin asked if he could have a word with you." He waited for Mother to catch up to him and then gave her his arm.

I wanted, more than anything, to go with them. After what I'd said about going to Hollywood, I didn't think Griff would ever want to speak to me again. I would have explained it all in the note, about how it wasn't him I didn't like and it wasn't him I was trying to run away from. It was me. But . . . how did you say something like that to someone, face-to-face?

He got up from his chair and came toward me, hands in his pockets. "I think it was kind of nice, you trying to save me and all."

Then why was he trying so hard not to laugh? I slouched down in the chair. "If I weren't so stupid, then I might have realized . . . everything. But I really thought that man was going to murder you."

"I know you did. So thanks." He reached a hand down to me, and I put mine in it. He pulled me to standing. "I thought you were really brave."

He wasn't going to make fun of me? "You—you did?"

He dropped my hand and shoved his hands back into his pockets. "I've always thought you were brave."

"You have?"

"Sure. You're always doing things no one else would ever think to do."

When my parents said things like that, it always sounded bad. But when Griff said them, it sounded entirely different. He made it seem as if he admired me.

"I just wanted to come over and . . . well . . ." He took his hands from his pockets and took up mine again. And then he looked down at me. "You know I've been trying to talk to you for a while now."

"Before you do, I just want you to know I'm sorry I didn't tell you sooner about that man. I wanted to, but I thought . . . I mean . . . it seemed like it would be better to figure out what was going on first. . . ."

"You could have been hurt, Ellis. Especially if they were planning to do what it was you thought they were."

"I know. But . . . I didn't want to hurt you by telling you I was going away. And then I did figure it out, kind of, but by that time it was almost too late. And then . . ."

He cupped my face with his hands. "And then?"

I dropped my gaze from his. "And then I decided I didn't want to go to Hollywood anymore." That's what I hadn't told my parents. I'd decided I wanted to stay.

He pushed a stray lock of hair behind my ear.

"And . . . I'm just not good at very many things, Griff." Why did I sound like I was pleading?

He bent and kissed my cheek.

"I always end up disappointing everyone."

"Ellis."

"And I don't want to disappoint you too." I felt my chin begin to tremble. Because that was the worst of it. That's what staying meant. If I stayed, then eventually I'd disappoint him too.

"You could never disappoint me."

Why wouldn't he listen! "But even if I try my best, I can't promise I'll always be good, because, well . . . we both know I won't be."

"But that doesn't mean you're bad." He planted a kiss on my nose. The softest, most delicate kiss.

It didn't? He was staring down at my lips and I almost gave in and lifted my mouth to his, but then I realized I had to be strong. Sometimes the truth hurt, but I had to do what was right for him. "I'm just no good for you, Griffin Phillips! Don't you know that?"

He just smiled that lazy Griff smile. "No."

He still wasn't listening. "Well, I'm not!"

"Why?"

"Because—because—because I *flunked economics*!" There. Surely now he would understand.

But his smile only grew wider. "I don't want some perfect co-ed or some bug-eyed Betty. I want *you*." He was . . . was he kneeling? "Ellis Eton, will you be my wife?"

"*Wife!* But I thought—I mean—I—" This wasn't right. "I thought you were going to *pin* me, not *propose* to me."

"I was. But it took so long to get you alone to talk to you, I don't want to waste any more time. So . . . will you?"

There was such confidence, such hope, such *love* as he looked up at me through those gorgeous blue eyes. And I knew then something I ought to have realized long ago: There was a perfect role that had been waiting for me practically my entire life, and I didn't have to run away to audition for it. I didn't have to go to Hollywood. I didn't even have to pretend to be somebody different. "There's no one else I'd rather be."

He stood and pushed an impossibly old-fashioned but perfectly right ring onto my finger. "You probably want something more modern, but—"

"It's perfect. Completely and utterly perfect!" I flung my arms around Griff's neck, causing him to stagger as I stood on tiptoe to kiss him. And from the front hall, a loud sigh went up from behind me.

My mother. "Oh, Ellis!"

Author's Note

I purposely gave Ellis Eton one of those impulsive, restless minds diagnosed by modern medicine as having ADHD. I was curious to see what her era would have done with a person who just couldn't concentrate no matter how hard she tried.

The Harvard Annex was created in 1879 for the private instruction of women by faculty from Harvard University. It took on the name Radcliffe College in 1894, when it was officially chartered by the state of Massachusetts. Radcliffe students were instructed, on their own campus, by professors from Harvard who essentially taught the same courses twice: once to the men at Harvard and once to the women at Radcliffe. Joint instruction in Harvard classrooms was instituted in 1943. Radcliffe women finally began to receive Harvard degrees in 1963, and in 1991, Radcliffe College was subsumed by Harvard University, although the name still lives on in the Radcliffe Institute of Advanced Study.

Griff's finance commission, supported by many of the first families of Boston, worked very hard throughout the 1920s to collect proof of Mayor Curley's wrongdoings. Supported by the underworld from his very first appearance on the political stage, allegations of ballot-stuffing, corruption, fraud, and misappropriation of government funds followed Curley wherever he went. Although he served a sentence for fraud in the early years of the century, it took until 1947 to convict him of wrongdoing, and even then it was only on mail fraud. Curley served four terms as mayor of Boston, one term as governor of Massachusetts, and two terms as a U.S. congressman as well as serving three prison sentences (during one of which he was re-elected mayor). President Truman later pardoned two of those convictions.

King Solomon controlled illegal activities in Boston and much of New England during the 1920s. He dealt in gambling and narcotics before expanding into bootlegging during Prohibition. Although he was arrested for his dealings in narcotics, he was acquitted. Later, when sentenced to jail in Atlanta for perjury during his previous trial, two congressmen intervened to have him transferred to a prison closer to home. Some of the inlets along Buzzards Bay were indeed used for smuggling liquor into the country, and college sports have always been of special interest to gamblers.

During the 1920s, nothing was done by halves. It was an era defined by its fads. It gave us the raccoon coat as well as bobbed hair and the kohl eye pencil. If the fringed flapper dress is still iconic, less well-known is the fact that flappers used to scorn all footwear but galoshes. In 1923 mah-jongg was the thing to do. In 1924 it was the crossword puzzle. And at one point, when the Charleston was all the rage, there were over four hundred different ways to dance it.

Self-improvement and psychoanalysis became prominent in that decade as well; the mania for auto-suggestion and a fervent belief in willpower swept the nation. Thousands of men and women across America started each day by reciting Emile Coué's mantra, "Every day, in every way, I am getting better and better." His thoughts find an echo in modern society's Law of Attraction.

So often we compartmentalize history. In textbooks, World War I starts in 1914 and ends in 1918. The Jazz Decade starts in 1920 and ends in 1930. On paper, there's a gap separating the two eras. When you think about it, however, how could the generation of young men who had survived the horrors of trench warfare *not* have influenced the decade to come? The careless, free and easy, anything-goes Roaring Twenties were a direct result of the war. Veterans came home wearied by war and burdened with survivor's guilt. The rules of polite, tradition-bound living had gotten them very little in a world gone mad. Questioning the value of the rules they'd grown up with, they determined to eat, drink, and be merry because in their experience, tomorrow they might very well die. For them, the Jazz Decade was a definite and quite deliberate march toward self-destruction.

The suffragettes of the late nineteenth and early twentieth centuries presented their crowning achievement of the vote to their daughters only to watch in horror as the jazz generation seemed to throw all that hard work away. Abstinence didn't stand a chance when confronted with a "tomorrow we die" philosophy. Sex and drugs were originally associated with jazz, not with rock and roll. Everything done in the '60s and '70s was first done in the 1920s. There truly is nothing new under the sun. Our modern culture, which loves to push the unprepared and, perhaps, undeserving up onto pedestals and then tut-tut when they topple, got its birth in the '20s. Countless

Hollywood actors and actresses crashed and burned during the decade when their dysfunctional upbringings left them unprepared for the dual spotlights of fame and fortune.

The slide in morality among the decade's youth can be blamed on two things: movies and the automobile. Many young men of the era freely volunteered that everything they knew about kissing, necking, and petting they learned from the movies. And the car changed everything. No longer did a man have to spend his time courting a girl within the confines of her family home at the invitation of her wary parents. Irene was right in some respects: If you were going to let a man buy you a drink or take you out to dinner, then you owed him something. This shift of control in the dating arena from the female to the male forever altered relations between the genders.

The golden age of movies began in the 1920s. Over 7.5 million Americans attended a movie every week, and an average of seven hundred feature films were produced each year. Ellis's dream of running away to Hollywood might seem naïve to us, but magazines like *Photoplay* and *Movie Mirror* enjoyed a monthly distribution in the hundreds of thousands and were filled with stories of ingénues who were discovered by happenstance and went on to storied careers. Many of our greats—Greta Garbo, Douglas Fairbanks, Katherine Hepburn, Joan Crawford, Jean Harlow—got their start on the Silent Screen. And speaking of movies, you might be surprised at what your grandmother or great-grandmother watched at the theater when she was a girl. Before the era of censorship, just about anything went!

Prohibition and the 1920s

Is it possible to legislate morality?

As I saw this book beginning to spiral around that theme, I tried my best to stop it. If you're like me, you probably hate that question, because let's be honest, if you answer "yes," others view you as naïve. If you answer "no," then you're suspected of having thrown your personal standards to the winds. But that was exactly the debate at the heart of the Eighteenth Amendment to the U.S. Constitution.

On January 17, 1920, Prohibition went into effect, and America declared itself to be a dry nation. The Volstead Act, which provided enforcement to the amendment, prohibited the manufacture, sale, and transportation of alcohol—except for medicinal, research, industrial, or religious purposes—although the actual *consumption* of alcohol was never prohibited. You couldn't make it or possess it or sell it, but you could drink it. Especially if you had a doctor's prescription! Federal enforcement of the amendment was tepid at best, and at least one state never passed laws to enforce the amendment at all.

Was Prohibition a success?

In many parts of rural America, drinking dropped by half. But in cities like Boston and Chicago, the number of tickets issued for driving while intoxicated went up substantially. As always happens when something is forbidden, the underworld gladly stepped up to provide alcohol, and crime increased as criminal networks were organized to meet the demand. By some estimates 100,000 speakeasies could be found in New York City alone. These far outnumbered the saloons that had existed previously.

Was there anyone during the 1920s who chose to obey the law? Of course there was. Many people never let a drop of liquor touch their lips. And some of the descendants of those people still don't today. Apparently, those who had abstained before Prohibition continued to do so . . . but those who enjoyed a drink before Prohibition was enacted still did, no matter what anybody said. It didn't change much of anything except to formally divide our nation into halves. Those who drank (mostly urban dwellers and immigrants) and those who did not (mostly those who lived in rural areas).

Prohibitionists saw the ravages alcohol had perpetrated on society in the form of violence, the destruction of the family unit, and ruined lives, and they tried to fix it by applying a broad solution. Many of those who supported Prohibition did it with the intention of helping their fellow man: those like the poor and immigrants, who ought to know better than to drink but couldn't seem to help themselves. A significant part of the population supported the law on other people's behalf; they didn't really think it applied to them. But for many others, the solution seemed more like a punishment.

In some ways, however, Prohibition was the great leveler. Speakeasies did what old-time suffragettes had all but given up on: more than promoting liquor, they brought into being true equality of the sexes. In speakeasies, women were finally able to drink beside men. And what's more, they were able to smoke too! Dubious achievements you might say, but those forums liberated a whole generation of women whose mothers had been raised to think men and women couldn't enjoy their leisure time together.

What's certain is that when Prohibition ended on December 5, 1933, gangsters and crime syndicates were firmly entrenched within society, there were more alcoholics than there had been before, a generation of Americans had grown up understanding it's okay to break the law, and the idea that politicians weren't to be trusted became imbedded in popular culture.

How could a law so well-intentioned have brought about so many horrible results? Perhaps it can be explained in the difference between an authoritarian approach, which encourages rebellion, and an authoritative approach, which encourages dialogue. Can you legislate morality? You can try, I suppose (and wouldn't the world be a better place if it worked?). But given the outcome of Prohibition, I would say it's unlikely to succeed.

So what is a person concerned with the moral welfare of a nation supposed to do? You can't force anyone to do anything, but you can try to influence their choices. You can talk about consequences, and you can make the benefits of your own choices more visible to other people.

It has been noted that the Eighteenth Amendment to the Constitution was the only amendment that restricted Americans' rights. All the other amendments actually expanded them. Am I a skeptic? Not exactly. There were many unintended consequences that resulted from the Eighteenth Amendment, but at least one of them was positive: It's much more difficult to buy a drink now than it was during Prohibition in the 1920s; we seem to have chosen self-correction as a society. I have to think that as tempting as it is to try to force people to do the right thing, we were designed for the freedom of choice. Laws have never been able to change human nature, and only God can change hearts.

Discussion Questions

1. Has doing a favor for a friend ever gotten you into trouble?

2. Has a misunderstanding ever caused you to take drastic measures or ended in a comic moment?

3. How would you describe Ellis? How did she describe herself? Is there a difference in the way you view her and the way she viewed herself? Why?

4. Through the course of the story, Ellis discovered that work is hard. How old were you when you came to that realization?

5. Ellis's professor and parents thought her problems could be solved if she would just buckle down and apply herself. Ellis, however, understood that she couldn't because she wasn't like everyone else. In what ways are you not

like "everyone else"? How have you dealt with this? And who exactly *is* "everyone else"?

6. This book was filled with faulty assumptions and unmet expectations. Which of them stood out to you? What has your experience with assumptions and expectations been?

7. What sort of expectations did your family have for you as you were growing up? Were you able to meet them?

8. Where do you draw a line on moral issues in the political sphere? Is it worth trying to legislate morality? Are there any alternatives?

9. Whose fault was it that Irene died? How far is it necessary to go in being your brother's keeper?

10. Ellis repeated Emile Coué's mantra, "Every day, in every way, I am getting better and better." What do you say to yourself? What effect are those words having on your life? On your relationships?

11. If you could help someone change their role in life, who would it be? How would you do it?

Also From Siri Mitchell

To learn more about Siri and her books, visit sirimitchell.com.

Falling in Love Could Be a Recipe for Disaster

Lucy Kendall returns from a tour of the Continent, her luggage filled with the latest fashions and a mind fired by inspiration. After tasting Europe's best confections, she's sure she'll come up with a recipe that will save her father's struggling candy business and reverse their fortunes. But she soon discovers that their biggest competitor, the cheat who swindled her father out of his prize recipe, has now hired a promotions manager—a cocky, handsome out-of-towner who gets under Lucy's skin.

Charlie Clarke's new role at Standard Manufacturing is the chance of a lifetime. He can put some rough times behind him and reconnect with the father he's never known. The one thing he never counted on, however, was tenacious Lucy Kendall. She's making his work life miserable. and making herself impossible for him to forget.

Unrivaled

◊ BethanyHouse

 Stay up-to-date on your favorite books and authors with our free e-newsletters. Sign up today at bethanyhouse.com.

 Find us on Facebook. facebook.com/bethanyhousepublishers

 Free exclusive resources for your book group! bethanyhouse.com/anopenbook

an open book